OXFORD WORLD'S CLASSICS

ROCHESTER: SELECTED POEMS

JOHN WILMOT, second Earl of Rochester, was born on 1 April 1647, at Ditchley in Oxfordshire. He inherited the earldom in 1658, when his father, a royalist war-hero, died in exile in Europe. When Charles II was restored to the throne in 1660, Rochester was at Wadham College, Oxford, and he subsequently completed his education on the Grand Tour in France and Italy. In 1664, he made his debut at court, where his charm and wit rapidly endeared him to Charles; his courage under fire in a naval engagement during the Second Anglo-Dutch War in 1665 was a further recommendation. In 1666, Rochester was appointed a Gentleman of the King's Bedchamber, a highly influential post, and he reached the summit of royal favour between 1667 and 1673, while his close friend George Villiers, Duke of Buckingham, was the king's chief minister. Also in 1667, Rochester married the heiress Elizabeth Malet; thereafter, he divided his time between London, the family home at Adderbury in Oxfordshire, which was shared with his pious and formidable mother, and summer visits to his wife's estates at Enmore in Somerset. At court, Rochester became a figurehead for the new culture of hedonism and irreligion, and after the Buckingham faction lost power his increasingly extreme behaviour led to extended periods of banishment in 1674, 1675, and 1676. These were the years of his greatest achievement as a poet, when his satirical masterpieces 'A Letter from Artemiza in the Town to Chloe in the Country', 'A Satire against Reason and Mankind', and 'An Allusion to Horace', as well as a number of his most accomplished lyrics, began to circulate in manuscript. In 1679, his health collapsed as a result of the venereal disease and alcohol-related illnesses which had first affected him in the mid-1660s. In his final months, Rochester engaged in a series of conversations about religion and morality with the churchman Gilbert Burnet, eventually undergoing a deathbed conversion in circumstances which remain controversial. He died on 26 July 1680, at the age of thirty-three.

PAUL DAVIS is Reader in English at University College London. He is the author of *Translation and the Poet's Life: The Ethics of Translating in English Culture, 1646–1726* (Oxford, 2008).

OXFORD WORLD'S CLASSICS

*For over 100 years Oxford World's Classics have brought
readers closer to the world's great literature. Now with over 700
titles—from the 4,000-year-old myths of Mesopotamia to the
twentieth century's greatest novels—the series makes available
lesser-known as well as celebrated writing.*

*The pocket-sized hardbacks of the early years contained
introductions by Virginia Woolf, T. S. Eliot, Graham Greene,
and other literary figures which enriched the experience of reading.
Today the series is recognized for its fine scholarship and
reliability in texts that span world literature, drama and poetry,
religion, philosophy, and politics. Each edition includes perceptive
commentary and essential background information to meet the
changing needs of readers.*

OXFORD WORLD'S CLASSICS

JOHN WILMOT,
EARL OF ROCHESTER

Selected Poems

Edited with an Introduction and Notes by
PAUL DAVIS

OXFORD
UNIVERSITY PRESS

OXFORD

UNIVERSITY PRESS

Great Clarendon Street, Oxford OX2 6DP
United Kingdom

Oxford University Press is a department of the University of Oxford.
It furthers the University's objective of excellence in research, scholarship,
and education by publishing worldwide. Oxford is a registered trade mark of
Oxford University Press in the UK and in certain other countries

Editorial material © Paul Davis 2013

The moral rights of the author have been asserted

First published as an Oxford World's Classics paperback 2013

Impression: 8

British Library Cataloguing in Publication Data

Data available

ISBN 978-0-19-958432-1

Printed in Great Britain by
Clays Ltd, Elcograf S.p.A.

ACKNOWLEDGEMENTS

LIKE all scholars of Rochester, I owe an immense debt to the late Harold Love, upon whose monumental *The Complete Works of John Wilmot, Earl of Rochester* (Oxford, 1999) the present edition is based. Henry Woudhuysen and Peter Beal guided my initial forays into seventeenth-century scribal culture. Conversations with my colleague John Mullan and successive generations of students have helped me find out what I think about Rochester. Akane has put up, more or less uncomplainingly, with the incursion of the 'libertine Earl' into our household. Judith Luna has been heroically patient in the face of interminable delays.

Shortly before his death in 2004, when I had not learned to share his passion for Rochester, Keith Walker passed on to me his copy of Harold Love's edition. For that and the many other generosities he showed me—academic, social, gastronomic—in the years immediately after I succeeded him in the English department at University College London, this edition is dedicated to Keith's memory.

CONTENTS

ABBREVIATIONS

1680	*Poems on Several Occasions By the Right Honourable the E. of R—* (Antwerp [London], 1680)
1691	*Poems, &c. on Several Occasions: with Valentinian, A Tragedy. Written by the Right Honourable John Late Earl of Rochester* (London, 1691)
Ellis	*John Wilmot, Earl of Rochester: Complete Poems*, ed. Frank H. Ellis (Harmondsworth, 1994)
Hammond	*John Wilmot, Earl of Rochester: Selected Poems*, ed. Paul Hammond (Bristol, 1982)
Johnson	Samuel Johnson, *A Dictionary of the English Language* (1755)
Love	*The Works of John Wilmot, Earl of Rochester*, ed. Harold Love (Oxford, 1999)
ODNB	*Oxford Dictionary of National Biography*
OED	*Oxford English Dictionary*
R.	Rochester
Thormählen	Mariänne Thormählen, *Rochester: The Poems in Context* (Cambridge, 1993)
Walker	*The Poems of John Wilmot, Earl of Rochester* (Oxford, 1984)

INTRODUCTION

IN the late summer or early autumn of 1680, a slim, shoddily produced octavo volume entitled *Poems on Several Occasions By the Right Honourable The E. of R*— appeared on the London bookstands. It was a smash, devoured so avidly by readers that few copies now survive intact. But apart from the date, all the information given on its title-page was lies. The place of publication was not 'Antwerp'—the printer was covering his tracks because so much of the volume's content was obscene, blasphemous or both. Most deceptive of all was the title itself. Those titillating initials, *E. of R*—, were intended to reveal not conceal—like the wisps of pelisse which veil the 'charms' of Nell Gwyn and other Restoration beauties in Peter Lely's famous age-defining portraits. But of the seventy-two items included in the volume, only just under half were in fact written by the scandalous John Wilmot, second Earl of Rochester, who had died weeks earlier, worn out by a life of drunkenness and debauchery, at the age of thirty-three. The remaining poems in the collection ranged from lyrics and satires now known to be by minor geniuses of the period such as Aphra Behn, George Etherege, and John Oldham, to throwaway squibs and ditties whose authorship will probably never be determined. What all the items in the volume had in common was that they were all to some degree representative of the new 'libertine' cultural temper of the 1660s and 1670s, that explosive release of sexual licentiousness, moral scepticism, and religious heterodoxy which swept away the spiritual authoritarianism of the Puritan era. *Poems on Several Occasions By the Right Honourable The E. of R*— was not so much an edition of Rochester as an anthology of the libertine literary culture which flourished during his short adult lifetime and of which he was then—and still remains today—the prime embodiment.

That anthology quickly came to look like a commemoration, for the world it describes passed away with Rochester. Even as he lay dying, his former partners in excess were being forced to sober up and take sides in a national political emergency, the Exclusion Crisis precipitated by the efforts of the Earl of Shaftesbury and his supporters in parliament to have Charles's brother James, Duke of York removed from the line of succession because he was a Roman Catholic.

In the event, James did take the throne when Charles died in 1685, but he was forced to give up the crown three years later as a 'Protestant wind' swept his son-in-law William of Orange across the Channel to power in the 'Glorious' Revolution. The regime of William and Mary was strongly reformist, defining itself in contrast with the profanity and perversion of the Restoration past; and yet it was in this climate that the next significant edition of Rochester appeared in 1691. Entitled like its predecessor *Poems on Several Occasions*, it was in all other respects a quite different production. The publisher was Jacob Tonson, already well on his way to cornering the market for high-end literature through his de luxe editions of *Paradise Lost* and Dryden's classical translations. Tonson's aim was to canonize Rochester as an English classic; it was in his edition that Rochester first emerged as an individual author responsible for a specific body of work. Gone now were the mass of spurious attributions, replaced by more than a dozen authentic love lyrics, giving a canon of forty-three poems virtually all of which are still reckoned to be by Rochester. However, these advances came at a price. In assembling his edition, Tonson apparently had help from Rochester's formidable mother, but the dowager Countess of Rochester had been raised a Puritan, and her motivation for co-operating with Tonson was a desire to rehabilitate her son's memory. In the new edition, 'exceeding care was taken', according to its preface, 'that every block of offence should be removed'.[1] This meant leaving out some poems now rated among Rochester's most definitive achievements—'The Imperfect Enjoyment', 'A Ramble in St. James's Park', 'A Satire on Charles II'—as well as cleaning up a welter of local obscenities in pieces which were salvaged: notably, the mentions of homosexuality in 'The Disabled Debauchee' and 'Love to a Woman', and the instance of female masturbation in the last stanza of 'Fair Chloris in a pig-sty lay' (the rape fantasy in the preceding stanzas was retained).

The precedent set by Tonson lasted for two hundred and fifty years. Re-issues of his sanitized edition dominated the market throughout the eighteenth century, and further surgery was required to make Rochester presentable to Victorian readers ('one cannot copy out even the titles of his poems', lamented the critic Hippolyte Taine

---

[1] David Farley-Hills (ed.), *John Wilmot, Earl of Rochester: The Critical Heritage* (London, 1972), 169.

in 1863). In 1953, when Vivian de Sola Pinto brought out the first modern scholarly edition, he still had to omit 'The Imperfect Enjoyment' and 'A Ramble in St. James's Park' to shield his publisher from prosecution. Not until that iconic year of revolt 1968 did it become possible to read Rochester in an unexpurgated edition, when David Vieth's *Complete Poems of John Wilmot, Earl of Rochester* was published by Yale University Press. British readers had to wait longer—scholars until 1984 when Keith Walker's old-spelling Blackwells edition came out, and the public at large another decade after that for Paddy Lyons's Everyman (1993) and Frank Ellis's Penguin (1994). The story of Rochester's publication history, then, has all the hallmarks of an exemplary episode in the history of censorship, and it has usually been presented as such. For Ellis and Lyons, every recuperated 'fuck', 'cunt', or 'bugger' was another nail in the coffin of what Lyons termed 'the text-police' (though he warned against declaring final victory until Rochester was universally acknowledged as the author of the scatological farce *Sodom*).[2] Twenty years on, the picture looks rather more complicated. Those years have seen a boom in research into the transmission of Rochester's texts, culminating in Harold Love's edition on which the present volume is based, and this new scholarship has cast doubt on the applicability of simple models of censorship to Rochester's case. Certainly the idea that by scraping away layers of bowdlerization we have recovered his original texts in all their pristine obscenity has been exposed as a simplification, born of the modern tendency to equate sexual candour with authenticity. It may even be that editors who saw themselves as liberating Rochester from the censors were in fact perpetuating 'censorship' of his work, in an expanded sense of the term—colluding in the dissemination of a demonic image of him which was itself a product of strategic rewriting.

With only a handful of exceptions, Rochester's poems were originally published not in print but in manuscript. As an Earl, he subscribed to the early-modern aristocrat's prejudice against print publication on the grounds that it was tainted by associations with money-mindedness, standardization, and professionalism. Only writers who needed to earn their living by their pens had dealings with printers; nobles kept to manuscript as the medium of disinterested amateurism. Typically, Rochester would pass copies of

[2] *Rochester: Complete Poems and Plays*, ed. Paddy Lyons (London, 1993), p. vii.

a poem to his family and friends, or members of his coterie at court, after which it would spread outwards to a wider readership through successive recopyings, a process which has come to be known as 'scribal publication'. In this way, poems could achieve a substantial circulation within a short space of time (the Surveyor of the Press, Roger L'Estrange, who was charged with tracking down the authors of politically oppositional manuscript works, complained that they spread as fast as the plague). But of course manuscript is an inherently unstable medium; scribally published texts were liable to alteration at every stage of recopying, and not only through slips of the pen—early-modern copyists had few qualms about deliberately rewriting their sources. Rochester's work particularly invited such scribal interventions: there are many hundreds of textual variants in the surviving manuscript copies of his poems. Only a minority of these changes, however, can be explained as acts of censorship; in fact, there is every reason to suppose that in the course of its scribal transmission, Rochester's work was spiced up as often as it was watered down, pornified as often as it was gentrified. Human nature suggests as much, but the particular conditions of scribal culture in Rochester's lifetime also played a part. In previous generations, manuscripts mainly circulated within delimited networks of readers, but in the Restoration, scribal publication became commercialized: non-elite readers were increasingly demanding access to notionally exclusive manuscript material, and enterprising booksellers set up consortiums of professional copyists—scriptoriums—to satisfy this demand. Within this emergent market, no commodity was more valuable than the name of the infamous Rochester, and since most scribal verse was anonymous, there was an obvious temptation to ascribe stray scandalous items to him, or else to 'sex up' whatever authentic pieces of his did come to hand which might otherwise have failed to live up to readers' expectations of the 'libertine Earl'.

Consider a famous textual variant from the ending of 'Upon his Drinking a Bowl', Rochester's imitation of Anacreon, the supposititious Greek poet whose lyrics advocating a life of wine, women, and song were staples of the Cavalier repertoire. This is the final stanza in *1680*:

> Cupid and Bacchus my saints are:
>   May drink and love still reign.
> With wine I wash away my cares
>   And then to cunt again.

But in Tonson's edition, the last line reads 'And then to Love again'. An open-and-shut case of censorship, according to Lyons: 'Tonson's four-letter word "Love" replacing Rochester's word "cunt"'.[3] But can we be sure that 'cunt' was 'Rochester's word'? Certainly it was an obscenity he and other libertine courtiers specially favoured, but for that very reason it was vulnerable to imitation—it was precisely Dryden's (alleged) habit of suddenly shouting out 'cunt!' when in company with the court wits that Rochester used to belittle him as a wannabe in 'An Allusion to Horace'. Furthermore, the choice is not simply between 'Cunt' and 'Love'. If we look behind the printed texts to the original scribal phase of the poem's publication, we discover alternative readings, the most well attested of which in the eight surviving manuscripts is simply 'Phill', short for Phyllis, a generic name for the mistress in many Restoration love lyrics. So while Tonson's 'Love' was doubtless a bowdlerization of 'Cunt', 'Cunt' itself may have resulted from a prior act of vulgarization, either on the part of the printer of *1680* or, more likely, of a copyist who wanted to accentuate the poem's transgressiveness, whether for reasons of personal taste or commercial advantage. It was established by the first scholar to pay attention to the manuscripts of Rochester—David Vieth—that the texts of *1680* were drawn from a scriptorium anthology, now preserved in the Beinecke Rare Books Library at Yale University (unfortunately, 'Upon his drinking a bowl' was torn out of the manuscript by a later reader). Known as the 'Hansen' manuscript, after the diplomat, Friedrich Adolphus Hansen, whose name appears on the title-page, this was indeed a luxury commercial product, made to order for a customer with a particular taste for libertine, highly explicit verse.

'Phill' is the reading adopted in this edition, but a final possibility is that Rochester was responsible for all three of 'Love', 'Cunt', and 'Phill'. Like most of his lyrics, 'Upon his drinking a bowl' was designed for performance, and by varying the level of politeness or obscenity in the final line Rochester could customize it for a range of social contexts—'Love' or 'Phill', if he were reciting it in polite company, 'Cunt' when it was sung at a drinking-bout with his fellow court wits in his apartments at Whitehall. Textual variations in Rochester's poems need to be understood in terms of the various

---

[3] *Rochester: Complete Poems and Plays*, p. viii.

cultural environments in which the poems circulated, and this edition has been designed to enable readers to make such connections: a selection of the most critically significant variants is recorded in the notes, and information needed to 'place' the sources in which they occur is recorded in an 'Index of Manuscripts'. Particular use has been made of two major scribal collections of work by Rochester uncovered in the early 1990s, the so-called 'Harbin' and 'Hartwell' manuscripts, which apparently originate from within the poet's Oxfordshire household. These collections lack the court lampoons and the libertine satires, centring instead on Rochester's songs and lyrics, sometimes in versions more polite than were published at court. The Rochester they preserve is a rather less lurid figure than modern audiences are used to, but matches the description of the poet given by some insightful contemporary readers. This is the Rochester whose love poems were so admired for their outstanding lyrical beauty, so prized as performance pieces by Restoration and eighteenth-century composers, that the poet John Oldham lamented that when Rochester died 'the art of graceful song' died with him.[4] It is the Rochester who was praised as the epitome of verbal refinement and an authority on courtly manners, particularly by the women readers who took such an interest in his work; who was praised by Aphra Behn for his 'softness' and 'sweetness', and by his niece Anne Wharton (yet more strikingly to modern ears) for having 'civilized the rude'.[5] If this was a partial, localized, view of the poet, the same could be said of its polar opposite, devilish 'rake Rochester'. There are no secure grounds for subordinating one to the other, and no signs that Rochester himself sought to do so. On the contrary, the uniquely chaotic state of the surviving manuscripts of his verse suggests he considered it either undesirable or impossible to homogenize his authorial self; he was apparently content to be a different type of poet in each of the communities to which he belonged, the various places between which he divided his time.

In this sense, understanding scribal publication brings us to the heart of Rochester's concerns as a poet. For the discontinuous or occasional aspects of human identity are a major subject in his verse. The basic idea was a commonplace of libertine writing: that human

---

[4] Farley-Hills (ed.), *Rochester: The Critical Heritage*, 95.
[5] Ibid. 105, 107.

beings cannot be expected to transcend their material susceptibility to change is an argument advanced in favour of promiscuity by dozens of male speakers in the so-called 'against constancy' lyrics which bulk so large in the Restoration repertoire. But for Rochester this was no mere convention: he explored its psychological and philosophical consequences with singular energy and rigour. For the speaker of what is perhaps his best-known lyric, 'Love and Life', who insists that 'All my past life is mine no more' and 'Whatever is to come is not', inconstancy is not so much a tactical convenience as an existential predicament—he 'balances in the void, sustaining himself on nothing whatever'.[6] In the major satires, several of which have place-names in their titles—'A Ramble in St. James's Park', 'Tunbridge Wells', 'A Letter from Artemiza in the Town to Chloe in the Country'—Rochester focuses again and again on characters who are variously liberated or threatened by changes of location. As an Earl, he himself shared his name with a place, and this conjunction is wittily activated in his extraordinary auto-satire, 'To the Post Boy', where 'Rochester' recounts the story of his disgraceful life, before finally enquiring of the boy 'The readiest way to Hell?' and receiving the response: 'The readiest way, my Lord,'s by Rochester'. Tellingly, this poetic confession takes place in a transitional environment, a coaching-inn somewhere between Epsom and London, where the poet is waiting to be supplied with a fresh horse in order to complete his escape after the drunken brawl on 17 June 1676 which led to the death of his friend Captain Downs. There is no single way to Rochester—he was a poet caught between places. The four remaining sections of this introduction seek to locate him in relation to the principal cultural domains of his age: the court, the theatre, the country, and the church.

Court

Throughout his lifetime and for generations of readers since his death, Rochester was indissolubly linked with the court. He was the leader of the so-called 'merry gang' of aristocratic wits, the savagest noble in Charles II's notoriously feral entourage. But this association

[6] Barbara Everett, 'The Sense of Nothing', in Jeremy Treglown (ed.), *Spirit of Wit: Reconsiderations of Rochester* (Oxford, 1982), 11.

has begun to weaken lately. The more Rochester is revered as an icon of subversion, the more inconvenient it becomes to recall his entitlement as a member of the social and political elite. The one four-letter word Rochester's twenty-first-century admirers may find it hard to stomach is 'Earl'. In the recent bio-pic, *The Libertine* (2004), with Hollywood's go-to bohemian Johnny Depp in the lead, Rochester was shown wading knee-deep in mud through London's streets, drinking in low-rent taverns, rowing with his Puritan mother at his Oxfordshire estate, and most of all at the theatre, giving his mistress Elizabeth Barry acting lessons backstage, and of course directing the first night of *Sodom*. But the film featured not a single scene set in the vast interlocking network of buildings, containing some two thousand rooms, which made up the labyrinthine palace of St James's at Whitehall. The audience were never allowed to see Rochester entertaining high-born friends or mistresses in his court apartments, located in a prime spot at the corner of the Stone Gallery, or listening to one of his love poems being sung to violin accompaniment by the King's expensively imported French musicians at a ceremonial banquet. Even the poet's most celebrated act of subversion—smashing up the King's much-prized glass sundial—was omitted, presumably because it took place in the exclusive surroundings of the Privy Garden.

Yet the court was Rochester's main habitat, and it remains the inescapable context for understanding his poetry. His father Henry Wilmot, upon whose death in 1658 he inherited the title, was a Cavalier legend, a dashing *bon viveur* and war-hero who single-handedly engineered the future Charles II's escape to the Continent (including the famous concealment in an oak tree) after the disastrous battle of Worcester in 1651. Along with that blue-chip pedigree, Rochester was possessed of quick wits and considerable personal charm, attributes guaranteed to endear him to the pleasure-loving and easily bored Charles. He made his debut at court in 1664, at the age of seventeen, and by 1666 he had risen to become a Gentleman of the King's Bedchamber. One week in every four, Rochester would help Charles get dressed in the morning and undressed at night, serve his meals if he chose to dine in private, and sleep on a makeshift bed at the foot of the royal four-poster. A precious commodity in any court, such access to the monarch in his privy apartments was especially valuable in Charles's case, given his propensity for mixing political business with sexual pleasure. By the end of 1667, Rochester's arrival at the centre of power was confirmed. In the autumn, he took his seat in the House of Lords, under a special licence from the King since he was not yet twenty-one, and duly performed the service Charles expected of him—signing the warrant of impeachment against the Lord Chancellor Edward Hyde, Earl of Clarendon, on charges of financial corruption and mismanaging the Second Anglo-Dutch War. Clarendon's replacement as Charles's leading counsellor was George Villiers, second Duke of Buckingham, twenty years Rochester's senior but a close personal friend. The next six years were the high point of Rochester's court career. In addition to his friendship with Buckingham, Rochester was close to Charles's new favourite mistress Nell Gwyn, which gave him further means of influencing the King through so-called 'petticoat diplomacy'. But once Buckingham had lost power at the end of 1673, and been replaced in the King's affections by his bitter rival Thomas Osborne, Earl of Danby, Rochester became increasingly marginalized. His growing rebelliousness issued in three extended periods of banishment: at the turn of 1674, after he accidentally showed the King a copy of his 'Satire on Charles II' during the Christmas festivities at Whitehall; in the summer of 1675 following his drunken assault on Charles's sundial; and again in the summer of 1676 after the Epsom affray in which his companion Captain Downs and a local constable received lethal wounds.

Those debacles have sometimes been seen as acts of self-sabotage on Rochester's part, the culmination of his progressive disillusionment with life in Charles's venal entourage. Certainly, the 'Satire on Charles II' looks wilfully self-destructive. Charles may have been 'the easiest king and the best-bred man alive', as it begins by saying, but not even he could shrug off Rochester's betrayal of his bedchamber secrets ('The painful tricks of the laborious Nelly, | Employing hands, arms, fingers, mouth and thighs | To raise that limb which she all night enjoys' would have been witnessed at first hand by the poet). However, it is important not to mistake Rochester's factional resentments in the aftermath of Buckingham's fall for a more general rejection of the court system. The newly authenticated 'An Allusion to Tacitus' shows that once the odious Danby was removed from power in 1679, Rochester was quite prepared to find excuses for Charles, employing the time-honoured courtly fiction that the King had been led astray by evil counsellors. With the court as an institution Rochester had, from first to last, a love–hate relationship. He arrived too late to witness the honeymoon period of the early 1660s, and incurred his first banishment as early as 1669; but even after his final period of disfavour in 1676, he was still seeking to consolidate his presence at Whitehall, securing permission from Charles to add a new wing and staircase to his apartment. In this ambivalence, Rochester was essentially no different from courtier-poets in previous ages—Wyatt and Surrey under Henry VIII, or Raleigh and Sidney in the reign of Elizabeth I—all of whom complained about life at court as often as they celebrated it. However, Rochester's conflicts over his role as courtier took place against the background of a larger institutional realignment in English culture, which was to result, within a generation of his death, in the court losing the primacy it had enjoyed since the Middle Ages. By the early eighteenth century, the idea of the court as the natural seeding ground for poetic genius had begun the long decline from which it has never recovered, and Alexander Pope, the champion of the emergent market-based model of professional authorship, could dismiss Rochester and the other Restoration court poets 'as holiday writers—as gentlemen that diverted themselves now and then with poetry, rather than as poets'.[7]

The roots of the transformation lay in the Interregnum, when the structures of court governance were dismantled, and replaced with quasi-republican institutions. Of course, those structures were reconstituted at the Restoration, but the disruption of the court's hegemony inevitably left behind an increased awareness of its artificiality. Its dominance was also being eroded by wider social developments. The mobilization of the London populace as a political entity during the 1640s and 1650s had led to the emergence of urban spaces which encouraged cultural participation among non-elite citizens, what historians term 'the public sphere'. Such spaces proliferated in Restoration London, particularly in the so-called 'town', the area around Covent Garden and Drury Lane which became the focus of a development boom after the Great Fire of 1666 had destroyed much of the old city within the walls. Known for its coffee-houses, theatres, and prostitutes, the town quickly came to rival the court as a site of cultural consumption and erotic adventure. Far from resisting these

[7] Farley-Hills (ed.), *Rochester: The Critical Heritage*, 193.

changes, the men and women of the court were complicit in them, up to and including the King himself. Highly affable by disposition, Charles presided over an unprecedentedly open court, giving out keys to his private apartments, never mind the staterooms, with reckless abandon; in the galleries of the palace and during his daily walks in St James's Park, one contemporary observer was alarmed to note, 'he would pull off his hat to the meanest' of his subjects.[8] The King's behaviour particularly helped blur the divide between town and court. For he was often to be seen at the Duke's playhouse in Lincoln's Inn Fields or the King's in Drury Lane, the first English monarch to visit the public theatres. And, of course, actresses who caught his eye—most famously, Nell Gwyn—found no bar in securing admission to the royal bedchamber.

The increasingly fluid intercourse between the court and London's other cultural locales clearly fascinated Rochester; transitions in and out of Whitehall are a recurrent theme of his verse. In 'Quoth the Duchess of Cleveland to Councillor Knight', the King's principal mistress is preparing, under cover of darkness, to slip out of her court apartments by the 'back stairs' leading down to the banks of the Thames, and be rowed upriver to go slumming in Sodom, the red-light district between what is now the Embankment and Fleet Street. The blazingly obscene lyric 'By all Love's soft yet mighty pow'rs', which it used to be thought was about a country conquest of Rochester's, 'one Nell Browne of Woodstock', has been shown by Harold Love to be addressed to a low-born woman recently introduced to court, almost certainly Nell Gwyn herself. The speaker, a Whitehall insider, is giving the new arrival a much-needed lesson in the standards of personal hygiene expected of a court lady. But the cultural traffic in the poem is not all one-way: Rochester's subtle manipulation of tone and lexis makes the ingénue's slovenliness seem charmingly innocent, and the habitué's obsession with physical cleanliness a mark of his moral degradation. (There is anecdotal evidence that Nell deliberately held on to her earthy personal style, as a salutary contrast to the precious French manners of her main rival, Louise de Kéroualle, the Duchess of Portsmouth.) The Rochesterian speaker who comes off worst in his dealings with the world beyond Whitehall, though, is the protagonist of 'A Ramble in St. James's Park'.

[8] Quoted in N. H. Keeble, *The Restoration: England in the 1660s* (Oxford, 2002), 61.

He has apparently taken a town whore as his mistress; arriving back at the fringes of the court after a foray to a tavern in Drury Lane, he is outraged to discover her encouraging the advances of three wannabe courtiers whose highest boast is that through a family connection in the Queen's (notoriously unfashionable) household they have eaten at the waiters' table in the Presence Chamber, the least restricted area of St James's. The contradictions of the speaker's cultural positioning are brilliantly embodied in the formal experimentalism of the poem. It is a hybrid of the expansive mode of Horatian satire, particularly associated with the description of encounters in urban public spaces, and the narrower mode of personal satire or 'lampoon' which was the vernacular of territorial conflict inside Whitehall (lampoons were court graffiti, often tagged to the doors of their victims' chambers). The urbane Horatian tone dominates in the opening section of the poem, as the speaker complacently surveys the scene in the park, but after the shock of Corinna's betrayal he closets himself in the brutality of lampoon to repair the damage to his courtly ego.

It would be a mistake to align Rochester too closely with the speaker of 'A Ramble' but the latter's predicament was one in which his creator was unavoidably implicated. Rochester was particularly brought to feel the waning of his power as a court poet by the writer who personified the emergent authority of the town, John Dryden. Their relationship started out as one of patron and client; in the early 1670s, Dryden would submit drafts of his plays for Rochester's approval. But soon Dryden's increasing confidence in his role as Poet Laureate, and his self-representation as an arbiter of taste in a series of groundbreaking critical essays, began to pique Rochester's courtly pride. The break came in 1675, and provoked Rochester to write one of his most influential poems, 'An Allusion to Horace', a major document in the history of English criticism. On a casual reading, the poem looks like a simple reaffirmation of court values. Rochester pulls rank, ridiculing Dryden's clumsy attempts to fit in with the court wits, and insisting that the proper measure of literary merit was not the 'unthinking laughter and poor praise' of the 'rabble' who flocked to Dryden's plays, but the approval of 'those few who know'—Rochester's own friends and acolytes at court. Yet the 'Allusion to Horace' was not entirely reactionary; there are signs in it that Rochester was attempting to create a new blend of court and town aesthetics. Dryden's notorious fluency and disinclination to revise his work gave Rochester the chance to paint him as a 'scribbling' author with a 'loose slattern Muse'—more or less how a professional writer might have stereotyped a 'court wit'. This in turn left some of the terrain of professionalism vacant, which Rochester was quick to occupy, exhorting Dryden to have more care for his craft: 'Compare each phrase, examine every line, | Weigh every word, and every thought refine'. Rochester's innovative critical project is reflected in the revolutionary mode of the poem. 'Allusion', which Samuel Johnson credited Rochester with pioneering, is a subcategory of classical imitation in which the names of people and places in the original poem are updated to modern equivalents. The particular poem by Horace which Rochester chose as his source was one Dryden had used to build his Augustan critical power-base; by imitating it in the informal vein of 'allusion', Rochester flourished his own classical credentials whilst avoiding the appearance—lethal to a courtier—of nit-picking erudition.

The final act of Rochester's life as a court poet was 'An Epistolary Essay, from M. G. to O. B. upon their Mutual Poems', the last and most enigmatic of his major poems. On the surface, it looks like a 'Defence of Poetry' as written by a Restoration court wit. M. G.'s verse has come under attack from 'saucy censurers' in the town; he dismisses their criticism with a classic display of aristocratic insouciance, declaring that he does not write 'with the vain hope to be admired' but only to 'beget' some 'pleasure' to his 'dear self'. Since Rochester was the most conspicuous public face of this ethic of courtly self-gratification, many copyists assumed the poem was an actual verse letter in his own voice, and so re-titled it 'A Letter from My Lord Rochester', 'From the E. of R.', or some equivalent. In *1680*, the poem was placed first in the running order, giving it the appearance of a programmatic introduction to Rochester's work. This confessional reading remained the norm for nearly three hundred years, until David Vieth proposed in his inaugural study *Attribution in Restoration Poetry* (1963) that the 'Epistolary Essay' was in fact not an exposition of Rochester's own aesthetic creed, but a ventriloquistic satire on his bitterest enemy at court, John Sheffield, third Earl of Mulgrave (hence 'M. G.'). Vieth's thesis has now gained almost universal acceptance, but it is not beyond dispute. Rochester certainly did attack Mulgrave in others of his poems, most notably

'A Very Heroical Epistle in Answer to Ephelia', a dazzling exercise in satiric impersonation also cast as a verse letter. The persona of the 'Epistolary Essay' is broadly continuous with that of 'A Very Heroical Epistle'; both are studies in self-conceit, a quality for which Mulgrave was notorious even among his noble peers. However, M. G. does appear to function not only as a cautionary example but as a touchstone. There remains something superb about his vanity; the unconscious ironies in his speech (if they are that) are as fine as anything found in the mature satires of Dryden and Marvell. Probably the generations of readers who saw the speaker as a Rochesterian self-portrait—among them Pope, who was probably remembering M. G.'s boast 'I write for my own ease' when he called Rochester a 'holiday writer' who 'diverted' himself 'now and then with poetry'—were not simply duped. At the very least, the 'Epistolary Essay' proves what is often said about satirists—that they share the vices they impute to their victims; that their attacks are always in some sense self-directed. But it may be that Rochester originally drafted the poem as an apology for his own courtly attitudes before transforming it at a later date into a satire, once those attitudes came to seem unsustainable. 'An Epistolary Essay, from M. G. to O. B. upon their Mutual Poems' is the suicide note of England's last great court poet.

Theatre

The idea that all forms of theatrical activity were prohibited during the Interregnum is something of a simplification, but the full-scale reopening of the playhouses after the Restoration was seen by most contemporary observers as defining the spirit of the new age. The lucrative rights to the play-starved market in London were split between two companies—the Duke's (patronized by the Duke of York), which initially operated out of a converted tennis-court in Lincoln's Inn Fields before moving into a new purpose-built theatre in Dorset Gardens, on the river near St Paul's, in 1671, and the King's, which had a number of temporary premises before its permanent home in Russell Street, just off Drury Lane, on the site of the present Theatre Royal, was finally completed in 1674. New developments in playhouse design and performance practice confirmed the theatre as an emblematic site of Restoration modernity. For the first time female roles were played not by boys, as they had been since Shakespeare's day, but by professional actresses, and the chance to observe women's bodies in states of semi-undress and postures of theatrical passion quickly became central to the appeal of playgoing. Meanwhile, technological advances pioneered at Dorset Gardens, such as hanging scenery and flying machines, fuelled a taste for the visually spectacular productions known as semi-operas which came to predominate in the repertoire from the mid-1670s. These twin innovations naturally suggested a view of Restoration culture as lubricious and sensationalist, and references to the theatre in oppositional writing of the period usually imply this analysis: in Milton's *Samson Agonistes* (1671), for instance, the Philistine temple demolished by Samson has more than a hint of a Restoration playhouse about it. But even in the work of dramatists who supported the restored monarchy, like George Etherege and William Wycherley, theatrical motifs suggest a view of the Restoration as an age of disguise, moral and political hypocrisy (on re-entering the capital in 1660, to a show of universal rejoicing, Charles II was heard to remark to the Earl of Clarendon that it must have been 'his own fault that he had been absent so long, for he saw nobody that did not protest he had ever wished for his return').[9]

The culturally symptomatic status of the theatre is fully reflected in Rochester's life and writing. He chose as his first residence in London (as opposed to Whitehall) a house on Portugal Row in Lincoln's Inn Fields, right next door to the Duke's playhouse. All the leading playwrights of the day were either his friends (Etherege, Wycherley) or clients (Dryden, Thomas Shadwell) and he had affairs with a number of actresses—not all of them, it should be noted, merely exploitative liaisons. Nell Gwyn, almost certainly Rochester's lover before she was the King's, became a lifelong friend and political associate. Most of all, there was Elizabeth Barry, whom Rochester tutored in acting technique, helping her to develop the naturalistic style which later brought her such success in tragic roles; their relationship lasted five years and produced a daughter, before collapsing into acrimony as Rochester came to resent her increasing fame. In his own theatre-going, Rochester conspicuously embodied the new mores of Restoration dramatic culture, in particular the progressive blurring of the divide between the onstage and offstage worlds. Restoration playhouses had no proscenium arch to mark the boundary between the stage and the auditorium, and since the latter remained fully lit throughout performances the playgoers watched each other as much as the action. The court wits often sat in the pit, immediately adjacent to the stage, from where their impromptu critical remarks meshed with the scripted dialogue, endorsing or trumping the playwright's own inventiveness. Rochester's interventions were not limited to throwaway bon mots: a number of dramatists deferred to him as an authority on dramatic taste, including Thomas Crowne, Nathaniel Lee, and Thomas Otway as well as Dryden in the early part of his career. At the height of his celebrity, he became a dramatic character in his own right, providing the model for at least two rake heroes—Don John in Shadwell's *The Libertine* (1675), and Dorimant in Etherege's *The Man of Mode* (1676), a role in which Thomas Betterton apparently mimicked Rochester's accent and mannerisms to a T.

Rochester's fragmentary works as a playwright, in particular his adaptation of Fletcher's tragedy *Valentinian*, lie outside the scope of this edition, but a sample of the prologues and epilogues he provided for plays by his friends and acquaintances is included. These were far from mere puffs: recent research has underscored their centrality in Rochester's canon. An unfinished piece ('What vain unnecessary things are men') preserved only in Rochester's handwritten draft in the 'Portland' manuscript, and previously taken to be the start of a major satire because of its strong links with 'A Letter from Artemiza to Chloe', has now been shown by Edward Saslow to be the sketch of an epilogue for a play to be performed by an all-female cast while the male actors of the King's company were on strike during the 1672 season. Rochester's epilogue to Francis Fane's *Love in the Dark* (1675) was already recognized as a significant piece, featuring as it does a closely technical comparison of ritualized and naturalistic acting styles which recalls the ambivalent treatment of artifice and informality in literary style in the immediately contemporaneous 'An Allusion to Horace'. But fresh complexity is added to the epilogue's weighing of those values by Paul Hopkins's recent discovery of a new fourteen-line passage (included in this edition) written alongside the text in the copy of the play owned by John Verney, Rochester's Oxfordshire neighbour and a close family friend. Beyond these explicitly theatrical pieces, dramatic characters and concerns recur in a number of Rochester's major satires. Cuff and Kick, two louts from Shadwell's comedy *Epsom Wells* (1673), turn up in 'Tunbridge Wells'; the 'fine Lady' in 'A Letter from Artemiza to Chloe' shares a catch-phrase ('Let me die!') with the equally affected Melantha in Dryden's *Marriage-à-la-Mode* (1671); and in 'Timon' much of the after-dinner conversation between Half-Wit, Huff, Ding-Boy, and Kickum is taken up with ham-fisted debate about the merits of contemporary dramatists.

Rochester's verse can also be seen as dramatic in a more fundamental sense. In *Some Passages of the Life and Death of John Earl of Rochester* (1680), the first and still most indispensable biography of the poet, the churchman Gilbert Burnet, who attended Rochester on his deathbed, reports that 'he took pleasure to disguise himself as a Porter, or as a Beggar' and to 'go about in odd shapes, in which he acted his part so naturally, that even those who were in the secret . . . could perceive nothing by which he might be discovered'.[10] During his banishment from court in the summer of 1676, the poet disguised himself as a quack doctor, 'Alexander Bendo', and set up shop selling bogus charms and nostrums from a temporary wooden stage near Tower Hill. In a seminal lecture delivered nearly fifty years ago, Anne Barton proposed that these actorly inclinations found an outlet in Rochester's poems; that the major satires in particular are written in dramatized voices, 'in character', as it were. This thesis has acquired the status of a critical truism, but it is important to ask what exactly we mean when we say that the speaker of a Rochester poem is dramatized. On a maximal understanding of the term, it would mean that their attitudes are to be clearly distinguished from Rochester's. Some commentators in the 1960s and 1970s took this view, as they sought to dislodge the naive biographical readings of Rochester's work which abounded in the eighteenth and nineteenth centuries. Yet it would be perverse to deny the resemblances between Rochester and his satirical protagonists. At the time he wrote 'The Disabled Debauchee', for instance, Rochester had, like the poem's speaker, recently retired from naval service, and, given the worsening of his syphilis, might well have suspected that his best days as a rake, like the debauchee's, were already behind him. What is needed in

[10] Farley-Hills (ed.), *Rochester: The Critical Heritage*, 54.

such cases is an approach which recognizes areas of overlap between Rochester and his libertine speakers whilst addressing the effects of his playful or analytic detachment from them. Conversely, it is worth exploring what aspects of Rochester's mentality found expression through those of his dramatized speakers who appear least like alter egos, particularly the female ones whose voices he adopted with such striking regularity, in 'The Platonic Lady' and 'A Young Lady to her Ancient Lover', in 'What vain unnecessary things are men' (which we now know was actually to have been spoken by an actress), and most of all in what is increasingly considered his satiric masterpiece, 'A Letter from Artemiza in the Town to Chloe in the Country'. These poems have much to tell us about Rochester's need for relief from the hyper-masculinism of his role as court rake—and also about his preparedness to explore the fears and fantasies about women which might stem from such a need.

Given the extent of the modern emphasis on Rochester's habits of ventriloquism and impersonation, it might be supposed that critics would be wary of attributing confessional sincerity to any of his utterances. Yet certain parts of Rochester's work have continued to be treated in recent studies as in effect statements of his personal convictions. The passages most often privileged in this way involve memorable articulations of libertine ethical positions: the sceptical maxims debunking man's moral pretensions in the final section of 'A Satire against Reason and Mankind' ('all men would be cowards if they durst' or 'Men must be knaves, 'tis in their own defence'), two lines affirming the material changeableness of human beings from 'Love and Life' ('All my past life is mine no more' and 'The present moment's all my lot'), and most of all the ringing denial of Christian eschatology in the opening line of 'Seneca's *Troas*. Act. 2. Chorus': 'After death nothing is, and nothing death'. Certainly these sound like statements of principle, but to credit them as sincere may be to succumb to an unexamined complicity with the rhetoric of libertinism. Libertines were fond of contrasting the merely acted or artificial character of conventional moral postures with the putative authenticity or naturalness of their own disabused positions. Theatrical conceits in Rochester's libertine lyrics regularly carry this implication; as when the speaker of 'Upon his Leaving his Mistress' refuses to 'design' a 'face' of monogamous commitment to 'damn' his beloved to be 'only mine', or that of 'To Corinna', seeing through her efforts to 'force' a 'frown', proceeds to uncover her true libidinous self. Some powerful tendencies within modern culture—Freud's insistence on the primacy of the sex drive, a Nietzschean sense of the constructedness of moral ideals—can make us now as prone to accept such libertine special pleading at face value as pious Williamite readers or high-minded Victorian ones were to reject it out of hand.

In fact, libertinism was itself essentially theatrical—'not so much a philosophy as a set of performances', in the words of James Grantham Turner, the leading modern authority on the topic.[11] Samuel Pepys gives an account in his *Diary* of one notorious libertine scene, involving Rochester's friends Sedley and Buckhurst, which was played out at the Cock Tavern in Covent Garden on 16 June 1663 when, after a drunken dinner, Sedley emerged on to the balcony and in front of the assembled crowd on the piazza below set about 'shewing his nakedness—acting all the postures of lust and buggery that could be imagined'.[12] This performative element is central to Rochester's explorations of the libertine as a cultural figure: in their differing ways, the disabled debauchee, the speaker of the 'Satire against Reason and Mankind', and M. G. are all self-dramatizing characters who, we feel, can only be themselves when they have an audience to impress or offend. The philosophical premises of libertinism—its emphasis on the materiality of human being, its rejection of obscurantist theories of spiritual essence—logically entailed a view of the self as actor, adopting a succession of discrete roles. Rochester confronted the ramifications of this logic head-on; in particular, the discomfiting fact that the theatricality of the libertine's transgressions made them vulnerable to imitation, thereby frustrating his desire to free himself from the toils of social convention. Rochester's libertine protagonists are beset by grotesque replicas of themselves: the three court wannabes who make up to Corinna in 'A Ramble in St. James's Park'; the latitudinarian cleric quoting lines from the libertine bible, Lucretius' *De Rerum Natura*, in 'A Satire against Reason and Mankind'; Dryden shouting 'cunt!' in 'An Allusion to Horace'. In Rochester's poetic world there is ultimately no escape from these ham actors. All that world is a stage, its men and women—including their creator—merely players.

---

[11] James Grantham Turner, *Libertines and Radicals in Early Modern London: Sexuality, Politics, and Literary Culture, 1630–1685* (Cambridge, 2002), p. x.

[12] Quoted in Keeble, *The Restoration*, 177.

Country

It would take an eccentric editor to think of including much work by
Rochester in an anthology of rural poetry. London, and especially the
environs of the court, is the home terrain of Rochester's verse; the
countryside hardly ever features. Of course, poetry of rural descrip-
tion of the kind we are familiar with today did not begin to be written
until the middle decades of the eighteenth century, and is particularly
a product of Romanticism. But Rochester's impatience with even
those more stylized poetic approaches to the country which were
current in his lifetime is palpable. His mock-pastorals are all mock
and no pastoral. 'A Dialogue between Strephon and Daphne' lacks
even a cursory scenic frame, not so much as a grazing sheep or
purling brook. The protagonists of 'As Chloris full of harmless
thought' and 'Fair Chloris in a pig-sty lay' seem to be having fantasies
about becoming court women; the former imagines herself being
wooed by 'princes', the latter dreams of having 'snowy arms' and
wielding 'ivory pails'. The only one of Rochester's major poems set in
the country is 'Tunbridge Wells', and its engagement with nature
extends no further than an introductory line and a half of mock-
Homeric description of the sunrise. All these pieces barely muster
enough respect for the rural fiction to allow it to function effectively
as a comic foil. Where rural elements occur in Rochester's urban
poetry, the illusions of pastoral come in for predictably rough treat-
ment. 'A Ramble in St. James's Park' graffities over Edmund Waller's
decorous 'On St. James's Park, as Lately Improved by His Majesty'
(1661) with 'bugg'ries, rapes and incests', and the plaints of the love-
lorn 'swain' Amintor in Sir Carr Scroope's 'A Letter' are given nasty,
brutish and short shift in Rochester's obscene 'Answer'. This is what
we expect Rochester to do with country material—reduce it to what
Hamlet, in the course of his cruel rejection of Ophelia, punningly
calls 'cuntry matters'.

Yet the place of the rural in Rochester's imaginary is worth further
thought. He actually spent as much of his life in the country as he did
in London. His family seat was at Adderbury in rural Oxfordshire,
where his wife and children had their permanent residence together
with his mother, the Dowager Countess. The surviving correspond-
ence between Elizabeth and Rochester shows that he did not visit
from London as regularly as she would have liked, but also that he

was rather more committed to domestic life than modern readers might suppose. From 1674, he was in Oxfordshire more regularly, if not at Adderbury itself then at his bachelor pad nearby, the hunting lodge in Woodstock Park which came as a perk of his appointment as Ranger, an office for which Rochester had been petitioning Charles for some years. Through his wife, Rochester also had substantial interests in the West Country, in the shape of the extensive Malet family estates around Enmore in Somersetshire. Between their marriage in 1667 and his death thirteen years later, the couple spent most summers in Enmore; from the mid-1670s, Rochester was active in local politics, serving as an alderman in Taunton and later as Deputy Lieutenant of Somerset, responsible for collecting the region's taxes on behalf of the crown. Some of Rochester's country poems can be connected with his trips to the West Country. 'A Pastoral Dialogue between Alexis and Strephon' (not included in this edition) was billed on the title-page of the printed edition as 'written at the Bath, 1674', Rochester having stopped off en route to Enmore that year to join the Duchess of Portsmouth's travelling court at the fashionable spa resort. Its companion piece, 'A Dialogue between Strephon and Daphne', and the spa satire 'Tunbridge Wells' probably also originated from this rural mini-break (not that the courtiers spent much time mixing with the locals or admiring the countryside).

But in fact quite a number of Rochester's other poems, including those with urban settings, were also written in the country, if a remark in Gilbert Burnet's biography is to be believed. According to Burnet, Rochester 'would often go into the Country, and be for some months wholly employed in Study, or the Sallies of his Wit, which he came to direct chiefly to satire'.[13] That punctures the illusion of spontaneous poetic fecundity which earned Rochester his reputation as a master of the courtly arts of improvisation, reminding us that the brilliant effects of explosive vocal immediacy he created in the signature passages of 'rant' in poems such as 'An Imperfect Enjoyment' and 'A Ramble in St. James's Park' are in fact the result of considerable craftsmanship. But Burnet's observation also queers the pitch of Rochester's Whitehall identity at a deeper level. Tacitly but unmistakably, he was evoking the widespread contemporary understanding of the country as a moral environment, the antidote to the smoke and

---

[13] Farley-Hills (ed.), *Rochester: The Critical Heritage*, 54.

stir of life in the metropolis, and more especially at court. He was inviting readers to connect Rochester with the ruralist ethos of 'retirement' particularly embodied by one of the Earl's favourite poets, Abraham Cowley who, disappointed in his hopes of preferment at the Restoration, had withdrawn to Barn Elms in Surrey, where he devoted himself to gardening and the composition of eruditely classical and philosophically high-minded verse. Of course, this was not a position Rochester could openly adopt; the place in Rochester's work where the ethic of rural withdrawal is most explicitly at issue is in 'The Disabled Debauchee', and there it receives a sceptical debunking. The debauchee's retirement from the sexual fray is announced in the opening lines with an echo of a passage from Book II of Lucretius' *De Rerum Natura* which had become a watchword in the Restoration for the country-dweller's putative condition of sage equanimity. However, as the debauchee freely admits (taking a leaf out of one of Rochester's favourite books, La Rochefoucauld's *Maximes*), it is only because he is old and impotent and so 'good for nothing else' that he is reduced to being 'wise'.

Yet if the country did not exactly make a moralist of Rochester, there is reason to believe that it enabled a broadening and deepening of his imaginative range as a poet. Following the debacle over his 'Satire on Charles II', Rochester withdrew to Oxfordshire for the first two months of 1674, and it was later that year that his three longest and most conceptually ambitious satires—'Timon', 'A Satire against Reason and Mankind', and 'A Letter from Artemiza to Chloe'—went into circulation. Rochester's revelation of his authorship of the 'Satire on Charles II' may not have been a drunken accident but deliberately engineered by the poet as a way of extricating himself from court, and two of his poems which can be dated to the months leading up to his banishment further suggest that he was looking to the country as a regenerative environment at this crisis point in his career. Both are translations from Lucretius' epic of natural philosophy *De Rerum Natura* ('On the Nature of Things'). The first ('The Gods, by right of Nature, must possess') describes how the gods dwell in cosmic bliss, 'far removed' from the turbulent world they created; when Dryden was given sight of the translation, he immediately applied it to Rochester's own case: 'You are that Rerum Natura of your own Lucretius', he told the Earl in a letter of April or May 1673; 'Your friends in town are ready to envy the leisure you have given yourself in the country'.[14] The other extract Rochester chose to translate ('Great mother of Aeneas and of Love') is still more revealing— Lucretius' invocation to Venus as the source of nature's fertility, entreating her to inspire his verse. This translation had no circulation beyond Rochester's private household (the only copy is in the 'Portland' manuscript) and can be linked to particular circumstances obtaining there around the time of its composition. Adderbury had for some years been a predominantly female environment. In addition to Rochester's wife and mother, and his first child, Anne, born in 1669, also resident there were the poet's two nieces from the Dowager Countess's first marriage, Ellen and Anne Lee. But for most of 1673 and the early months of 1674, Rochester's family home was emphatically a place of female fecundity. Ellen Lee, aged fourteen and already married to James Bertie, son of the Earl of Abingdon, returned to live at Adderbury for the duration of her first pregnancy between the spring and winter. Towards the end of that period, Rochester's own wife also became pregnant—with a second daughter, as it turned out: Elizabeth Wilmot, named after her mother, was born in the spring or early summer of 1674. When Rochester returned to Oxfordshire in need of new inspiration, he was surrounded on all sides by evidence of Venus's regenerative power.

But his own hopes of rebirth were bedevilled with complications. Already his version of Lucretius' prayer to Venus was conspicuously awkward, closer to Latin than English in its grammatical construction, as if he were signalling some discomfort in singing the praises of natural eroticism. He certainly had good reason. Elizabeth Wilmot's pregnancy in late 1673 marked her recovery of sexual health after a bout of syphilis given her by her husband; in the spring (of all seasons) Rochester had taken her to London to undergo the excruciating mercury treatment which was then the only cure. According to John Aubrey, Rochester 'was wont to say that when he came to Brentford'—that is, when he rode back into London from Oxfordshire—'the devil entered into him and never left him till he came into the country again to Adderbury or Woodstock',[15] but in 1673 the poet had made a metropolitan hell of his rural heaven. The prospect of rural redemption receded further in subsequent years, as

[14] *The Letters of John Wilmot, Earl of Rochester*, ed. Jeremy Treglown (Oxford, 1980), 87–8.

[15] Farley-Hills (ed.), *Rochester: The Critical Heritage*, 178.

he was drawn back into the court's polluted embrace. Lucretius' paean to Venus continued to haunt his imagination—two of his mature lyrics, 'Upon his Leaving his Mistress' and 'A Young Lady to her Ancient Lover', feature clear allusions to it. But both are crucially unstable in tone, their conceits of natural sensuality beset with intimations of promiscuity, prime examples of the compound of idealism and cynicism in Rochester's most distinctive love poems. Thus, the speaker of the first poem gives as his reason for leaving his mistress that only 'meaner beauties' should be the possession of 'one happy man', whereas she like 'the kind seed-receiving earth, | To every grain affords a birth'. But is he in fact respecting her natural liberty, as a true free-thinker should, or merely mouthing libertine pieties as a means of ridding himself of a slut? Contemporary readers were divided on this question, to judge from the various placements of the poem in manuscript miscellanies: some put it next to the 'Strephon' pastorals; in others it is grouped with the brutally misogynistic lampoons 'Love to a Woman' and the pseudo-Rochesterian 'Of Marriage'. A similar quandary arises in 'A Young Lady to her Ancient Lover'. Is the lady's self-presentation as an erotic force of nature able to 'restore' the 'youthful heat' of her ageing lover with 'Brooding kisses', as 'showers in autumn fall | And a second spring recall', to be trusted, or is their unlikely union actually based on a cruder calculus of sexual and economic interests? Again, Rochester's contemporaries were apparently unsure—variants between the manuscript and printed texts make the lady seem more or less ingenuous or artful. Vigorous debate among modern critics, much of it strongly gendered, shows the poem retains its unsettling power to engage the sexual prejudices of its readers, both male and female.

Rochester's internal conflicts about the country are most intricately given form in 'A Letter from Artemiza in the Town to Chloe in the Country'. The poem adapts the mode of the Horatian verse epistle to the new cultural circumstances of the 1670s when improvements to the road network and the advent of a regular postal service meant that country-dwellers in all but the most outlying regions could receive newsletters from relatives or agents in the metropolis within twenty-four hours. Traffic between London and the country is also the poem's principal thematic concern. Artemiza begins by giving a satirical account of a 'fine Lady' newly arrived in the capital, a representative of the new wave of well-to-do rural gentry whose habit it was becoming at this period to decamp to London for the whole parliamentary and theatrical season (October to March), renting lodgings in the fashionable squares and piazzas of the town. Attacks on the vulgarity and philistinism of these wannabe urbanites were a staple of 'sex comedies' like Wycherley's *The Country Wife*, which was running as Rochester's poem went into circulation. The fine Lady conforms to type in her ham-fisted imitations of metropolitan manners. However, complication is introduced when she herself adopts an anti-rural posture, recounting the story of a young country squire who migrates to town and becomes infatuated with the whorish Corinna, debauching himself and bankrupting his family for generations to come. This loathing of her own kind exacerbates the satire on the fine Lady, but its larger consequence lies in discouraging the reader from simply identifying with an anti-ruralist viewpoint. So where should we position ourselves? The obvious answer is with Artemiza, the over-arching consciousness of the poem and ostensibly the positive standard against which the deficiencies of the fine Lady and Corinna are to be measured. But in a poem so preoccupied with location as an ethical marker, it is notable how hard Artemiza herself is to place. Rochester leaves it unclear whether she is visiting from the country or resident full-time in London. Her most famous lines, in praise of love, hover uncertainly between rural idealism and courtly world-weariness:

> Love, the most gen'rous passion of the mind,
> The softest refuge innocence can find,
> The safe director of unguided youth,
> Fraught with kind wishes, and secured by Truth,
> That cordial drop Heav'n in our cup has thrown,
> To make the nauseous draught of Life go down,
> On which one only blessing God might raise,
> In lands of atheists, subsidies of praise (ll. 40–7)

It may be that in the self-divided tone of those lines—half-Adderbury ('softest refuge'), half-Whitehall ('nauseous draught'), as it were—we are hearing something close to Rochester's own voice. When Pope quoted 'The Cordial Drop of Life is Love alone' in one of his own Horatian epistles, he attributed the sentiment not to Artemiza but to 'Wilmot'.[16]

---

[16] *The Sixth Epistle of the First Book of Horace Imitated*, ll. 126–7.

In 1679, with Rochester safely on his deathbed, 'A Letter from Artemiza to Chloe' reached print in a pirated edition. By this time, the formulation employed in its title had taken on sharp ideological connotations. The word 'country' had come to stand for a platform of political, religious, and cultural values opposed to those of the court, and *A Letter from a Person of Quality to his Friend in the Country* (1675), an explosive pamphlet attacking the policies of the Danby administration, had initiated a vogue for such mock-newsletters to country correspondents in the run-up to the Exclusion Crisis. The party groupings forged in the heat of this crisis later came to be known by the familiar terms 'Tory' and 'Whig', but while Rochester was still alive the current labels were 'court' and 'country'. Whoever was responsible for printing 'Artemiza to Chloe' may have hoped to capitalize on the uncertainty over Rochester's political affiliation, at a time when the escalation of his syphilis-related illnesses kept him out of the public eye for increasingly long periods. After the poet's death, his friend Robert Wolseley claimed that Rochester supported the campaign against 'arbitrary oppression',[17] a phrase with strong 'country' associations (as in the title of Marvell's dynamite pamphlet of 1677 *An Account of the Growth of Popery and Arbitrary Government*). This claim has been endorsed by some modern commentators, but the only one of Rochester's later poems which invites a 'country' reading is the newly authenticated 'An Allusion to Tacitus', and even there a nascent sense of political engagement coexists with the court libertine's traditional cynicism about affairs of state. Politically as well as morally, the country remained to the last a place Rochester could not fully inhabit, to which he sometimes thought of escaping but where he never fully belonged.

Church

The hell-raising Earl of Rochester died in the bosom of the Anglican church. He had begun exploring the prospects of a reconciliation in the autumn of 1679, in a series of conversations with the churchman Gilbert Burnet. A former chaplain to the King, Burnet had recently ministered to the dying Jane Roberts, a past mistress of both

---

[17] Farley-Hills (ed.), *Rochester: The Critical Heritage*, 140.

Rochester and Charles; now he was summoned to the deathbed of the arch-libertine himself. Over the course of the next six months, Burnet and Rochester conducted a rolling dialogue about 'Natural and Revealed Religion, and . . . Morality', the last of their discussions taking place two days before Rochester's death on 26 July 1680. Afterwards, Burnet wrote up his notes into *Some Passages of the Life and Death of John Earl of Rochester*, cementing an image of the poet as the 'greatest of sinners' who became 'the greatest of penitents'. But the circumstances of Rochester's conversion have always been controversial. When news of his encounters with Burnet broke in London, it was met with widespread amazement and incredulity; the budding libertine William Fanshaw returned from a visit to Woodstock to report that the Earl had not reformed but gone mad. Modern sceptics point to evidence that Rochester was no longer fully in charge of his own affairs. A particular focus of doubt has been the poet's final letter to Burnet, dated 25 June 1680, in which he formally professed 'how much I abhor what I so long loved, & how much I glory in repentance in God's service'.[18] By then Rochester was too ill to write, and though the letter is signed by him, the body of the text is in the hand of his pious mother. With the assistance of her chaplain Robert Parsons, who preached the sermon at Rochester's funeral, the Dowager Countess has been suspected of mounting a campaign to launder her son's memory, culminating in the publication of Jacob Tonson's purged 1691 edition of Rochester's verse.

One reason to take Burnet's version of events seriously is that he does not pretend to have convinced Rochester on every question. On two subjects in particular the poet kept up his defiance: 'the belief of Mysteries in the Christian Religion; which he thought no man could do, since it is not in a man's power to believe that which he cannot comprehend'; and the 'aspirings that he had observed at Court, of some of the Clergy, with the servile ways they took to attain to Preferment' (Burnet's refusal of a bishopric in 1671 may have recommended him to Rochester).[19] These two objections were regularly twinned throughout the seventeenth century by 'Erastian' thinkers, most notably Thomas Hobbes, to produce a powerful critique of the church's meddling in political affairs. Most of the anti-religious

---

[18] *The Letters of John Wilmot*, 244.
[19] Farley-Hills (ed.), *Rochester: The Critical Heritage*, 72, 77.

sentiment in Rochester's poems takes this form: in 'Seneca's *Troas*. Act. 2. Chorus', for instance, where 'Hell and the foul fiend that rules | God's everlasting fiery jails' are 'Devised by rogues' (that is, rogues in surplices), and most of all in 'A Satire against Reason and Mankind', which exposes the 'holy cheats and formal lies' (specious rituals and doctrinal innovations) power-hungry churchmen use to 'tyrannize' over their superstitious congregations. Both those poems date from 1674, following the defeat of the latest in a line of parliamentary attempts, sponsored by the Buckingham faction, to secure 'toleration' for dissenters from Anglican orthodoxy. Another poem from the same period, 'Tunbridge Wells', offers explicit support for that lost cause, mounting an unmistakably Hobbesian attack on the priest who had come to personify resistance to toleration, Samuel Parker. But once the clericalist Danby had replaced Buckingham as Charles's principal counsellor, men like Parker were in the ascendant; efforts to break the hegemony of the established church did not resume until some years after Rochester's death.

Erastian or anticlerical views should not be confused with 'atheism' in the modern sense of the term. Parker and other defenders of uniformity made a habit of referring to those outside the Anglican mainstream as 'atheists', but most were in fact strong Protestants who believed the established church was tainted with 'Popery'. A stripe of such Calvinistic or Puritan rigour is visible in the Dowager Countess of Rochester's religious writings; in arguing for toleration, then, Rochester was showing himself to be his mother's son, spiritually speaking. Outright disbelief in God was widely considered unfeasible in this period, and the anecdotal evidence associating Rochester with such disbelief needs to be interpreted with care. For example, he told Parsons that once 'at an Atheistical Meeting at a person of Quality's . . . [he] undertook to manage the Cause, and was the principal Disputant against God and Piety, and for [his] performances received the applause of the whole company'.[20] But disputing 'against God' might mean not denying his existence but criticizing his conduct, and 'piety' could be 'religiose canting' rather than simply 'belief'; in any case, Rochester's theatrical language makes it plain that he was playing up to his devilish reputation. Similar caveats apply to ostensibly atheist statements in his poems.

[20] Robert Parsons, *A Sermon Preached at the Earl of Rochester's Funeral* (1680), 23.

The case most often cited is 'After death nothing is, and nothing death', but Cowley produced a version of the same passage, and he is never credited with atheism. It is not even safe to say that Rochester's writing is implicitly atheist. Some of his contemporaries probably did use anticlerical views as a cover for radical scepticism verging on atheism: Hobbes would be an example, as well as Charles Blount, the philosopher and free-thinker with whom Rochester exchanged letters, possibly including a copy of the Seneca translation, towards the end of his life. Hobbes and Blount, though, were commoners and print-publishing authors, and thus had to be mindful of the censor (Blount's pioneering deist works appeared during the lapse of the Licensing Act in 1679) and the possibility that they might be prosecuted for blasphemy (the statute which provided for the burning of heretics was not repealed until 1677, and the bishops apparently contemplated using it against Hobbes). Rochester's situation was entirely different: a high aristocrat who enjoyed royal protection and whose work circulated anonymously in manuscript, he had little need to mask the heterodoxy of his religious views.

In fact, it is possible to argue that Rochester had less in common with sceptics like Hobbes and Blount than with their enemies at the opposite end of the spectrum of contemporary religious belief—the members of the radical sects whose irrational and solipsistic theologies they blamed for the disintegration of the polity during the Civil War era. The contemporary term for those theologies—'enthusiasm'—was applied to Rochester by his friend Francis Fane in the dedication to *Love in the Dark*. 'Others, by wearisome steps, and regular gradations, climb up to Knowledge', Fane wrote; 'your Lordship is flown up to the top of the Hill: you are an Enthusiast in Wit; a Poet and Philosopher by Revelation.'[21] That affects a contempt for human learning, attributing the power of Rochester's verse to divine inspiration, what the self-declared prophets of the 1640s and 1650s termed 'the inner light'. Of course, Fane was being rhetorically extravagant, but his analogy repays further thought. Centrally at issue here is Rochester's most famous and controversial poem, 'A Satire against Reason and Mankind'. This form of title is not necessarily authorial; several manuscript copies bill the poem as a satire 'on' or 'against' just 'Man'. But if copyists experienced it as an

---

[21] Farley-Hills (ed.), *Rochester: The Critical Heritage*, 37.

attack on reason, they were not entirely mistaken. To be sure, the libertine speaker insists ''Tis not true Reason I despise' but rather the 'false' version promulgated by his clerical adversary, an 'exalted power whose business lies | In non-sense and impossibilities'; that is, the neo-Aristotelian hybrid of rationality and faith which Hobbes and other sceptics regularly attacked as obscurantist. However, in ridiculing that rarefied notion, the speaker is led to the opposite extreme, a reductively sensationalist understanding of reason that would not have been dignified with the name by Hobbes. The overall effect of the 'Satire', a reader might well feel, is to render all human pretensions to rationality suspect. The 'Addition' abandons the idea altogether. Originally circulated separately from the main body of the poem, as a response to denunciations of its cynicism and misanthropy by Edward Stillingfleet and other leading churchmen, this defence of the 'Satire' is written in something closer to Rochester's own voice. It describes an ideal priest, the opposite of the clerical interlocutor in the 'Satire', and reason is not one of his distinguishing features; on the contrary, he must 'believe | Mysterious Truths, which no man can conceive'—transcendent doctrines so contrary to human ways of thinking ('conceive' = 'understand') that they could not possibly have been fabricated ('conceive' = 'invent') for political ends. The nearest equivalents to this model of otherworldly fideism in Restoration terms were the Quakers and other radicals whose refusal to abandon their nonconformist beliefs in the face of legal and social persecution was recognized, even by many who considered the beliefs themselves ludicrous, as a standing reproof to the hypocrisy and self-interest of the age.

Libertinism in general has been convincingly interpreted as the continuation of Civil War religious radicalism by other means. Many of the definitive practices of the libertine—swearing and profanity, sexual licentiousness, parodying liturgical forms—were pioneered by the 'antinomian' sects as marks of their having been emancipated by Christ from the moral law. When Sedley engaged in 'shewing his nakedness' on the balcony of the Cock Tavern on the evening of 16 June 1663, and (as Pepys's account goes on) 'abusing of scripture and, as it were, from thence preaching a Mountebank [i.e. mock] sermon from that pulpit', he was not doing anything that had not already been done by the Ranters twenty years earlier. The appropriation of sectarian behaviours by the court wits has generally been explained in class terms—as part of their rearguard action in defence of their status as the political elect. But in the case of Rochester, there are grounds for taking literally the idea of libertinism as a mode of spirituality. In a famous passage of his funeral sermon for the poet, Robert Parsons drew attention to a particular quality of excess in Rochester's transgressiveness, which he represented as an inverted form of religious zeal:

this was the heightening and amazing circumstance of his sins that he was so diligent and industrious to recommend and propagate them . . . framing arguments for Sin, making Proselytes to it, and writing Panegyrics upon Vice; singing Praises to the great enemy of God, and casting down Coronets and Crowns before his Throne.[22]

The singular virulence and dynamism of Rochesterian profanity readily emerges from comparison with the work of his libertine peers. But what particularly supports Parsons's intuition is the tendency for violent episodes of 'scoffing' and cursing in Rochester's poems to accompany intimations of transcendence. Two prominent cases are in 'A Ramble in St. James's Park', where the speaker's invective against Corinna escalates steeply after he remembers 'leaning' on her 'breast | Wrapped in security and rest', and in 'A Letter from Artemiza to Chloe', where Artemiza's famous description of Love as 'That cordial drop Heav'n in our cup has thrown, | To make the nauseous draught of Life go down' crosses spiritual idealism with gross eucharistic parody ('drop' as 'sperm', 'cup' as 'vagina') in a single couplet.

But the master-instance of the pattern is 'Upon Nothing', for generations of readers the archetypal expression of Rochester's spirituality. Here the suggestion of transcendence and its aggressive cancellation are not merely adjacent but coterminous. The poem's denial of the possibility of meaning in the face of an all-consuming nothingness is so absolute that it takes on a quality of metaphysical affirmation—Rochester's 'Nothing', as Samuel Johnson was only the first to observe, 'must be considered as having not only a negative but a kind of positive signification'.[23] The result is a kind of devout nihilism, disbelief escalated to such a pitch of intensity that it comes

[22] Ibid. 46.
[23] 'Rochester', in *The Lives of the Poets*, ed. Roger Lonsdale and John Mullan (Oxford, 2009), 117.

to sound like fundamentalist piety. But to judge from the poem's contemporary popularity with religious readers, it could also be directly assimilated to Christian styles of thought. Our only indication of the poem's date of composition comes from a note on the copy in the 'personal miscellany' of the nonconformist John Pye, and a number of Anglican churchmen also kept copies. In particular, we now know that Rochester's mother took a keen interest in the poem, going to the trouble of collating two textually discrepant manuscript versions, probably in the run-up to the publication of *1691*. Such readers might have seen 'Upon Nothing' as a throwback to medieval Christianity's loathing of all things earthly, 'contemptus mundi'; or the poem's violent energies of negation might have reminded them of the iconoclastic extremism of the 1640s, when faith meant annihilating human representations of the divine. Or perhaps they just remembered that for any true believer in the crucified Christ absence and abnegation is the way to God. Rather than any of Burnet's arguments or his mother's strong-arm tactics, it was contemplation of the mystery of the crucifixion (which 'no man can conceive') that provided the final impetus for Rochester's conversion. A few days before his death, Parsons read to him the verses from Isaiah 53 about the 'suffering servant' who prefigures Christ in submitting to revilement and brutalization in the cause of human redemption. As he listened, Rochester 'felt an inward force upon him, which did so enlighten his mind, and convince him, that he could resist it no longer', according to Burnet's report; 'For the words had an authority which did shoot like Rays or Beams in his Mind'.[24] The words were these:

He is despised and rejected of men; a man of sorrows, and acquainted with grief; and we hid as it were our faces from him; he was despised, and we esteemed him not.

Surely he hath borne our griefs, and carried our sorrows: yet we did esteem him stricken, smitten of God, and afflicted.

But he was wounded for our transgressions, he was bruised for our iniquities: the chastisement of our peace was upon him; and with his stripes we are healed.

[24] Farley-Hills (ed.), *Rochester: The Critical Heritage*, 82.

NOTE ON THE TEXT

ONLY a few of Rochester's poems were printed with his approval in his lifetime. Once his health had broken down, broadside printings of some of his politer satires began creeping out, followed within weeks of his death by a surreptitious edition of *Poems on Several Occasions by the E. of R—* (1680). The establishment printer Jacob Tonson brought out a second edition in 1691. *1680* and *1691* have formed the basis of all previous modern editions of Rochester aimed at the general reader. Yet both are in different ways unreliable. *1680* was rushed out in a bid to capitalize on Rochester's notoriety by a printer whom agents acting on behalf of the poet's immediate family subsequently sought to unmask and prosecute. About half the poems it contains are not by Rochester at all. *1691*, almost certainly instigated by Rochester's pious mother, excluded or bowdlerized his most scandalous verse to make him fit for the new age of moral reform under William III and Mary. Rochester himself published his work in manuscript, by circulating copies to members of his coterie at court. The texts then radiated outwards through successive acts of copying. Interpreting the mass of often contradictory textual evidence which results from such 'scribal publication' was a task to which Harold Love devoted much of his scholarly life, culminating in his monumental Oxford English Texts edition of *The Works of John Wilmot, Earl of Rochester* which appeared in 1999. The texts in this new selected edition are modernized versions of Love's, and my aim more largely is to transmit the fruits of his textual scholarship beyond the narrow coterie of specialists to general readers of Rochester's work.

Scholars before Love who edited Rochester from manuscript applied copy-text theory. They selected a 'best manuscript' for each poem, emending it from other sources more or less freely when it was in obvious error or otherwise unsatisfactory. But Love came to believe that this approach was tenable only for a handful of Rochester's poems, those of his polite lyrics which did not circulate far beyond his immediate family. (I have recorded Love's choices of copy-text in the headnotes to these poems.) For the majority of Rochester's poems, however, Love established his texts through 'recensional editing'.

Having collated all the available copies, he mapped out the systemic relations between them, before using this overall 'transmission history' to reconstruct a text featuring those of the variants he judged closest to the readings of the lost authorial archetype. This method is not entirely failsafe, but it does provide the surest available foundation for approaching Rochester's texts. Love documented his reasonings in his exhaustive textual notes, with the stated intention of enabling scholars to reassess his verdicts for themselves. No evidence emerged during my own research to contradict his transmission histories, although I have been able to examine only a small minority of the two hundred or so manuscripts worldwide he and his research assistant Meredith Sherlock collated. Further endorsement of Love's approach was provided by a group of new sources I uncovered while preparing this edition. They include two copies of 'Upon Nothing', a systematically paradoxical piece which circulated widely but flummoxed many of its copyists, with the result that its 'textual tradition offers', according to Love, 'every conceivable kind of editorial problem'. The new copies are entirely orthodox members of two of the four textual sub-groups discriminated in his transmission history of the poem.

However, I have not accepted Love's decisions wholesale. For all its cogency and comprehensiveness, his method did not free him from having to make marginal judgements in particular cases where respectable sources offer contradictory evidence. His conclusions in such cases, by his own admission, 'cannot claim finality', and I have my doubts about some of them. As a matter of principle, though, I have refrained from altering the substantives of Love's texts. The one exception is in the matter of titles: where poems which Rochester probably just called 'Song' or 'Satire' later acquired more descriptive handles I have retained them for their readerly convenience. These cases are documented in the headnotes. Otherwise, it seemed best not to add a further layer of eclecticism to Love's reconstructed texts (readers interested in the detail of their genesis must refer to his edition). Instead, a selection of cases where his readings are disputable are addressed in the notes, by recording variants from other sources. The cases have been selected for their direct critical interest, because they raise provocative questions not only about the poems in which they appear but also Rochester's writing more generally. Readers should not, of course, suppose that a passage for which no variants are specified in the notes is therefore textually stable. The only comprehensive account of Rochester's texts is in Love's edition. I have, though, sought to provide readers with the means of engaging in informed debate about the variants which are recorded here. Since this involves not just weighing up the readings themselves but also comparing the different types of sources in which they occur, information about the provenance and character of those manuscripts referred to by name in the notes is laid out in an 'Index of Manuscripts' at the back of the edition.

All the poems in this edition can now be confidently assigned to Rochester. I have included only three Love thought suspect. 'An Allusion to Tacitus' has since been confirmed as Rochester's by new manuscript evidence, while 'Timon' was shown by stylometric analyses conducted by Love's colleague John Burrows to be 'primarily Rochester's'; the case of 'Tunbridge Wells' remains more problematic (see the headnote) but I concur with the many editors and commentators who have felt that parts of it at least are simply too good to have been written by any poet at work in 1674 other than Rochester. The task of selection has not been too arduous. More than two-thirds of the canon as defined by Love is included (52 out of 71 poems), and no substantial work omitted. The matter of arrangement was more problematic. Chronological order is the default choice in selections of this kind, but evidence about the dates of Rochester's poems is available only for the theatre epilogues, a couple of the translations, and those of the major satires which feature topical references. Like Love and his predecessor Keith Walker, I have preferred to organize the poems by genre. This approach too has its disadvantages. Generic experimentation is a central feature of Rochester's best work (discussed in the Introduction). In particular, he persistently eroded the distinction between lyric and dramatic verse. Hence, the most contentious of my designations, 'Dramatic Monologues' (defended in the headnote to 'The Disabled Debauchee'). But all my categorizations are to some degree provisional, and I hope readers will contemplate alternatives. Within each category, the sequencing is chronological wherever possible. For the 'Songs and Love Lyrics' I have taken my lead from the compilers of Restoration manuscript miscellanies. Generally they grouped lyrics by theme, and I have kept some of their linkages (e.g. the two absence poems 'The Mistress' and 'Absent from thee I languish still'), but they also tried out riskier conjunctions, in particular between polite and obscene lyrics. My own arrangements are meant to be debatable, if not frankly provocative; contemporary alternatives are recorded in the headnotes. Readers are invited to think of others, to re-make these *Selected Poems of Rochester* into their own 'personal miscellany' of his work.

The degree sign (°) indicates a note at the back of the book.

SELECT BIBLIOGRAPHY

Editions of Rochester

The Gyldenstolpe Manuscript Miscellany of Poems by John Wilmot, Earl of Rochester, and other Restoration Authors, ed. Bror Danielsson and David Vieth (New Haven, 1968).

Singing to Phillis: Settings of Poems by the Earl of Rochester (1647–80), ed. Steven Devine and Nicholas Fisher (Huntingdon, 2009).

The Complete Works of John Wilmot, Earl of Rochester, ed. Harold Love (Oxford, 1999).

The Letters of John Wilmot, Earl of Rochester, ed. Jeremy Treglown (Oxford, 1980).

John Wilmot, Earl of Rochester: The Poems and Lucina's Rape, ed. Keith Walker and Nicholas Fisher (Oxford, 2010).

Biography

Burnet, Gilbert, *Some Passages of the Life and Death of the Right Honourable John Earl of Rochester* (1680).

Fisher, Nicholas, '"I abhorr what I soe long lov'd: An Exploration of Rochester's "death bed repentance"', *The Seventeenth Century*, 26 (2011), 323–49.

Johnson, J. W., *A Profane Wit: The Life of John Wilmot, Earl of Rochester* (Rochester, NY, 2004).

Johnson, Samuel, 'Life of Rochester', in *Lives of the English Poets: A Selection*, ed. Roger Lonsdale and John Mullan (Oxford, 2009).

Lamb, Jeremy, *So Idle a Rogue: The Life and Death of Lord Rochester* (London, 1993).

Love, Harold, 'Hamilton's *Mémoires de la vie du comte de Grammont* and the reading of Rochester', *Restoration: Studies in English Literary Culture, 1660–1700*, 20 (1996), 95–102.

Parsons, Robert, *A Sermon Preached at the Funeral of the Rt Honourable John Earl of Rochester* (Oxford, 1680).

Scribal Publication and Editorial History

Davis, Paul 'An Unrecorded Collection of Restoration Scribal Verse, Including Three New Rochester Manuscripts', *English Manuscript Studies 1100–1700*, 18 (2013).

Fisher, Nicholas, 'Jacob Tonson and the Earl of Rochester', *The Library*, 7th series, 6 (2005), 133–60.

Fisher, Nicholas, 'Manuscript Miscellanies and the Rochester Canon', *English Manuscript Studies 1100–1700*, 13 (2007), 270–95.

Hammond, Paul, 'Censorship in the Manuscript Transmission of Restoration Poetry', in *The Making of Restoration Poetry* (Woodbridge, 2006).

——'Rochester and his Editors', in *The Making of Restoration Poetry* (Woodbridge, 2006).

Harold Love, 'Scribal Texts and Literary Communities: The Rochester Circle and Osborn b 105', *Studies in Bibliography*, 42 (1989), 219–35.

——*Scribal Publication in Seventeenth-Century England* (Oxford, 1993).

——'Refining Rochester: Private Texts and Public Readers', *Harvard Library Bulletin*, 7 (1996), 40–9.

——'Rochester: A Tale of Two Manuscripts', *Yale University Library Gazette*, 72 (1997), 41–53.

Vieth, David, *Attribution in Restoration Poetry: A Study of Rochester's Poems of 1680* (New Haven, 1963).

Historical and Cultural Contexts

Chernaik, Warren, *Sexual Freedom in Restoration Literature* (Cambridge, 1995).

Goldie, Mark, 'Danby, the Bishops and the Whigs', in Tim Harris, Paul Seaward, and Mark Goldie (eds.), *The Politics of Religion in Restoration England* (Oxford, 1990).

Hammond, Paul, 'The King's Two Bodies: Representations of Charles II', in Jeremy Black (ed.), *Culture, Politics and Society in Britain, 1660–1800* (Manchester, 1991).

Harris, Brice (ed.), *The Poems of Charles Sackville, Sixth Earl of Dorset* (New York, 1979).

Harris, Tim, *Restoration: Charles II and His Kingdoms 1660–1685* (London, 2005).

Howe, Elizabeth, *The First English Actresses* (Cambridge, 1992).

Keeble, N. H., *The Restoration: England in the 1660s* (Oxford, 2002).

Lord, George deForest (ed.), *Poems on Affairs of State: Augustan Satirical Verse, 1660–1714*. Volume I: 1660–1678 (New Haven, 1963).

Love, Harold, 'Who were the Restoration Audience?', *Yearbook of English Studies*, 10 (1980), 21–44.

——'Dryden, Rochester, and the Invention of the "Town"', in Claude Rawson and Aaron Santesso (eds.), *John Dryden (1631–1700): His Politics, His Plays, and His Poets* (Newark, NJ, 1994).

——*English Clandestine Satire, 1660–1702* (Oxford, 2004).

——and Hume, Robert D. (eds.), *Works associated with George Villiers, 2nd Duke of Buckingham* (Oxford, 2007).

Marshall, Alan, *The Age of Faction: Court Politics, 1660–1702* (Manchester, 1999).

Mengel, Jr., E. F. (ed.), *Poems on Affairs of State: Augustan Satirical Verse, 1660–1714*. Volume II: 1678–1681 (New Haven, 1965).

Owen, Susan (ed.), *A Companion to Restoration Drama* (Oxford, 2002).

Picard, Liza, *Restoration London* (1997).

Spurr, John, *The Restoration Church of England, 1646–1689* (Oxford, 1991).

—— *England in the 1670s: 'This Masquerading Age'* (Oxford, 2000).

Tilmouth, Christopher, *Passion's Triumph over Reason: A History of the Moral Imagination from Spenser to Rochester* (Oxford, 2007).

Treglown, Jeremy, 'Scepticism and Parody in the Restoration', *Modern Language Review*, 75 (1980), 18–47.

Wilson, John Harold (ed.), *Court Satires of the Restoration* (Columbus, OH, 1976).

Yardley, Bruce, 'George Villiers, Second Duke of Buckingham, and the Politics of Toleration', *Huntington Library Quarterly*, 55 (1992), 317–37.

Zwicker, Steven N., 'Virgins and Whores: The Politics of Sexual Misconduct in the 1660s', in Conal Condren and A. D. Cousins (eds.), *The Political Identity of Andrew Marvell* (Aldershot, 1990).

General Studies and Anthologies of Criticism

Burns, Edward (ed.), *Reading Rochester* (Liverpool, 1995).

Erskine-Hill, Howard, 'Rochester: Augustan or Explorer?', in G. R. Hibbard (ed.), *Renaissance and Modern Essays Presented to Vivian de Sola Pinto in Celebration of his Seventieth Birthday* (New York, 1972).

Farley-Hills, David, *Rochester's Poetry* (London, 1978).

—— (ed.), *John Wilmot, Earl of Rochester: The Critical Heritage* (London, 1972).

Fisher, Nicholas (ed.), *That Second Bottle: Essays on John Wilmot, Earl of Rochester* (Manchester, 2000).

Greer, Germaine, *John Wilmot, Earl of Rochester* (Horndon, 2000).

Gunn, Thom, 'Saint John the Rake', in Jonathan F. S. Post (ed.), *Green Thoughts, Green Shades: Essays by Contemporary Poets on the Early Modern Lyric* (Berkeley and Los Angeles, 2000).

Righter, Anne, 'John Wilmot, Earl of Rochester', *Proceedings of the British Academy*, 53 (1967), 46–69.

Thormählen, Marianne, *Rochester: The Poems in Context* (Cambridge, 1993).

Treglown, Jeremy (ed.), *The Spirit of Wit: Reconsiderations of Rochester* (Oxford, 1982).

Vieth, David (ed.), *John Wilmot, Earl of Rochester: Critical Essays* (New York, 1988).

Studies of Particular Aspects of Rochester's Work

Alsop, D. K., '"An Epistolary Essay from M. G. to O. B. upon Their Mutuall Poems" and the Problem of the Persona in Rochester's Poetry', *Restoration: Studies in English Literary Culture, 1660–1700*, 12 (1988), 61–8.

Baines, Paul, 'From "Nothing" to "Silence": Rochester and Pope', in Burns (ed.), *Reading Rochester*.

Carver, Larry, 'Rascal before the Lord: Rochester's Religious Rhetoric', in Vieth (ed.), *Rochester: Critical Essays*.

Ellenzweig, Sarah, '*Hitherto Propertied*: Rochester's Aristocratic Alienation and the Paradox of Class Formation in Restoration England', *English Literary History*, 69 (2002), 703–25.

——'The Faith of Unbelief: Rochester's "Satyre", Deism, and Religious Freethinking in Restoration England', *Journal of British Studies*, 44 (2005), 27–45.

Everett, Barbara, 'The Sense of Nothing', in Treglown (ed.), *Spirit of Wit*.

Fabricant, Caole, 'Rochester's World of Imperfect Enjoyment', *Journal of English and Germanic Philology*, 73 (1974), 338–50.

Fisher, Nicholas, 'Love in the Ayre: Rochester's Songs and their Music', in Fisher (ed.), *That Second Bottle*.

——'Rochester's Contemporary Reception: The Evidence of the Memorial Verses', *Restoration: Studies in Literary Culture, 1660–1700*, 30 (2006), 1–14.

——'The Contemporary Reception of Rochester's *A Satyr against Mankind*', *Review of English Studies*, 57 (2006), 185–220.

——'Rochester's *An Allusion to Tacitus*', *Notes & Queries*, 255 (2010), 503–7.

——and Jenkinson, Matt, 'Rochester and the Specter of Libertinism', *Huntington Library Quarterly*, 70 (2007), 537–52.

Griffin, Dustin, 'Rochester and the "Holiday Writers"', in Dustin Griffin and David Vieth (eds.), *Rochester and Court Poetry: Papers Presented at a Clark Library Seminar, 11 May 1985* (Los Angeles, 1988).

Hammond, Brean, 'An Allusion to Horace', Jonson's Ghost and the Second Poets' War', in Burns (ed.), *Reading Rochester*.

——and Kewes, Paulina, '*A Satyre against Reason and Mankind* from Page to Stage', in Fisher (ed.), *That Second Bottle*.

Hammond, Paul, 'Rochester's Homoeroticism', in Fisher (ed.), *That Second Bottle*.

Hopkins, Paul, '"As it was not spoke by Mr. Haines": An Unpublished Attack on Shadwell in an Epilogue by Rochester', in R. C. Alston (ed.), *Order and Connexion: Studies in Bibliography and Book History: Selected Papers from The Munby Seminar, Cambridge, July 1994* (Cambridge, 1997).

Love, Harold, 'Rochester and the Traditions of Satire', in Harold Love (ed.), *Restoration Literature: Critical Approaches* (London, 1972).

—— 'Shadwell, Rochester and the Crisis of Amateurism', *Restoration: Studies in Literary Culture, 1660–1700*, 20 (1996), 119–34.

—— 'Nell Gwyn and Rochester's "By all Love's soft, yet mighty Pow'rs"', *Notes & Queries*, 247 (2002), 355–7.

Manning, Gillian, 'Rochester's *Satyr against Reason and Mankind* and Contemporary Religious Debate', *The Seventeenth Century*, 8 (1993), 99–122.

—— '*Artemiza to Chloe*: Rochester's "Female" Epistle', in Fisher (ed.), *That Second Bottle*.

Miller, Henry Knight, 'The Paradoxical Encomium with Special Reference to its Vogue in England, 1600–1800', *Modern Philology*, 53 (1956), 145–78.

Paulson, Ronald, 'Rochester: The Body Politic and the Body Private', in Louis Landa and Aubrey Williams (eds.), *The Author in His Work: Essays on a Problem in Criticism* (New Haven, 1978).

Quaintance, Richard E., 'French Sources of the Restoration "Imperfect Enjoyment" Poem', *Philological Quarterly*, 42 (1963), 190–9.

Rawson, Claude, 'Lordly Accents: Rochester', in *Satire and Sentiment 1660–1830: Stress Points in the Augustan Tradition* (New Haven, 1994).

Robinson, K. E., 'The Art of Violence in Rochester's Satire', in Claude Rawson and Jenny Mecziems (eds.), *English Satire and the Satiric Tradition* (Oxford, 1984).

Rogers, Pat, '*An Allusion to Horace*', in Treglown (ed.), *Spirit of Wit*.

Saslow, Edward, 'A "New" Epilogue by Rochester', *Restoration: Studies in Literary Culture, 1660–1700*, 20 (1996), 1–9.

Selden, Raman, 'Rochester and Oldham: "High Rants in Profaneness"', in Burns (ed.), *Reading Rochester*.

Thormählen, Marianne, 'Rochester and "The Fall": The Roots of Discontent', *English Studies*, 69 (1988), 396–409.

—— 'Rochester and Jealousy: Consistent Inconsistencies', *Durham University Journal*, 80 (1988), 213–18.

—— 'Dissolver of Reason: Rochester and the Nature of Love', in Fisher (ed.), *That Second Bottle*.

Treglown, Jeremy, 'The Satirical Inversion of Some English Sources in Rochester's Poetry', *Review of English Studies*, 24 (1973), 42–8.

Vieth, David, '"Pleased with the contradiction and the sin": The Perverse Artistry of Rochester's Lyrics', *Tennessee Studies in Literature*, 25 (1980), 35–56.

Wilcox, Helen, 'Gender and Artfulness in Rochester's "Song of a Young Lady to Her Ancient Lover"', in Burns (ed.), *Reading Rochester*.

Wilcoxon, Reba, 'Pornography, Obscenity and Rochester's "The Imperfect Enjoyment"', *Studies in English Literature*, 15 (1975), 375–90.

Wilcox, Helen, 'The Rhetoric of Sex in Rochester's Burlesque', *Papers in Language and Literature*, 12 (1976), 273–84.

Wintle, Sarah, 'Libertinism and Sexual Politics', in Treglown (ed.), *Spirit of Wit*.

Further Reading in Oxford World's Classics

Four Restoration Libertine Plays, ed. Deborah Payne Fisk.

Restoration Literature: An Anthology, ed. Paul Hammond.

Wycherley, William, *The Country Wife and Other Plays*, ed. Peter Dixon.

A CHRONOLOGY OF JOHN WILMOT, EARL OF ROCHESTER

1647 Born at Ditchley House, Oxfordshire (1 April), son of Henry, Lord Wilmot and his second wife, Anne St John, widow of Sir Henry Lee.

1651 Henry Wilmot helps Charles II escape to France following the defeat of the royalist army at the Battle of Worcester.

1652 Henry Wilmot created Earl of Rochester (13 December).

1658 John Wilmot becomes second Earl of Rochester, following the death of his father in Ghent (19 April).

1660 Rochester enters Wadham College, Oxford (18 January). Charles II returns to London as King (29 May). Barbara Palmer, later Duchess of Cleveland, becomes Charles II's mistress (June).

1661–4 Rochester travels on the Continent with his tutor, Dr Andrew Balfour.

1664 Makes his formal debut as a courtier (25 December), delivering a letter to the King from his sister Henrietta, wife of Louis XIV's brother, the Duc D'Orléans.

1665 Botched attempt to abduct and marry the Somerset heiress Elizabeth Malet (26 May) leads to Rochester being imprisoned in the Tower of London for three weeks.

1665–6 Enlists in the navy during the Second Anglo-Dutch War, distinguishing himself by his bravery at Solebay (September 1665) and the 'St James's Fight' (July 1666).

1666 Appointed Gentleman of the Bedchamber to Charles II (21 March) with pension of £1,000 a year (c.£120,000 now) and lodgings within Whitehall Palace.

1667 Marries Elizabeth Malet (29 January). Takes up his seat in the House of Lords (10 October). Dutch fleet invades the Medway, towing away the *Royal Charles* (13 June). Clarendon goes into exile in France (29 November).

1669 Strikes Thomas Killigrew in the presence of the King (16 February). Sent to Paris to deliver a letter to Charles II's sister (12 March), remaining until July. First child, Anne Wilmot, baptized (30 April). Nell Gwyn becomes Charles II's mistress. Rochester undergoing mercury treatment for urinary disorder caused by kidney stones or possibly syphilis (November).

1670 Charles signs secret Treaty of Dover with Louis XIV (22 May). Rochester takes a house next door to the Lincoln's Inn playhouse on Portugal Row (summer).

1671 Only son, Charles Wilmot, baptized (2 January). Louise de Kéroualle, later Duchess of Portsmouth, replaces the Duchess of Cleveland as Charles II's principal mistress (probably October).

1672 Charles II issues Declaration of Indulgence (15 March). 'The Imperfect Enjoyment' (possibly). 'What vain unnecessary things are men', probably as epilogue for all-female revival of Fletcher's *The Bloody Brother*.

1673 Begins training the actress Elizabeth Barry. 'The Disabled Debauchee' (circulating in February), 'A Ramble in St. James's Park' (circulating in March), 'Translation from Lucretius, *De Rerum Natura*, ii. 646–51' (spring), 'Upon his drinking a bowl' (summer?). Flees court after accidentally showing the King his 'Satire on Charles II' during the Christmas festivities at Whitehall.

1674 In disgrace at Adderbury until mid-February. Fall of Buckingham (January). Rochester appointed Ranger of Woodstock Park (27 February). Spends the summer in Bath as a member of the Duchess of Portsmouth's retinue. 'A Dialogue between Strephon and Daphne.' Second daughter, Elizabeth Wilmot, baptized (13 July). 'Timon.' Collapse of the 'Cabal' ministry (September). Earl of Danby becomes Charles II's chief minister. 'Seneca's *Troas*. Act. 2. Chorus' (possibly circulating). 'Tunbridge Wells', 'A Satire against Reason and Mankind.'

1675 Granted permission by the King to begin building new apartments at Whitehall (4 January). Appointed Master, Surveyor, and Keeper of the King's hawks (24 January). Takes possession of the High Lodge at Woodstock, thereafter his bachelor retreat. 'A Letter from Artemiza in the Town to Chloe in the Country' (circulating by spring 1675?). Begins affair with Elizabeth Barry. 'Epilogue to *Love in the Dark*' (May). Flees court after smashing the King's glass sundials in the Privy Garden (25 June). 'An Allusion to Horace' (winter).

1676 In disgrace at Adderbury and Woodstock. Partially blind and urinating blood from advanced syphilis. Third daughter, Malet Wilmot, baptized (6 January). Rumours of his death circulating at Whitehall (February). Some of Rochester's lyrics begin appearing in printed songbooks. The Epsom 'affray' in which his friend Captain Downs is killed defending him (17 June). 'To the Post Boy.' Banished from court, Rochester spends the summer selling remedies as the quack doctor 'Alexander Bendo' in London's suburbs.

1677 'Epilogue to *Circe*' (May). Elected Alderman of Taunton, near his wife's estates at Enmore in Somerset. 'Love and Life' anonymously published in *Songs for 1, 2 & 3 Voyces*. Birth of Elizabeth Clerke, Rochester's daughter by Elizabeth Barry.

1678 Reported by his Oxfordshire neighbour John Verney as 'very ill and very penitent' (spring). 'Upon Nothing' (circulating in May). Titus Oates's allegations launch the 'Popish Plot' crisis (August). Impeachment of Danby (December).

1679 'My Lord All-pride', 'A very heroical epistle in answer to Ephelia' probably in circulation. 'An Allusion to Tacitus' (spring?). Parliament dissolved to prevent the Exclusion Bill from becoming law (12 July). Anonymous printed editions of 'A Satire against Reason and Mankind', 'A Letter from Artemiza in the Town to Chloe in the Country', and 'Upon Nothing'. 'An essay on satire', by Mulgrave and Dryden, begins circulating (autumn). 'An Epistolary Essay, from M. G. to O. B. upon their mutual Poems.' Weekly conversations between Rochester and Gilbert Burnet begin (October).

1680 Reconciliation with the Church of England. Final conversations with Burnet (20–24 July). Dies at High Lodge, Woodstock (26 July). Unauthorized edition of *Poems on Several Occasions by the E. of R—* (autumn). Publication of *Some Passages of the Life and Death of John Earl of Rochester* by Gilbert Burnet (November).

SELECTED POEMS

SONGS AND LOVE LYRICS

The Discovery

Celia, that faithful servant you disown
Would in obedience keep his love unknown;
But bright ideas, such as you inspire,°
We can no more conceal than not admire.
My heart at home in my own breast did dwell,   5
Like humble hermit in a peaceful cell.
Unknown and undisturbed it rested there,
Stranger alike to hope and to despair.
Now Love with a tumultuous train invades
The sacred quiet of those hallowed shades.   10
His fatal flames shine out to every eye,
Like blazing comets in a winter sky.
How can my passion merit your offence,
That challenges so little recompence:°
For I am one born only to admire;   15
Too humble e'er to hope, scarce to desire,
A thing whose bliss depends upon your will,
Who would be proud you'd deign to use him ill.
Then give me leave to glory in my chain,
My fruitless sighs, and my unpitied pain.   20
Let me but ever love, and ever be
Th'example of your pow'r and cruelty.
Since so much scorn does in your breast reside,
Be more indulgent to its mother, pride.
Kill all you strike, and trample on their graves;   25
But own the fates of your neglected slaves:°
When in the crowd yours undistinguished lies,
You give away the triumph of your eyes.
Perhaps (obtaining this) you'll think I find
More mercy than your anger has designed: 30
But Love has carefully contrived for me
The last perfection of misery.

For to my state the hopes of common peace,°
Which every wretch enjoys in death, must cease:
My worst of fates attends me in my grave,   35
Since, dying, I must be no more your slave.

Song

Give me leave to rail at you,
(I ask nothing but my due),
To call you false, and then to say
You shall not keep my heart a day.
But (alas!) against my will,   5
I must be your captive still.
Ah! be kinder then, for I
Cannot change, and would not die.°

Kindness has resistless charms,
All besides but weakly move;   10
Fiercest Anger it disarms,
And clips the wings of flying Love.°
Beauty does the heart invade,
Kindness only can persuade;
It gilds the lover's servile chain   15
And makes the slave grow pleased and vain.

The Answer
[*by Elizabeth Wilmot, Countess of Rochester*]

Nothing adds to your fond fire°
More than scorn and cold disdain:
I to cherish your desire
Kindness used, but 'twas in vain.
You insulted on your slave,°   5
Humble love you soon refused:
Hope not then a pow'r to have
Which ingloriously you used.

Think not, Thyrsis, I will e'er
By my love my empire lose.   10
You grow constant through despair;
Love returned you would abuse.
Though you still possess my heart,
Scorn and rigour I must feign.
Ah! forgive that only art   15
Love has left your love to gain.°

You that could my heart subdue,
To new conquests ne'er pretend:°
Let your example make me true
And of a conquered foe, a friend.   20
Then if e'er I should complain
Of your empire, or my chain,
Summon all your pow'rful charms,
And kill the rebel in your arms.°

Song

While on these lovely looks I gaze,
    To see a wretch pursuing°
In raptures of a blest amaze
    His pleasing, happy ruin,
'Tis not for pity that I move:°   5
    His fate is too aspiring
Whose heart, broke with a load of love,
    Dies wishing and admiring.

But if this murder you'd forgo,
    Your slave from death removing,   10
Let me your art of charming know
    Or learn you mine of loving.
But whether life or death betide
    In love 'tis equal measure:
The victor lives with empty pride,   15
    The vanquished dies with pleasure.°

Song

Phyllis, be gentler I advise,
    Make up for time misspent;
When beauty on its death-bed lies,
    'Tis high time to repent.°

Such is the malice of your fate°   5
    That makes you old so soon,°
Your pleasure ever comes too late,
    How early e'er begun.

Think what a wretched thing is she
    Whose stars contrive in spite   10
The morning of her love should be
    Her fading beauty's night.

Then if to make your ruin more
    You'll peevishly be coy,
Die with the scandal of a whore,°   15
    And never know the joy.

The Mistress

An age in her embraces passed
Would seem a winter's day,
Where life and light with envious haste
Are torn and snatched away.

But oh! how slowly minutes roll   5
When absent from her eyes
That feed my love, which is my soul,
It languishes and dies;

For then, no more a soul but shade,
It mournfully does move   10
And haunts my breast, by absence made
The living tomb of love.

You wiser men, despise me not
Whose lovesick fancy raves
On shades of souls and heav'n knows what,   15
Short ages, living graves.°

Whene'er those wounding eyes so full°
Of sweetness you did see,
Had you not been profoundly dull
You had gone mad like me.°   20

Nor censure us, you who perceive
My best belov'd and me
Sigh and lament, complain and grieve:
You think we disagree—

Alas! 'tis sacred Jealousy,   25
Love raised to an extreme,
The only proof 'twixt her and me
We love and do not dream.

Fantastic fancies fondly move°
And in frail joys believe,   30
Taking false pleasure for true love;
But pain can ne'er deceive.

Kind jealous doubt, tormenting fear
And anxious cares (when past)
Prove our hearts' treasure fixed and dear,   35
And make us blest at last.°

God does not Heav'n afford until
In purgatory we
Have felt the utmost pains of Hell—
Then why the devil should she?   40

Song

Absent from thee I languish still;
Then ask me not when I return:
The straying fool 'twill plainly kill
To wish all day, all night to mourn.

Dear, from thine arms then let me fly,   5
That my fantastic mind may prove°
The torments it deserves to try
That tears my fixed heart from my love.

When wearied with a world of woe
To thy safe bosom I retire,   10
Where love and peace and truth do flow,
May I contented there expire

Lest, once more wand'ring from that heav'n,
I fall on some base heart unblest,
Faithless to thee, false, unforgiv'n,   15
And lose my everlasting rest.

[Song]
[Version 1]

How happy, Chloris, were they free,
    Might our enjoyments prove,
But you with formal jealousy°
    Are still tormenting love.

Let us, since wit instructs us how,   5
    Raise pleasure to the top;
If rival Bottle you'll allow,°
    I'll suffer rival Fop.

There's not a brisk insipid spark°
    That flutters in the Town°   10
But with your wanton eyes you mark
    The coxcomb for your own.

You never think it worth your care
   How empty nor how dull
The heads of your admirers are,   15
   So that their purse be full.

All this you freely may confess,
   Yet we'll not disagree;
For did you love your pleasures less
   You were not fit for me.   20

[Song]
[Version 2]

How perfect, Chloris, and how free
Would these enjoyments prove,
But you with formal jealousy
Are still tormenting love.

Let us (since wit instructs us how)   5
Raise pleasure to the top;
If rival bottle you'll allow
I'll suffer rival fop.

There's not a brisk insipid spark
That flutters in the Town   10
But with your wanton eyes you mark
Him out to be your own.

You never think it worth your care
How empty nor how dull
The heads of your admirers are,   15
So that their purse be full.

All this you freely may confess,
Yet we'll not disagree,
For did you love your pleasures less
You were not fit for me.   20

Whilst I, my passion to pursue,
Am whole nights taking in
The lusty juice of grapes, take you
The juice of lusty men.

Upbraid me not that I design   25
Tricks to delude your charms,
When running after mirth and wine
I leave your longing arms;

For wine (whose power alone can raise
Our thoughts so far above)   30
Affords ideas fit to praise°
What we think fit to love.

To a Lady, in a Letter

Such perfect bliss, fair Chloris, we
    In our enjoyment prove,
'Tis pity restless jealousy
    Should mingle with our love.

Let us (since wit has taught us how)   5
    Raise pleasure to the top:
You rival Bottle must allow,
    I'll suffer rival Fop.

Think not in this, that I design
    A treason 'gainst Love's charms,   10
When following the god of wine
    I leave my Chloris' arms;

Since you have that, for all your haste°
    (At which I'll ne'er repine),
Will take his liquour off as fast   15
    As I can take off mine.

There's not a brisk insipid spark
    That flutters in the Town
But with your wanton eyes you mark
    Him out to be your own.   20

Nor do you think it worth your care
    How empty and how dull
The heads of your admirers are,
    So that their cods be full.°

All this you freely may confess   25
    Yet we ne'er disagree,
For did you love your pleasure less
    You were no match for me.

Whilst I my pleasure to pursue
    Whole nights am taking in   30
The lusty juice of grapes, take you
    The juice of lusty men.

Against Constancy

Tell me no more of constancy,
    The frivolous pretence°
Of cold age, narrow jealousy,
    Disease, and want of sense.°

Let duller fools on whom kind chance   5
    Some easy heart hath thrown,
Since they no higher can advance,
    Be kind to one alone.

Old men and weak, whose idle flame°
    Their own defects discovers,   10
Since changing does but spread their shame,
    Ought to be constant lovers.

But we whose hearts do justly swell
  With no vainglorious pride,
Knowing how we in love excel,   15
  Long to be often tried.

Then bring my bath, and strew my bed,
  As each kind night returns:
I'll change a mistress till I'm dead,
  And fate change me to worms.   20

Love and Life

All my past life is mine no more,
  The flying hours are gone
Like transitory dreams given o'er
Whose images are kept in store
  By memory alone.   5

What ever is to come is not:
  How can it then be mine?
The present moment's all my lot
And that as fast as it is got°
  Phyllis is wholly thine.   10

Then talk not of inconstancy,
  False hearts and broken vows:
If I by miracle can be
This livelong minute true to thee°
  'Tis all that Heaven allows.   15

Song

As Chloris full of harmless thought
  Beneath the willows lay,
Kind love a comely shepherd brought
  To pass the time away.

She blushed to be encountered so 5
   And chid the amorous swain;
But as she strove to rise and go
   He pulled her down again.

A sudden passion seized her heart
   In spite of her disdain, 10
She found a pulse in ev'ry part
   And love in ev'ry vein.
'Ah youth', quoth she, 'what charms are these
   That conquer and surprise?
Ah let me! for unless you please° 15
   I have no power to rise.'

She faintly spoke and trembling lay
   For fear he should comply,
But virgins' eyes their hearts betray,
   And give their tongues the lie. 20
Thus she who princes had denied,
   With all their pompous train,
Was in the lucky minute tried
   And yielded to a swain.

A Dialogue between Strephon and Daphne

STRE: Prithee now, fond fool, give o'er;
     Since my heart is gone before
  To what purpose should I stay?
     Love commands another way.

DAPH: Perjured swain, I knew the time 5
     When dissembling was your crime;
  In pity now employ that art
     Which first betrayed, to ease my heart.

STRE: Women can with pleasure feign;
     Men dissemble still with pain. 10
  What advantage will it prove
     If I lie who cannot love?

DAPH: Tell me then the reason why
    Love from hearts in love does fly;
  Why the bird will build a nest   15
    Where he ne'er intends to rest.

STRE: Love like other little boys°
    Cries for hearts as they for toys
  Which when gained in childish play
    Wantonly are thrown away.   20

DAPH: Still on wing or on his knees
    Love does nothing by degrees,
  Basely flying when most prized,
    Meanly fawning when despised,

  Flatt'ring or insulting ever,   25
    Generous and grateful never;
  All his joys are fleeting dreams,
    All his woes severe extremes.

STRE: Nymph, unjustly you inveigh:
    Love like us must fate obey.   30
  Since 'tis Nature's law to change,
    Constancy alone is strange.

  See the heav'ns in lightnings break,
    Next in storms of thunder speak
  Till a kind rain from above   35
    Makes a calm—so 'tis in love.

  Flames begin our first address,
    Like meeting thunder we embrace;
  Then you know the show'rs that fall
    Quench the fire and quiet all.   40

DAPH: How should I these show'rs forget?
    'Twas so pleasant to be wet.
  They killed love, I know it well:
    I died all the while they fell.

Say at least what nymph it is 45
　Robs my breast of so much bliss.
If she is fair I shall be eas'd,
　Through my ruin you'll be pleased.

STRE: Daphne never was so fair,
　　Strephon scarcely so sincere; 50
　Gentle, innocent and free,
　　Ever pleased with only me.

　Many charms my heart enthrall
　　But there's one above 'em all:
　With aversion she does fly 55
　　Tedious trading constancy.°

DAPH: Cruel shepherd, I submit:
　　Do what Love and you think fit.
　Change is fate and not design—
　　Say you would have still been mine. 60

STRE: Nymph, I cannot: 'tis too true
　　Change has greater charms than you.
　Be by my example wise:
　　Faith to pleasure sacrifice.

DAPH: Silly swain I'll have you know 65
　　'Twas my practice long ago:°
　Whilst you vainly thought me true
　　I was false in scorn of you.

　By my tears, my heart's disguise,
　　I thy love and thee despise. 70
　Womankind more joy discovers
　　Making fools than keeping lovers.

Song

Fair Chloris in a pig-sty lay,
   Her tender herd lay by her;
She slept; in murm'ring gruntlings they,
   Complaining of the scorching day,
Her slumbers thus inspire.   5

She dreamt whilst she with busy pains
   Her snowy arms employed
In ivory pails to fill up grains°
   One of her love-convicted swains°
Thus hasting to her cried.   10

'Fly nymph, oh fly, ere't be too late
   A dear-loved life to save!
Rescue thy bosom pig from fate°
   That now expires hung on the gate°
That leads to yonder cave.   15

My self had gone to set him free
   Rather than brought the news;
But I am so abhorred by thee
   That even thy darling's life from me
I know thou would'st refuse.'   20

Frighted at this away she flies:
   Not blushes to her face
Nor the bright lightning from the skies
   Nor love shot by her brighter eyes
Flew half so swift a pace.   25

This plot it seems the amorous slave
   Had laid against her honour
Which not one god took care to save,
   For he pursued her to the cave
And threw himself upon her.   30

Now pierced in her virgin's zone,
    She feels the foe within it;
She hears an amorous broken groan,
    The striving lover's fainting moan,
Just in the happy minute. 35

Frighted she wakes, and waking frigs:
    Nature thus kindly eased°
In dreams raised by her grunting pigs
    And her own thumb betwixt her legs,
She's innocent and pleased. 40

A Letter [*by Sir Carr Scroope*]

Madam.
I cannot change as others do
    Though you unjustly scorn,
Since that poor swain that sighs for you°
    For you alone was born; 5
No, Phillis, no, your heart to move
    A surer way I'll try,
And to revenge my slighted love
    Will still love on, will still love on, and die.

When killed with grief Amintor lies 10
    And you to mind shall call
The sighs that now unpitied rise,
    The tears that vainly fall,
That welcome hour that ends his smart
    Will then begin your pain, 15
For such a faithful tender heart
    Can never break, can never break, in vain.

Answer

I fuck no more than others do,
   I'm young and not deformed,
My tender heart sincere and true
   Deserves not to be scorned;
Why, Phillis, then, why will you swive   5
   With forty lovers more?°
Can I, said she, with nature strive?
   Alas I am, alas I am, a whore.

Were all my body larded o'er
   With darts of love so thick   10
That you might find in every pore
   A well-stuck standing prick,
While yet alone my eyes were free
   My heart would never doubt
In amorous rage and ecstasy°   15
   To wish those eyes, to wish those eyes, fucked out.

To Corinna

What cruel pains Corinna takes
   To force that harmless frown,°
When not one charm her face forsakes:
   Love cannot lose his own.°

So sweet a face, so soft a heart,   5
   Such eyes so very kind
Betray (alas) the silly art
   Virtue had ill designed.

Poor feeble tyrant who in vain°
   Would proudly take upon her   10
Against kind Nature to maintain
   Affected rules of honour.°

The scorn she bears so helpless proves°
  When I plead passion to her
That much she fears, but more she loves,   15
  Her vassall should undo her.

[*Song*]

At last you'll force me to confess
You need no arts to vanquish:
Such charms from nature you possess,
'Twere dullness not to languish;
Yet spare a heart you may surprise°   5
And give my tongue the glory
To scorn, while my unfaithful eyes°
Betray a kinder story.

Grecian Kindness

The utmost grace the Greeks could show
When to the Trojans they grew kind
Was with their arms to let 'em go
And leave their ling'ring wives behind.
  They beat the men and burnt the town,   5
  Then all the baggage was their own.°

There the kind deity of wine
Kissed the soft wanton god of love:
This clapped his wings, that pressed his vine°
And their blest pow'rs united move,   10
  While each brave Greek embraced his punk,°
  Lulled her asleep and then grew drunk.

Love to a Woman

  Love a woman! Th'rt an ass:
    'Tis a most insipid passion
  To choose out for thy happiness
    The dullest part of God's creation.

Let the porter and the groom,   5
  Things designed for dirty slaves,°
Drudge in fair Aurelia's womb°
  To get supplies for age and graves.

Farewell Woman!—I intend
  Henceforth every night to sit   10
With my lewd well-natured friend,
  Drinking to engender wit.

Then give me health, wealth, mirth, and wine,
  And if busy love intrenches°
There's a sweet soft page of mine   15
  Can do the trick worth forty wenches.°

The Platonic Lady

I could love thee till I die,
  Would'st thou love me modestly
And never press, whilst I live,°
  For more than willingly I'd give;
Which should sufficient be to prove,   5
  I'd understand the art of love.°
I hate the thing is called enjoyment;°
  Besides it is a dull employment:
It cuts off all that's life and fire
  From that which may be termed desire,   10
Just like the bee whose sting being gone,
  Converts the owner to a drone.
I love a youth will give me leave
  His body in my arms to wreathe,
To press him gently and to kiss,   15
  To sigh and look with eyes that wish
For what if I could once obtain,
  I would neglect with flat disdain.°
I'd give him liberty to toy,
  And play with me and count it joy;   20

Our freedoms should be full complete,
   And nothing wanting but the feat.
Let's practise then and we shall prove
   These are the only sweets of love.

The Fall

How blest was the created state
   Of man and woman ere they fell
Compared to our unhappy fate:
   We need not fear another hell.°

Naked beneath cool shades they lay: 5
   Enjoyment waited on desire.°
Each member did their wills obey
   Nor could a wish set pleasure higher.°

But we poor slaves to hope and fear
   Are never of our joys secure: 10
They lessen still as they draw near
   And none but dull delights endure.

Then, Chloris, while I duly pay°
   The nobler tribute of a heart,
Be not you so severe to say°   15
   You love me for a frailer part.

Upon his Leaving his Mistress

'Tis not that I am weary grown
Of being yours, and yours alone;
But with what face can I design°
To damn you to be only mine?
You whom some kinder Pow'r did fashion,   5
By merit or by inclination,°
The joy at least of one whole nation.

Let meaner spirits of your sex
With humbler aims their thoughts perplex,°
And boast, if by their arts they can   10
Contrive to make one happy man,
Whilst, moved by an impartial sense,°
Favours, like Nature, you dispense
With universal influence.

See the kind seed-receiving earth   15
To ev'ry grain affords a birth,
On her no show'rs unwelcome fall,
Her willing womb retains 'em all;
And shall my Celia be confined?
No!—live up to thy mighty mind,   20
And be the mistress of mankind.

A Young Lady to her Ancient Lover

Ancient person for whom I°
All the flutt'ring youth defy,°
Long be it ere thou grow old,
Aching, shaking, crazy, cold;
But still continue as thou art,   5
Ancient person of my heart.

On thy withered lips and dry
Which like barren furrows lie
Brooding kisses I will pour
Shall thy youthful heat restore   10
(Such kind showers in autumn fall
And a second spring recall);
Nor from thee will ever part,
Ancient person of my heart.

Thy nobler parts which but to name   15
In our sex would be counted shame,
By age's frozen grasp possessed,
From their ice shall be released
And soothed by my reviving hand
In former warmth and vigour stand.   20

All a lover's wish can reach°
For thy joy my love shall teach,
And for thy pleasure shall improve
All that art can add to love;
Yet still I'll love thee without art°   25
Ancient person of my heart.

Song

By all Love's soft yet mighty pow'rs,
    It is a thing unfit
That men should fuck in time of flow'rs°
    Or when the smock's beshit.

Fair nasty nymph, be clean and kind°   5
    And all my joys restore,
By using paper still behind
    And sponges for before.°

My spotless flames can ne'er decay
    If after ev'ry close°   10
My smoking prick escape the fray
    Without a bloody nose.

If thou would'st have me true, be wise
    And take to cleanly sinning:°
None but fresh lovers' pricks can rise,°   15
    At Phyllis in foul linen.

[*Song*]

Leave this gaudy gilded stage,
From custom more than use frequented,°
Where fools of either sex and age°
Crowd to see themselves presented!°
To Love's theatre the bed   5
Youth and Beauty fly together
And act so well it may be said
The laurel there was due to either.
'Twixt strifes of Love and War the difference lies in this:°
When neither overcomes Love's triumph greater is.   10

STAGE ORATIONS AND
DRAMATIC MONOLOGUES

[*Could I but make my wishes insolent*]

Could I but make my wishes insolent
And force some image of a false content!°
But they, like me, bashful and humble grown
Hover at distance about Beauty's throne,
There worship and admire, and then they die,   5
Daring no more lay hold of her than I.
Reason to worth bears a submissive spirit
But fools can be familiar with merit:°
Who but that blundering blockhead Phaeton°
Could e'er have thought to drive about the Sun?   10
Just such another durst make love to you
Whom not ambition led but dulness drew:
No am'rous thought could his dull heart incline
But he would have a passion, for 'twas fine;°
That, a new suit, and what he next must say,   15
Runs in his idle head the livelong day.°
Hard-hearted saint!—since 'tis your will to be
So unrelenting pitiless to me,°
Regardless of a love so many years
Preserved 'twixt ling'ring hopes and awful fears.   20
Such fears in lovers' breasts high value claims°
And such expiring martyrs feel in flames.
My hopes your self contrived, with cruel care,
Through gentle smiles to lead me to despair;°
'Tis some relief in my extreme distress   25
My rival is below your power to bless.

[*What vain unnecessary things are men!*]

What vain unnecessary things are men!
How well we do with out 'em; tell me then
Whence comes that mean submissiveness we find
This ill-bred age has wrought on womankind?
Fall'n from the rights their sex and beauties gave   5
To make men wish, despair, and humbly crave,
Now 'twill suffice if they vouchsafe to have.
To the Pall Mall, playhouse and the drawing-room°
(Their women-fairs) these women coursers come°
To chaffer, choose, and ride their bargains home.°   10
At the appearance of an unknown face
Up steps the arrogant, pretending ass,°
Pulling by th'elbow his companion Huff,°
Cries: 'Look, de God that wench is well enough,°
Fair and well-shaped, good lips and teeth: 'twill do.   15
She shall be tawdry for a month or two°
At my expense, be rude, and take upon her,°
Show her contempt of quality and honour
And with the general fate of errant Woman
Be very proud awhile, then very common.'   20
Ere bear this scorn, I'd be shut up at home
Content with humouring my self alone,°
Force back the humble Love of former days°
In pensive madrigals and ends of plays°
When, if my lady frowned, th'unhappy knight   25
Was fain to fast and lie alone that night.°
But whilst th'insulting wife the breeches wore°
The husband took her clothes to give his—°
Who now maintains it with a gentler art:
Thus tyrannies to commonwealths convert.   30
Then, after all, you find what e'er we say°
Things must go on in their lewd natural way;
Besides the beastly men we too oft see
Can please themselves alone as well as we.
Therefore, kind ladies of the Town, to you   35
For our stol'n, ravished men we hereby sue.°

By this time you have found out, we suppose,
That they're as errant tinsel as their clothes,°
Poor broken properties that cannot serve°
To treat such persons so as they deserve.   40
Mistake us not, we do not here pretend
That like your young sparks you can condescend
To love a beastly playhouse creature, foh!
We dare not think so meanly of you, no—
'Tis not the player pleases but the part;   45
She may like Rollo who despises Hart.°
To theatres as temples you are brought
Where Love is worshipped and his precepts taught.
You must go home and practise; for 'tis here°
Just as in other preaching places where   50
Great eloquence is shown 'gainst sin and papists
By men who live idolators and atheists.°
These two were dainty trades indeed could each°
Live up to half the miracles they teach:°
Both are a   55

The Disabled Debauchee

As some brave admiral, in former war
 Deprived of force but pressed with courage still,°
Two rival fleets appearing from afar,
 Crawls to the top of an adjacent hill

From whence, with thoughts full of concern, he views   5
 The wise and daring conduct of the fight,°
And each bold action to his mind renews
 His present glory and his past delight;°

From his fierce eyes flashes of rage he throws,
 As from black clouds when lightning breaks away,   10
Transported, thinks himself amidst his foes,
 And, absent, yet enjoys the bloody day:

So, when my years of impotence approach,
   And I'm by pox and wine's unlucky chance
Forced from the pleasing billows of Debauch   15
   On the dull shore of lazy Temperance,°

My pains at least some respite shall afford
   While I behold the battles you maintain,
When fleets of glasses sail about the board,
   From whose broad sides volleys of wit shall rain.   20

Nor shall the sight of honourable scars,°
   Which my too forward valour did procure,
Frighten new-listed soldiers from the wars:
   Past joys have more than paid what I endure.

Should hopeful youths, worth being drunk, prove nice,°   25
   And from their fair inviters meanly shrink,
'Twill please the ghost of my departed Vice°
   If, at my counsel, they repent and drink.°

Or should some cold-complexioned sot forbid,
   With his dull morals, your bold night-alarms,   30
I'll fire his blood by telling what I did
   When I was strong, and able to bear arms.

I'll tell of whores attacked, their lords at home,°
   Bawd's quarters beaten up, and fortress won,°
Windows demolished, watches overcome;   35
   And handsome ills by my contrivance done.°

Nor shall our love-fits, Chloris, be forgot,
   When each the well-looked link-boy strove t'enjoy,
And the best kiss was the deciding lot
   Whether the boy fucked you, or I the boy.°   40

With tales like these, I will such thoughts inspire
   As to important mischief shall incline;
I'll make them long some ancient church to fire,
   And fear no lewdness they're called to by wine.

Thus, statesman-like, I'll saucily impose   45
   And safe from action, valiantly advise;
Sheltered in impotence, urge you to blows,
   And being good for nothing else, be wise.

Epilogue to Love in the Dark

As charms are nonsense, nonsense seems a charm°
Which hearers of all judgment does disarm;
For songs and scenes a double audience bring,°
And dogg'rel takes which two-eyed Cyclops sing.°
Now to machines and a dull masque you run,°   5
We find that wit's the monster you would shun,
And by my troth 'tis most discreetly done;°
For since with vice and folly wit is fed,
Through mercy 'tis, most of you are not dead.
Players turn puppets now at your desire,   10
In their mouths nonsense, in their tails a wire,
They fly through clouds of clouts, and showr's of fire.°
A kind of losing loadum is their game,°
Where the worst writer has the greatest fame.
To get vile plays like theirs shall be our care;   15
But of such awkward actors we despair:°
False taught at first—
Like bowls ill-biased, still the more they run
They're further off than when they first begun.
In comedy their unweighed action mark:°   20
There's one is such a dear familiar spark
He yawns as if he were but half awake,
And fribbling for free speaking does mistake.°
False accent and neglectful action too—°
They have both so nigh good, yet neither true,°   25
That both together, like an ape's mock face,°
By near resembling man do man disgrace.
Th'rough-paced ill actors perhaps may be cured;°
Half-players, like half-wits, can't be endured.
Yet these are they who durst expose the age   30
Of the great wonder of our English stage,°

Whom Nature seemed to form for your delight,
And bid him speak, as she bid Shakespeare write.
Those blades indeed are cripples in their art,
Mimic his foot but not his speaking part.°   35
Let them the *Traitor* or *Volpone* try!°
Could they
Rage like Cethegus, or like Cassius die,°
They ne'er had sent to Paris for such fancies
As monsters' heads and Merry Andrew's dances.°   40
Withered perhaps, not perished, we appear,
But they were blighted, and ne'er came to bear.°
Th'old poets dressed your mistress wit before;°
These draw you on with an old painted whore,
And sell, like bawds, patched plays for maids twice o'er.°   45
Old wit we have, they on new may live
Of their own poet at-all-positive.°
To *Epsom Wells*°
'Tis known his interlining friends lent wit;
Some doubt if he writ that, all grant he writ   50
The *Humorists*, the *Shepherdess*, and *Hypocrite*;°
And by the style of *Tempest* masque we know
That none but he could write the *Psyche* too.
Each day now adds new vigour to his pen,
Since Samson-like his locks are grown again.°   55
Such wit with us must needs be scarce and dear,
Unless he'd write another *Miser* here.°
But hold! our wishes need not make such haste—
Our house was burnt for playing of his last.°
Yet they may scorn our house and actors too,   60
Since they have swelled so high to hector you.°
They cry, 'Pox o'these Covent Garden men,
Damn'em, not one of them but keeps out ten!°
Were they once gone, we for those thundering blades
Should have an audience of substantial trades,°   65
Who love our muzzled boys and tearing fellows,
My Lord great Neptune, and great nephew Aeolus.°
Oh how the merry citizen's in love°
With—
"Psyche, the goddess of each field and grove."°   70

He cries, "I'faith, methinks 'tis well enough",
But you roar out and cry, "'Tis all damned stuff.'"
So to their house the graver fops repair,
While men of wit find one another here.

Epilogue to Circe

Some few from wit have this true maxim got,°
That 'tis still better to be pleased than not,
And therefore never their own torment plot,
While the malicious critics still agree
To loathe each play they come and pay to see.   5
The first know 'tis a meaner part of sense
To find a fault than taste an excellence;
Therefore they praise and strive to like, while these
Are dully vain of being hard to please.
Poets and women have an equal right   10
To hate the dull, who dead to all delight
Feel pain alone, and have no joy but spite.
'Twas impotence did first this vice begin:
Fools censure wit, as old men rail of sin,
Who envy pleasure which they cannot taste,   15
And good for nothing, would be wise at last.°
Since therefore to the women it appears,
That all these enemies of wit are theirs,°
Our poet the dull herd no longer fears:
What e'er his fate may prove, 'twill be his pride   20
To stand or fall, with Beauty on his side.°

TRANSLATIONS AND IMITATIONS

[*Translation from Lucretius,* De Rerum Natura, *ii. 646–51*]

The Gods, by right of Nature, must possess
An everlasting age of perfect peace:
Far off removed from us and our affairs,
Neither approached by dangers, or by cares,
Rich in themselves, to whom we cannot add,   5
Not pleased by good deeds nor provoked by bad.

[*Translation from Lucretius,* De Rerum Natura, *i. 1–4*]

Great mother of Aeneas and of Love,°
Delight of mankind, and the powers above,
Who all beneath those sprinkled drops of light°
Which slide upon the face of gloomy night,
Whither vast regions of that liquid world   5
Where groves of ships on wat'ry hills are hurled,
Or fruitful earth, dost bless, since 'tis by thee°
That all things live, which the bright sun does see.

Upon his Drinking a Bowl

Vulcan, contrive me such a cup°
As Nestor used of old;°
Show all thy skill to trim it up,
Damask it round with gold.°

Make it so large that filled with sack   5
Up to the swelling brim
Vast toasts on the delicious lake°
Like ships at sea may swim.

Engrave no battle on its cheek
(With war I've nought to do):   10
I'm none of those that took Maastricht°
Nor Yarmouth leaguer knew.°

Let it no name of planets tell,
Fixed stars or constellations,
For I am no Sir Sidrophel°   15
Nor none of his relations.

But carve thereon a spreading vine,
Then add two lovely boys;
Their limbs in amorous folds entwine,
The type of future joys.°   20

Cupid and Bacchus my saints are,
May Drink and Love still reign:
With wine I wash away my cares
And then to Phill again.°

Seneca's Troas. *Act 2. Chorus.*

Thus Englished by a Person of Honour:

After death nothing is, and nothing death,
The utmost limit of a gasp of breath.
Let the ambitious zealot lay aside
His hopes of Heaven, whose faith is but his pride;
Let slavish souls lay by their fear,   5
Nor be concerned which way, nor where,
After this life they shall be hurled.
Dead, we become the lumber of the world,
And to that mass of matter shall be swept
Where things destroyed with things unborn are kept.   10
Devouring Time swallows us whole;
Impartial death confounds body and soul.
For Hell and the foul fiend that rules°
God's everlasting fiery jails

(Devised by rogues, dreaded by fools),   15
With his grim grisly dog that keeps the door,°
Are senseless stories, idle tales,
Dreams, whimsies, and no more.°

An Allusion to Horace.
The Tenth Satire of the First Book
Nempe incomposito dixi etc.

Well sir, 'tis granted I said Dryden's rhymes
Were stolen, unequal, nay dull many times.
What foolish patron is there found of his°
So blindly partial to deny me this?
But that his plays embroidered up and down   5
With wit and learning justly pleased the Town,
In the same paper I as freely own.°
Yet having this allowed, the heavy mass
That stuffs up his loose volumes must not pass;°
For by that rule I might as well admit   10
Crowne's tedious scenes for poetry and wit.°
   'Tis therefore not enough when your false sense
Hits the false judgment of an audience°
Of clapping fools, assembling a vast crowd
Till the thronged playhouse crack with the dull load.°   15
Tho' even that talent merits in some sort,
That can divert the rabble and the court,
Which blundering Settle never could attain°
And puzzling Otway labours at in vain.°
   But within due proportions circumscribe   20
What e'er you write, that with a flowing tide
The style may rise, yet in its rise forbear
With useless words to oppress the wearied ear:
Here be your language lofty, there more light,
Your rhetoric with your poetry unite.°   25
For elegance sake sometimes allay the force
Of epithets, 'twill soften the discourse:

A jest in scorn points out and hits the thing
More home than the morosest satire's sting.
Shakespeare and Jonson did herein excel,   30
And might in this be imitated well,
Whom refined Etherege copies not at all,°
But is himself a sheer original;°
Nor that slow drudge in swift pindaric strains,°
Flatman, who Cowley imitates with pains,°   35
And rides a jaded muse whipped with loose reins.°
When Lee makes temperate Scipio fret and rave,°
And Hannibal a whining amorous slave,
I laugh, and wish the hot-brained fustian fool°
In Busby's hands to be well lashed at school.°   40
Of all our modern wits none seems to me
Once to have touched upon true comedy,
But hasty Shadwell and slow Wycherley.°
Shadwell's unfinished works do yet impart°
Great proofs of force of nature, none of art: 45
With just bold strokes he dashes here and there,
Showing great mastery with little care,
And scorns to varnish his good touches o'er
To make the fools and women praise them more.
But Wycherley earns hard what e'er he gains,   50
He wants no judgment, nor he spares no pains;°
He frequently excels, and at the least
Makes fewer faults than any of the best.
Waller, by nature for the bays designed,°
With force, and fire, and fancy unconfined   55
In panegyrics does excel mankind:°
He best can turn, inforce, and soften things°
To praise great conquerors or to flatter kings.°
     For pointed satires, I would Buckhurst choose:°
The best good man, with the worst-natured muse.   60
     For songs and verses mannerly obscene°
That can stir nature up by springs unseen,°
And without forcing blushes warm the queen,°
Sedley has that prevailing gentle art°
That can with a resistless charm impart°   65
The loosest wishes to the chastest heart,

Raise such a conflict, kindle such a fire
Betwixt declining virtue and desire,°
Till the poor vanquished maid dissolves away
In dreams all night, in sighs and tears all day.　　　　　70

　　Dryden in vain tried this nice way of wit,°
For he to be a tearing blade thought fit.°
But when he would be sharp he still was blunt:
To frisk his frolic fancy he'd cry 'cunt!';
Would give the ladies a dry bawdy bob,°　　　　　75
And thus he got the name of Poet Squab.°
But to be just, 'twill to his praise be found,
His excellencies more than faults abound;
Nor dare I from his sacred temples tear
That laurel which he best deserves to wear.　　　　　80
But does not Dryden find even Jonson dull,
Fletcher and Beaumont uncorrect and full°
Of lewd lines (as he calls 'em), Shakespeare's style°
Stiff and affected; to his own the while°
Allowing all the justness that his pride　　　　　85
So arrogantly had to these denied?
And may not I have leave impartially
To search and censure Dryden's works, and try
If those gross faults his choice pen does commit°
Proceed from want of judgment or of wit,°　　　　　90
Or if his lumpish fancy does refuse°
Spirit and grace to his loose slattern muse?°

　　Five hundred verses every morning writ
Proves you no more a poet than a wit.
Such scribbling authors have been seen before:　　　　　95
Mustapha, *The English Princess*, forty more°
Were things perhaps composed in half an hour.

　　To write what may securely stand the test
Of being well read over thrice at least,
Compare each phrase, examine every line,　　　　　100
Weigh every word, and every thought refine;
Scorn all applause the vile rout can bestow
And be content to please those few who know.

　　Can'st thou be such a vain mistaken thing
To wish thy works might make a playhouse ring　　　　　105

With the unthinking laughter and poor praise
Of fops and ladies factious for thy plays?
Then send a cunning friend to learn thy doom°
From the shrewd judges in the drawing-room.°
    I've no ambition on that idle score,   110
But say with Betty Morris heretofore,°
When a court Lady called her Buckley's whore:°
I please one man of wit, am proud on't too;
Let all the coxcombs dance to bed to you.
    Should I be troubled when the purblind knight°   115
Who squints more in his judgment than his sight
Picks silly faults, and censures what I write?
Or when the poor led poets of the Town°
For scraps and coach-room cry my verses down?
I loathe the rabble; 'tis enough for me   120
If Sedley, Shadwell, Sheppard, Wycherley,°
Godolphin, Butler, Buckhurst, Buckingham°
And some few more whom I omit to name
Approve my sense: I count their censure fame.

An Allusion to Tacitus. De Vita Agricolae

The freeborn English, generous and wise,°
Hate chains but do not government despise:
Rights of the crown, tributes and taxes they,
When lawfully exacted, freely pay.
Force they abhor, and wrongs they scorn to bear,   5
More guided by their judgment than their fear:
Justice with them is never held severe.°
Here pow'r by tyranny was never got,
Laws may perhaps enslave 'em, force cannot.
Rash counsels here have still the worst effect:°   10
The surest way to reign is to protect.
Kings are least safe in their unbounded will,°
Joined with the wretched pow'r of doing ill;
Forsaken most when they're most absolute:
Laws guard the man and only bind the brute.   15

To force that guard, with the worst foe to join
Can never be a prudent king's design.
What king would change to be a Catiline,°
Break his own laws, stake an unquestioned throne,°
Conspire with vassals to usurp his own?°   20
'Tis rather some base favourite's vile pretence°
To tyrannize at the wronged king's expense.°
Let France grow proud beneath their tyrant's lust
While the racked people crawl and lick the dust;°
The mighty genius of this isle disdains°   25
Ambitious slavery and golden chains.°
England to servile yokes did never bow:°
What conquerors ne'er presumed, who dare do now?
Roman nor Norman ever could pretend°
To have enslaved, but made this isle their friend.   30

Song

Quoth the Duchess of Cleveland to councillor Knight,°
'I'd fain have a prick, knew I how to come by't;
I desire you'll be secret, and give your advice:
Though cunt be not coy, reputation is nice.'°

'To some cellar in Sodom your Grace must retire,°   5
Where porters, with black pots, sit around a coal-fire;°
There open your case, and your Grace cannot fail°
Of a dozen of pricks for a dozen of ale.'

'Is't so?', quoth the Duchess; 'Ay, by God', quoth the whore.
'Then give me the key that unlocks the back-door;°   10
For I had rather be fucked by porters and car-men
Than thus be abused by Churchill and Jermyn.'°

The Imperfect Enjoyment

Naked she lay clasped in my longing arms,
I filled with love and she all over charms,
Both equally inspired with eager fire,
Melting through kindness, flaming in desire.
With arms, legs, lips close clinging to embrace   5
She clips me to her breast and sucks me to her face.
Her nimble tongue (love's lesser lightning) played
Within my mouth and to my thoughts conveyed
Swift orders that I should prepare to throw
The all-dissolving thunderbolt below.   10
My fluttering soul, sprung with the pointed kiss,°
Hangs hovering o'er her balmy brinks of bliss;°
But whilst her busy hand would guide that part
Which should convey my soul up to her heart

In liquid raptures I dissolve all o'er,   15
Melt into sperm and spend at every pore.
A touch from any part of her had done't:
Her hand, her foot, her very look's a cunt.°
Smiling she chides in a kind, murm'ring noise
And from her body wipes the clammy joys,   20
When with a thousand kisses wand'ring o'er
My panting bosom, 'Is there then no more?'
She cries; 'All this to love, and rapture's due—
Must we not pay a debt to pleasure too?'
But I the most forlorn lost man alive   25
To show my wished obedience vainly strive:
I sigh, alas, and kiss, but cannot swive.°
Eager desires confound the first intent,
Succeeding shame does more success prevent
And rage at last confirms me impotent.   30
Even her fair hand which might bid heat return
To frozen Age and make cold hermits burn,
Applied to my dead cinder warms no more
Than fire to ashes could past flames restore.
Trembling, confused, despairing, limber, dry,°   35
A wishing, weak, unmoving lump I lie.
This dart of love whose piercing point oft tried
With virgin blood ten thousand maids has dyed,°
Which Nature still directed with such art
That it through every cunt reached every heart,   40
Stiffly resolved 'twould carelessly invade
Woman, nor man, nor ought its fury stayed—°
Where'er it pressed a cunt it found or made—
Now languid lies in this unhappy hour,
Shrunk up and sapless like a withered flower.   45
Thou treacherous, base deserter of my flame,
False to my passion, fatal to my fame,
Through what mistaken magic dost thou prove
So true to lewdness, so untrue to love?
What oyster, cinder, beggar, common whore°   50
Did'st thou e'er fail in all thy life before?
When vice, disease, and scandal lead the way
With what officious haste dost thou obey!

Like a rude roaring hector in the streets°
Who scuffles, cuffs and justles all he meets 55
But if his king or country claim his aid
The rake-hell villain shrinks and hides his head,
Even so thy brutal valour is displayed,
Breaks every stew, does each small whore invade,°
But when great Love the onset does command, 60
Base recreant to thy prince, thou durst not stand.°
Worst part of me and henceforth hated most,
Through all the Town a common fucking post,°
On whom each whore relieves her tingling cunt
As hogs on gates do rub themselves and grunt, 65
May'st thou to ravenous shankers be a prey°
Or in consuming weepings waste away;°
May strangury and stone thy days attend;°
May'st thou ne'er piss who didst refuse to spend°
When all my joys did on false thee depend. 70
And may ten thousand abler pricks agree
To do the wronged Corinna right for thee.

A Ramble in St. James's Park

Much wine had passed with grave discourse
Of who fucks who, and who does worse,
Such as you usually do hear
From them that diet at the Bear,°
When I, who still take care to see 5
Drunkenness relieved by lechery,°
Went out into St. James's Park
To cool my head, and fire my heart.
But though St. James has the honour on't,°
'Tis consecrate to Prick and Cunt. 10
There by a most incestuous birth
Strange woods spring from the teeming earth,
For they relate how heretofore,
When ancient pict began to whore,°
Deluded of his assignation 15
(Jilting it seems was then in fashion),

Poor pensive lover, in this place,
Would frig upon his Mother's face,°
Whence rows of mandrakes tall did rise°
Whose lewd tops fucked the very skies.   20
Each imitative branch does twine
In some loved fold of Aretine,°
And nightly now beneath their shade
Are bugg'ries, rapes, and incests made.
Unto this all-sin-shelt'ring grove,   25
Whores of the bulk and the alcove,°
Great Ladies, chamber-maids, and drudges,
The rag-picker, and heiress trudges;°
Car-men, divines, great Lords, and tailors,°
Prentices, poets, pimps and gaolers,   30
Foot-men, fine fops, do here arrive
And here promiscuously they swive.°

      Along these hallowed walks it was
That I beheld Corinna pass.
Who ever had been by to see   35
The proud disdain she cast on me
Through charming eyes, he would have swore
She dropped from Heav'n that very hour,
Forsaking the divine abode
In scorn of some despairing god;   40
But mark what creatures women are,
How infinitely vile and fair.

      Three knights o'th'elbow and the slur,°
With wriggling tails, made up to her.

      The first was of your Whitehall blades,°   45
Near kin to th'Mother of the Maids,°
Graced by whose favour he was able
To bring a friend to th'waiters' table,°
Where he had heard Sir Edward Sutton°
Say how the King loved Banstead mutton;°   50
Since when he'd ne'er be brought to eat,
By's good will any other meat.
In this, as well as all the rest,
He ventures to do like the best;

But wanting common sense, th'ingredient   55
In choosing well not least expedient,
Converts abortive imitation,
To universal affectation:
So he not only eats and talks,
But feels, and smells, sits down and walks,   60
Nay looks, and lives, and loves by rote,
In an old tawdry birthday coat.°
    The second was a Gray's Inn wit,°
A great inhabiter of the pit,
Where critic-like he sits and squints,   65
Steals pocket-handkerchiefs and hints
From's neighbour and the comedy,
To court and pay his landlady.
    The third a Lady's eldest son,
Within few years of twenty-one,   70
Who hopes from his propitious fate,
Against he comes to his estate,°
By these two worthies to be made
A most accomplished tearing blade.°
One in a strain 'twixt tune and nonsense   75
Cries, 'Madam, I have loved you long since,
Permit me your fair hand to kiss'—
When at her mouth her cunt says yes.
    In short, without much more ado,
Joyful and pleased, away she flew   80
And with these three confounded asses
From park to hackney coach she passes:
So a proud bitch does lead about
Of humble curs the amorous rout,
Who most obsequiously do hunt   85
The sav'ry scent of salt-swoll'n cunt.°
Some Pow'r more patient now relate°
The sense of this surprising fate.
Gods! that a thing admired by me
Should taste so much of infamy.°   90
Had she picked out to rub her arse on
Some stiff-pricked clown, or well-hung parson,°

Each job of whose spermatic sluice°
Had filled her cunt with wholesome juice,
I the proceeding should have praised,　　　　　　　95
In hope she had quenched a fire I raised:
Such nat'ral freedoms are but just;
There's something gen'rous in mere lust.°
But to turn damned abandoned jade°
When neither head nor tail persuade;　　　　　　　100
To be a whore in understanding,
A passive pot for fools to spend in!
The devil played booty, sure, with thee°
To bring a blot on infamy.
But why was I of all mankind　　　　　　　105
To so severe a fate designed?
Ungrateful! why this treachery
To humble fond, believing me,
Who gave you privilege above
The nice allowances of love?°　　　　　　　110
Did I ever refuse to bear
The meanest part your lust could spare?
When your lewd cunt came spewing home,
Drenched with the seed of half the Town,
My dram of sperm was supped up after,　　　　　　　115
For the digestive surfeit-water.°
Full gorged at another time
With a vast meal of nasty slime,
Which your devouring cunt had drawn
From porters' backs, and foot-men's brawn,°　　　　　　　120
I was content to serve you up
My bollockfull for your grace-cup;°
Nor ever thought it an abuse,
While you had pleasure for an excuse.
You that could make my heart away°　　　　　　　125
For noise and colours, and betray°
The secrets of my tender hours
To such knight-errant paramours,
When leaning on your faithless breast,
Wrapped in security and rest,°　　　　　　　130

Soft kindness all my pow'rs did move,
And Reason lay dissolved in Love—
May stinking vapours choke your womb,
Such as the men you dote upon;
May your depraved appetite, 135
That could in whiffling fools delight,°
Beget such frenzies in your mind
You may go mad for the north wind,°
And fixing all your hopes upon't,
To have him bluster in your cunt 140
Turn up your longing arse to th'air,
And perish in a wild despair.
But cowards shall forget to rant,°
Schoolboys to frig, old whores to paint,
The Jesuits' fraternity 145
Shall leave the use of buggery,
Crab-louse, inspired with grace divine,
From earthly cod to Heav'n shall climb,°
Physicians shall believe in Jesus,°
And disobedience cease to please us,° 150
Ere I desist with all my pow'r
To plague this woman and undo her.
But my revenge will best be timed
When she is married that is limed.°
In that most lamentable state,° 155
I'll make her feel my scorn and hate,
Pelt her with scandals (truth or lies)
And her poor cur with jealousies,
Till I have torn him from her breech,
While she whines like a dog-drawn bitch,° 160
Loathed and despised, kicked out of Town
Into some dirty hole alone
To chew the cud of misery,
And know she owes it all to me.
And may no woman better thrive, 165
That dares profane the Cunt I swive.°

On Mrs Willis

Against the charms our bollocks have
    How weak all human skill is!
Since they can make a man a slave
    To such a bitch as Willis.

Whom that I may describe throughout   5
    Assist me, bawdy powers:
I'll write upon a double clout°
    And dip my pen in flowers.°

Her look's demurely impudent,
    Ungainly beautiful;   10
Her modesty is insolent,
    Her wit both pert and dull.

A prostitute to all the town
    And yet with no man friends,
She rails and scolds when she lies down   15
    And curses when she spends.°

Bawdy in thoughts, precise in words,°
    Ill-natured though a whore,
Her belly is a bag of turds,
    And her cunt a common shore.°   20

A Satire on Charles II

I'th'isle of Great Britain (long since famous grown
For breeding the best cunts of Christendom)
There not long since lived (oh! may he live, and thrive)
The easiest king, and best-bred man alive.°
Him no ambition moved to get renown   5
Like the French fool who wanders up and down,°
Starving his people and hazarding his crown.
Peace is his aim, his gentleness is such,°
And's love, for he loves fucking much.

Nor are his high desires above his strength,   10
His sceptre and's prick are both of one length,
And she may sway the one who plays with th'other,
And make him little wiser than his brother.°
    I hate all monarchs and the thrones they sit on,
From the hector of France to the cully of Britain:°   15
The hector wins towns by money, not trenches, °
The cully he conquers all the pretty wenches;
He victory, and honour refuses,
And, rather than a crown, a cunt he chooses.
    Pricks, like buffoons at court,°   20
Will govern us, because they make us sport.
His was the sauciest that e'er did swive,
The proudest peremptory prick alive:
Though safety, religion, life lay on't,
'Twould break through all, to make its way to cunt.   25
With dog and bastard always going before,°
Restless he roves from whore to whore,
An easy monarch, scandalous, and poor.°
'Ah! My dear Carwell, dear'st of all my dears,°
Thou blest relief of my declining years,°   30
Ah! how I mourn thy fortune, and my fate,
To love so well, and to be loved so late';
For though in her he settled well his tarse,°
Yet still his graceless bollocks hang an arse.°
This to evince, 'twill be too long to tell you   35
The painful tricks of the laborious Nelly,°
Employing hands, arms, fingers, mouth, and thighs
To raise that limb which she all night enjoys.
Ah, generous sir! long may you survive,
For we shall never have such liberty to swive.   40

Timon °

A. What, Timon! does old age begin t'approach,°
That thus thou droop'st under a night's debauch?
Hast thou lost deep to needy rogues on tick°
Who ne'er could pay, and must be paid next week?

Tim: Neither, alas, but a dull dining sot   5
Seized me i'th'Mall, who just my name had got.
He runs upon me, cries, 'Dear rogue, I'm thine,
With me some wits of thy acquaintance dine.'
I tell him I'm engaged, but as a whore
With modesty enslaves her spark the more,   10
The longer I denied, the more he pressed;
At last, I e'en consent to be his guest.
    He takes me in his coach, and as we go
Pulls out a libel of a sheet or two,°
Insipid as the praise of pious queens   15
Or Shadwell's unassisted former scenes,°
Which he admired and praised at ev'ry line;
At last, it was so sharp it must be mine.
I vowed I was no more a wit than he,
Unpractised and unblest in poetry:°   20
A song to Phyllis I perhaps might make
But never rhymed but for my pintle's sake;°
I envied no man's fortune nor his fame,
Nor ever thought of a revenge so tame.°
He knew my style (he swore) and 'twas in vain   25
Thus to deny the issue of my brain.
Choked with his flatt'ry, I no answer make
But, silent, leave him to his dear mistake
Which he, by this, has spread o'er the whole Town
And me with an officious lie undone.   30
Of a well-meaning fool I'm most afraid,
Who sillily repeats what was well said.
But this was not the worst: when he came home
He asked, 'are Sedley, Buckhurst, Savile come?'°
No, but there were above Half-Wit and Huff,°   35
Kickum, and Ding-Boy. 'Oh 'tis well enough,°
They're all brave fellows', cries mine host; 'let's dine,°
I long to have my belly full of wine.
They'll write and fight, I dare assure you,
They're men *tam Marte quam Mercurio*.'°   40
I saw my error, but 'twas now too late:
No means nor hopes appear of a retreat.

Well, we salute, and each man takes his seat.°
'Boy', (says my sot) 'is my wife ready yet?'
A wife, good gods! A fop and bullies too!   45
For one poor meal what must I undergo?
In comes my lady straight; she had been fair,
Fit to give love and to prevent despair,
But age, beauty's incurable disease,
Had left her more desire than pow'r to please.   50
As cocks will strike although their spurs be gone,°
She with her old blear-eyes to smite begun.
Though nothing else, she (in despite of time)
Preserved the affectation of her prime:
How ever you begun, she brought in Love,   55
And hardly from that subject would remove.
We chanced to speak of the French king's success;°
My Lady wondered much how Heav'n could bless
A man that loved two women at one time,°
But more, how he to them excused his crime.   60
She asked Huff if Love's flame he never felt?
He answered bluntly—'Do you think I'm gelt?'°
She at his plainness smiled, then turned to me:
Love, in young minds, precedes ev'n poetry;
You to that passion can no stranger be,   65
But wits are given to inconstancy.
She had run on, I think, till now but meat
Came up, and suddenly she took her seat.
I thought the dinner would make some amends,
When my good Host cries out, 'Y'are all my friends,   70
Our own plain fare and the best tierce the Bull°
Affords I'll give you—and your bellies' full.
As for French kickshaws, Sellery, and Champoone,°
Ragouts, and fricasses, in troth w'have none.'
Here's a good dinner towards, thought I, when straight   75
Up comes a piece of beef, full horseman's weight,
Hard as the arse of Moseley, under which°
The coach-man sweats as ridden by a witch,°
A dish of carrots, each of 'em as long
As tool that to fair countess did belong,°   80

Which her small pillow could not so well hide
But visitors his flaming head espied.°
Pig, goose, and capon followed in the rear,°
With all that country bumpkins call good cheer,
Served up with sauces all of eighty-eight,°   85
When our tough youth wrestled and threw the weight.
And now the bottle briskly flies about,
Instead of ice, wrapped up in a wet clout.°
A brimmer follows the third bit we eat,°
Small beer becomes our drink, and wine our meat.°   90
The table was so large that in less space
A man might safe six old Italians place:°
Each man had as much room as Porter, Blunt,°
Or Harris had in Cullen's bushel cunt.°
And now the wine began to work: mine Host   95
Had been a Colonel, we must hear him boast
Not of towns won, but an estate he lost
For the King's service, which indeed he spent
Whoring and drinking, but with good intent.
He talked much of a plot, and money lent   100
In Cromwell's time. My Lady, she°
Complained our love was coarse, our poetry
Unfit for modest ears: small whores and players°
Were of our hair-brained youth the only cares,
Who were too wild for any virtuous league,   105
Too rotten to consummate the intrigue.°
Falkland she praised, and Suckling's easy pen,°
And seemed to taste their former parts again.°
Mine Host drinks to the best in Christendom,°
And decently my Lady quits the room.   110
    Left to our selves, of several things we prate;
Some regulate the stage, and some the state.
    Half-Wit cries up my Lord of Orrery;°
'Ah how well Mustapha, and Zanger die!°
His sense so little forced that by one line   115
You may the other easily divine.
    And which is worse, if any worse can be,
    He never said one word of it to me.°

There's fine Poetry! you'd swear 'twere prose,
So little on the sense the rhymes impose.'   120
'Damn me! (says Ding-Boy) in my mind, God zounds,°
Etherege writes airy songs and soft lampoons
The best of any man; as for your nouns,
Grammar, and rules of art, he knows 'em not
Yet writ two talking plays without one plot.'°   125
   Huff was for Settle, and *Morocco* praised,°
Said rumbling words, like drums, his courage raised:
   '*Whose broad-built Bulks the Boistrous Billows bear;*
   Zaphee, and Sally, Mugadore, Oran,
   The famed Arzile, Alcazer, Tituan.°   130
Was ever braver language writ by man?'°
   Kickum for Crowne declared, said in romance°
He had outdone the very wits of France;
'Witness *Pandion*, and his *Charles the Eight*,°
Where a young monarch, careless of his fate   135
Though foreign troops and rebels shock his state,
Complains another sight afflicts him more.
Viz *The Queen's Galleys Rowing from the Shore*,
   Fitting their Oars, and Tackling to be gone,
   Whilst sporting Waves smiled on the rising Sun.°   140
"Waves smiling on the sun!" I'm sure that's new,
And 'twas well thought on, give the devil his due.'
   Mine Host, who had said nothing in an hour,
Rose up and praised *The Indian Emperor*.°
   '*As if our Old World modestly withdrew,*   145
   And here in private had brought forth a new.°
There are two lines! who but he durst presume
To make the old world a new withdrawing room°
Where of another world she's brought to bed?
What a brave midwife is a Laureate's head!   150
But pox of all these scribblers, what d'ee think,
Will Zouches this year any Champoone drink?°
Will Turene fight him?'. 'Without doubt' (says Huff)°
'When they two meet, their meeting will be rough.'
'Damn me', (says Ding-Boy) 'the French cowards are: 155
They pay, but the English, Scots, and Swiss make war.°

In gaudy troops, at a review, they shine,
But dare not with the Germans battle join.
What now appears like courage is not so;
'Tis a short pride which from success does grow.   160
On their first blow they'll shrink into those fears
They showed at Cressy, Agincourt, Poitiers.
Their loss was infamous; honour so stained
Is by a nation not to be regained.'
'What they were then, I know not—now th'are brave;   165
He that denies it lies and is a slave'
(Says Huff, and frowned). Says Ding-Boy, 'That do I!
And, at that word, at t'other's head let fly
A greasy plate; when suddenly they all
Together by the ears in parties fall.   170
Half-Wit with Ding-Boy joins, Kickum with Huff.°
Their swords were safe, and so we let 'em cuff°
Till they, mine Host and I had all enough.
Their rage once over, they begin to treat,°
And six fresh bottles must the peace complete.   175
I ran down stairs, with a vow never more
To drink beer-glass and hear the hectors roar.

A Satire against Reason and Mankind

Were I (who to my cost already am
One of those strange prodigious creatures, man)
A spirit free to choose for my own share
What case of flesh and blood I pleased to wear,
I'd be a dog, a monkey, or a bear;   5
Or any thing but that vain animal
Who is so proud of being rational.
The senses are too gross, and he'll contrive°
A sixth to contradict the other five,
And before certain instinct will prefer   10
Reason, which fifty times for one does err.
Reason, an *ignis fatuus* of the mind,°
Which leaving light of nature, sense, behind,

Pathless and dangerous wand'ring ways it takes
Through Error's fenny bogs and thorny brakes,°   15
Whilst the misguided follower climbs with pain
Mountains of whimsies heaped in his own brain,
Stumbling from thought to thought, falls headlong down
Into Doubt's boundless sea where, like to drown,°
Books bear him up a while, and make him try   20
To swim with bladders of Philosophy,°
In hopes still to o'ertake th'escaping light;
The vapour dances in his dazzled sight,
Till spent, it leaves him to eternal night.
Then old Age and Experience hand in hand   25
Lead him to death, and make him understand,
After a search so painful and so long,
That all his life he has been in the wrong.
Huddled in dirt the reasoning engine lies,
Who was so proud, so witty and so wise.   30
Pride drew him in (as cheats their bubbles catch)°
And made him venture to be made a wretch.
His wisdom did his happiness destroy,
Aiming to know that world he should enjoy;
And wit was his vain frivolous pretence,   35
Of pleasing others at his own expense:
For wits are treated just like common whores,
First they're enjoyed and then kicked out of doors.
The pleasure past, a threat'ning doubt remains,
That frights th'enjoyer with succeeding pains: 40
Women and men of wit are dangerous tools,
And ever fatal to admiring fools.
Pleasure allures, and when the fops escape,
'Tis not that they're belov'd, but fortunate;
And therefore what they fear, at heart they hate.   45
    But now methinks some formal band and beard°
Takes me to task. Come on, sir, I'm prepar'd.
'Then, by your favour, any thing that's writ
Against this gibing, jingling knack called wit,
Likes me abundantly, but you take care°   50
Upon this point not to be too severe.

Perhaps my muse were fitter for this part,
For, I profess, I can be very smart°
On wit, which I abhor with all my heart.
I long to lash it in some sharp essay,   55
But your grand indiscretion bids me stay,
And turns my tide of ink another way.
What rage ferments in your degenerate mind,
To make you rail at Reason and Mankind?
Blest, glorious Man! to whom alone kind Heaven   60
An everlasting soul has freely given;
Whom his creator took such care to make,
That from himself he did the image take,
And this fair frame in shining reason drest,
To dignify his nature above beast.   65
Reason, by whose aspiring influence
We take a flight beyond material sense,
Dive into mysteries, then soaring pierce
The flaming limits of the universe,°
Search Heaven and Hell, find out what's acted there,   70
And give the world true grounds of hope and fear.'
  'Hold, mighty man!', I cry; 'all this we know
From the pathetic pen of Ingelo,°
From Patrick's *Pilgrim*, Sibbes' *Soliloquies*,°
And 'tis this very Reason I despise.   75
This supernatural gift that makes a mite°
Think he's the image of the infinite,
Comparing his short life, void of all rest,
To the eternal and the ever blest.
This busy puzzling stirrer up of doubt,   80
That frames deep mysteries, then finds them out,
Filling with frantic crowds of thinking fools
Those reverend Bedlams, Colleges and Schools;°
Born on whose wings each heavy sot can pierce
The limits of the boundless universe.   85
So charming ointments make an old witch fly,°
And bear a crippled carcass through the sky.
'Tis this exalted power whose business lies
In non-sense and impossibilities.

This made a whimsical philosopher°   90
Before the spacious world his tub prefer.
And we have modern cloistered coxcombs who
Retire to think 'cause they have nought to do:
But thoughts are given for action's government,
Where action ceases, thought's impertinent.   95
Our sphere of action is life's happiness,
And he who thinks beyond, thinks like an ass.
Thus, whilst against false reasoning I inveigh,
I own right reason, which I would obey:
That reason which distinguishes by sense,   100
And gives us rules of good and ill from thence,
That bounds desires with a reforming will,
To keep them more in vigour, not to kill.
Your Reason hinders, mine helps to enjoy,
Renewing appetites yours would destroy.   105
My reason is my friend, yours is a cheat:
Hunger calls out, my reason bids me eat;
Perversely yours your appetites does mock,
They ask for food, that answers "what's a clock?".
This plain distinction, sir, your doubt secures:°   110
'Tis not true reason I despise, but yours.

    Thus I think reason righted, but for man,°
I'll ne'er recant; defend him if you can.
For all his pride and his philosophy,
'Tis evident beasts are, in their degree,   115
As wise at least, and better far than he.
Those creatures are the wisest who attain
By surest means the ends at which they aim:
If therefore Jowler finds and kills his hares,°
Better than Meres supplies committee chairs,°   120
Though one's a statesman, th'other but a hound,
Jowler in justice would be wiser found.
You see how far man's wisdom here extends;
Look next if human nature makes amends:
Whose principles most generous are and just,   125
And to whose morals you would sooner trust.

Be judge your self, I'll bring it to the test,°
Which is the basest creature, man or beast.
Birds feed on birds, beasts on each other prey,
But savage man alone does man betray: 130
Pressed by necessity they kill for food,
Man undoes man to do himself no good.
With teeth and claws by nature armed, they hunt
Nature's allowance to supply their want.
But man with smiles, embraces, friendship, praise,   135
Inhumanly his fellow's life betrays;
With voluntary pains works his distress,
Not through necessity, but wantonness.
For hunger or for love they fight and tear,
Whilst wretched man is still in arms for fear: 140
For fear he arms, and is of arms afraid,
By fear to fear successively betrayed.
Base fear! The source whence his best passion came,
His boasted honour, and his dear-bought fame:
That lust of power, to which he's such a slave,   145
And for the which alone he dares be brave,°
To which his various projects are designed,
Which makes him generous, affable and kind;
For which he takes such pains to be thought wise
And screws his actions in a forced disguise,°   150
Leading a tedious life in misery
Under laborious mean hypocrisy.
Look to the bottom of his vast design,
Wherein man's wisdom, power and glory join:
The good he acts, the ill he does endure,   155
'Tis all from fear to make himself secure.
Merely for safety after fame we thirst;
For all men would be cowards if they durst.
And honesty's against all common sense;
Men must be knaves, 'tis in their own defence.   160
Mankind's dishonest; if you think it fair
Among known cheats to play upon the square,°
You'll be undone—
Nor can weak Truth your reputation save:
The knaves will all agree to call you knave.   165

Wronged shall he live, insulted o'er, oppressed,
Who dares be less a villain than the rest.
    Thus, sir, you see what human nature craves:
Most men are cowards, all men should be knaves.
The difference lies, as far as I can see,   170
Not in the thing it self, but the degree;
And all the subject matter of debate,
Is only who's a knave of the first rate.'

Addition

All this with indignation have I hurled
At the pretending part of the proud world,°
Who swoll'n with selfish vanity, devise
False freedoms, holy cheats and formal lies,°
Over their fellow slaves to tyrannize.   5
    But if in a court so just a man there be
(In court a just man yet unknown to me)
Who does his needful flattery direct°
Not to oppress and ruin, but protect
(Since flattery, which way so ever laid,   10
Is still a tax on that unhappy trade);°
If so upright a statesman you can find,
Whose passions bend to his unbiased mind,
Who does his arts and policies apply
To raise his country, not his family,   15
Nor while his pride owned avarice withstands,
Receives close bribes through friends' corrupted hands.°
    Is there a churchman who on God relies,
Whose life his faith and doctrine justifies;
Not one blown up with vain prelatic pride,°   20
Who for reproof of sins does man deride,°
Whose envious heart makes preaching a pretence°
With his obstreperous saucy eloquence°
To chide at kings, and rail at men of sense,
Who from his pulpit vents more peevish lies,   25
More bitter railings, scandals, calumnies,

Than at a gossiping are thrown about°
When the good wives get drunk and then fall out;
None of that sensual tribe, whose talents lie
In avarice, pride, sloth and gluttony,   30
Who hunt good livings, but abhor good lives,°
Whose lust exalted to that height arrives
They act adultery with their own wives,
And ere a score of years completed be,
Can from the lofty pulpit proudly see   35
Half a large parish their own progeny.
Nor doting bishop, who would be adored
For domineering at the council board,
A greater fop in business at fourscore,
Fonder of serious toys, affected more   40
Than the gay glittering fool at twenty proves,
With all his noise, his tawdry clothes and loves.

　　But a meek humble man of honest sense,
Who preaching peace does practise continence,
Whose pious life's a proof he does believe   45
Mysterious truths which no man can conceive.°
If upon earth there dwell such God-like men,
I'll here recant my paradox to them,°
Adore those shrines of virtue, homage pay,
And with the rabble world, their laws obey.   50

　　If such there be, yet grant me this at least,
Man differs more from man, than man from beast.

A Letter from Artemiza in the Town
to Chloe in the Country

Chloe, in verse by your command I write;
Shortly you'll bid me ride astride and fight.°
These talents better with our sex agree
Than lofty flights of dang'rous Poetry.
Amongst the men (I mean the men of wit—   5
At least they passed for such before they writ)

How many bold advent'rers for the bays,°
Proudly designing large returns of praise,
Who durst that stormy pathless world explore,
Were soon dashed back, and wrecked on the dull shore,   10
Broke of that little stock they had before!
How would a woman's tott'ring bark be tossed,
Where stoutest ships (the men of wit) are lost?
When I once reflect on this, I straight grow wise,
And my own self thus gravely I advise,   15
Dear Artemiza, poetry's a snare;
Bedlam has many mansions—have a care:°
Your muse diverts you, makes the reader sad;
You fancy you're inspired, he thinks you mad.
Consider too, 'twill be discreetly done   20
To make yourself the fiddle of the Town,°
To find th'ill-humoured pleasure at their need,
Cursed if you fail, and scorned though you succeed.
Thus, like an arrant woman as I am,°
No sooner well convinced writing's a shame—   25
That whore is scarce a more reproachful name
Than Poetess—
As men that marry, or as maids that woo,
Because 'tis the worst thing that they can do,
Pleased with the contradiction and the sin,   30
Methinks I stand on thorns till I begin.°
    Y'expect at least to hear what loves have passed
In this lewd town since you and I met last.
What change has happened of intrigues, and whether
The old ones last, and who and who's together.   35
But how, my dearest Chloe, shall I set
My pen to write what I would fain forget,
Or name that lost thing (Love) without a tear,
Since so debauched by ill-bred customs here?
Love, the most gen'rous passion of the mind,   40
The softest refuge innocence can find,
The safe director of unguided youth,
Fraught with kind wishes, and secured by Truth,
That cordial drop Heav'n in our cup has thrown,°
To make the nauseous draught of Life go down,   45

On which one only blessing God might raise,°
In lands of atheists, subsidies of praise°
(For none did e'er so dull and stupid prove
But felt a god and blest his pow'r in Love).
This only joy, for which poor we were made,   50
Is grown, like play, to be an arrant trade;°
The rooks creep in, and it has got of late°
As many little cheats and tricks as that.
But what yet more a woman's heart would vex,
'Tis chiefly carried on by our own sex,   55
Our silly sex who, born like monarchs free,
Turn gypsies for a meaner liberty,°
And hate restraint, though but from infamy.°
They call whatever is not common, nice,°
And deaf to Nature's rule, or Love's advice,   60
Forsake the pleasure, to pursue the vice.
To an exact perfection they have wrought
The action love; the passion is forgot.°
'Tis below wit, they tell you, to admire,
And e'en without approving they desire.   65
Their private wish obeys the public voice,
'Twixt good and bad whimsy decides, not choice.
Fashions grow up for taste, at forms they strike;°
They know what they would have, not what they like.°
Bovey's a beauty if some few agree°   70
To call him so; the rest to that degree
Affected are, that with their ears they see.

    Where I was visiting the other night,
Comes a fine Lady with her humble knight,
Who had prevailed on her, through her own skill,   75
At his request, though much against his will,
To come to London.
As the coach stopped, we heard her voice more loud
Than a great-bellied woman's in a crowd,
Telling the knight that her affairs require   80
He for some hours obsequiously retire.
I think she was ashamed to have him seen
(Hard fate of husbands)—the gallant had been,°
Though a diseased ill-favoured fool, brought in.°

'Dispatch', says she, 'that bus'ness you pretend,   85
Your beastly visit to your drunken friend;
A bottle ever makes you look so fine!
Methinks I long to smell you stink of wine.
Your country drinking breath's enough to kill—
Sour ale corrected with a lemon pill.°   90
Prithee farewell—we'll meet again anon';
The necessary thing bows, and is gone.°
She flies up stairs, and all the haste does show
That fifty antic postures will allow,°
And then bursts out—'Dear Madam, am not I   95
The alter'dst creature breathing? Let me die,°
I find my self ridiculously grown
Embarrassé with being out of Town,
Rude, and untaught, like any Indian queen;°
My country nakedness is strangely seen.°   100
How is Love governed—Love that rules the state,
And, pray, who are the men most worn of late?
When I was married, fools were a la mode,
The men of wit were then held incommode:°
Slow of belief, and fickle in desire,   105
Who ere they'll be persuaded, must inquire,
As if they came to spy, not to admire.
With searching wisdom, fatal to their ease,
They still find out why what may should not please;°
Nay, take themselves for injured when we dare   110
Make 'em think better of us than we are,
And if we hide our frailties from their sights,
Call us deceitful jilts, and hypocrites.
They little guess, who at our arts are grieved,
The perfect joy of being well deceived;   115
Inquisitive as jealous cuckolds grow:
Rather than not be knowing they will know
What, being known, creates their certain woe.
Women should these of all mankind avoid;
For wonder by clear knowledge is destroyed.   120
Woman, who is an arrant bird of night,
Bold in the dusk, before a fool's dull sight,
Should fly, when reason brings the glaring light.

But the kind easy fool, apt to admire°
Himself, trusts us: his follies all conspire   125
To flatter his and favour our desire.
Vain of his proper merit, he with ease°
Believes we love him best who best can please.
On him our gross dull common flatt'ries pass:
Ever most joyful when most made an ass,   130
Heavy to apprehend, though all mankind
Perceive us false, the fop concerned is blind,
Who doting on himself,
Thinks ev'ry one that sees him of his mind.

      These are true women's men.'—Here forced to cease,   135
Through want of breath (not will) to hold her peace,
She to the window runs, where she had spied
Her much esteemed dear friend the monkey tied.°
With forty smiles, as many antic bows,
As if't had been the lady of the house,   140
The dirty chatt'ring monster she embraced,
And made it this fine tender speech at last.
'Kiss me, thou curious miniature of man;
How odd thou art! How pretty! How japan!°
Oh! I could live, and die with thee'—then on   145
For half an hour in compliment she run.
I took this time to think what Nature meant
When this mixed thing into the world she sent,
So very wise, yet so impertinent.
One who knew ev'ry thing, whom God thought fit   150
Should be an ass through choice, not want of wit;
Whose foppery, without the help of sense,
Could ne'er have rose to such an excellence.
Nature's as lame, in making a true fop
As a philosopher: the very top   155
And dignity of folly we attain
By studious search, and labour of the brain,
By observation, counsel, and deep thought;
God never made a coxcomb worth a groat.
We owe that name to industry and arts: 160
An eminent fool must be a fool of parts;°

And such a one was she, who had turned o'er
As many books, as men, loved much, read more,
Had a discerning wit, to her was known
Ev'ry one's fault, and merit, but her own.   165
All the good qualities that ever blest
A woman, so distinguished from the rest,
Except discretion only, she possessed.
'But now, mon cher, dear Pug,' she cries, 'adieu',°
And the discourse broke off does thus renew.   170
   'You smile to see me (whom the world perchance
Mistakes to have some wit) so far advance
The interest of fools that I approve
Their merit more than men's of wit, in love.
But in our sex too many proofs there are   175
Of such whom wits undo, and fools repair.
This in my time was so observed a rule,
Hardly a wench in Town but had her fool.
The meanest common slut who long was grown
The jest and scorn of ev'ry pit-buffoon,°   180
Had yet left charms enough to have subdued
Some fop or other, fond to be thought lewd:°
Foster could make an Irish Lord a Nokes,°
And Betty Morris had her City-Cokes.°
A woman's ne'er so ruined but she can   185
Be still revenged on her undoer Man:
How lost so e'er, she'll find some lover more
A lewd abandoned fool than she a whore.°
That wretched thing Corinna, who had run
Through all the several ways of being undone,   190
Cozened at first by Love, and living then°
By turning the too-dear-bought trick on men—°
Gay were the hours, and winged with joy they flew,
When first the Town her early beauties knew:
Courted, admired, and loved, with presents fed,   195
Youth in her looks, and pleasure in her bed,
Till Fate, or her ill angel, thought it fit
To make her dote upon a man of wit,

Who found 'twas dull to love above a day,°
Made his ill-natured jest, and went his way.   200
Now scorned by all, forsaken and oppressed,
She's a *memento mori* to the rest.
Diseased, decayed, to take up half a crown,
Must mortgage her long scarf and mantua gown.°
Poor creature! who, unheard of, as a fly,   205
In some dark hole must all the winter lie,
And want and dirt endure a whole half year,
That for one month she tawdry may appear.°
In Easter term she gets her a new gown,°
When my young master's worship comes to Town,°   210
From pedagogue and mother just set free,
The heir and hopes of a great family,
Which with strong ale and beef the country rules,
And ever since the Conquest have been fools.°
And now with careful prospect to maintain   215
This character, lest crossing of the strain°
Should mend the booby-breed, his friends provide°
A cousin of his own to be his bride.
And thus set out
With an estate, no wit, and a young wife   220
(The solid comforts of a coxcomb's life),
Dunghill and pease forsook, he comes to Town,°
Turns spark, learns to be lewd, and is undone.
Nothing suits worse with vice than want of sense;
Fools are still wicked at their own expense.   225
This o'ergrown schoolboy lost Corinna wins,
And at first dash, to make an ass begins;
Pretends to like a man who has not known°
The vanities nor vices of the Town:
Fresh in his youth, and faithful in his love,   230
Eager of joys which he does seldom prove;°
Healthful and strong, he does no pains endure
But what the fair one he adores can cure;°
Grateful for favours does the sex esteem,
And libels none, for being kind to him.°   235
Then of the lewdness of the times complains,
Rails at the wits and atheists, and maintains

'Tis better than good sense, than pow'r, or wealth,
To have alone untainted youth and health.
The unbred puppy, who had never seen°   240
A creature look so gay, or talk so fine,
Believes, then falls in love, and then in debt,
Mortgages all, e'en to th'ancient seat,
To buy his mistress a new house for life,
To give her plate and jewels robs his wife;   245
And when to the height of fondness he is grown,
'Tis time to poison him, and all's her own.
Thus meeting in her common arms his fate,
He leaves her bastard heir to his estate,
And as the race of such an owl deserves,°   250
His own dull lawful progeny he starves.
Nature, who never made a thing in vain,
But does each insect to some end ordain,
Wisely provides kind-keeping fools, no doubt,°
To patch up vices men of wit wear out.'°   255
Thus she ran on two hours, some grains of sense
Still mixed with volleys of impertinence.
But now 'tis time I should some pity show
To Chloe, since I cannot choose but know
Readers must reap the dulness writers sow.   260
By the next post such stories I will tell
As, joined with these, shall to a volume swell,
As true as Heaven, more infamous than Hell;
But you are tired, and so am I. Farewell.

Tunbridge Wells

At five this morn, when Phoebus raised his head°
From Thetis' lap, I raised my self from bed°
And mounting steed, I trotted to the waters,
The rendezvous of fools, buffoons, and praters,°
Cuckolds, whores, citizens, their wives and daughters.°   5
My squeamish stomach I with wine had bribed
To undertake the dose it was prescribed;

But turning head, a sudden cursed view
That innocent provision overthrew
And without drinking made me purge and spew.   10
From coach and six a thing unwieldy rolled
Whose lumber cart more decently would hold:
As wise as calf it looked, as big as bully,°
But handled proves a mere Sir Nicholas Cully,°
A bawling fop, a natural Nokes, and yet°   15
He dares to censure as if he had wit.
To make him more ridiculous, in spite
Nature contrived the fool should be a knight.
Grant ye unlucky stars this o'ergrown boy
To purchase some inspiring pretty toy   20
That may his want of sense and wit supply
As buxom crabfish does his lechery.°
Though he alone were dismal sight enough,
His train contributed to set him off:
All of his shape, all of the self same stuff.   25
No spleen or malice need on them be thrown:
Nature has done the bus'ness of lampoon,
And in their looks their characters has shown.
Thrice blest be he who dildo did invent
To ram the neighbouring hole to fundament,°   30
Which may be lengthened, thickened in its measure,
And used at lecherous ugly Trulla's pleasure;°
For ne'er was bulk or stomach given to tarses°
Either to fill or smell such foggy arses.°
Endeavouring this irksome sight to balk   35
And a more irksome noise, their silly talk,
I silently slunk down t'th'lower walk.°
But often when one would Charybdis shun
Down upon Scylla 'tis one's fate to run,°
For here it was my cursed luck to find   40
As great a fop, though of another kind:
A tall stiff fool that walked in Spanish guise;°
The buckram puppet never stirred its eyes°
But grave as owl it looked, as woodcock wise.°
He scorns the empty talking of this mad age   45
And speaks all proverbs, sentences, and adage;

Can with as much solemnity buy eggs
As a cabal can talk of their intrigues;°
Master of ceremonies, yet can dispense
With the formality of talking sense.   50
From hence unto the upper end I ran,°
Where a new scene of foppery began:
A tribe of curates, priests, canonical elves,°
Fit company for none besides themselves,
Were got together; each his distemper told—   55
Scurvy, stone, strangury; some were so bold°
To charge the spleen to be their misery°
And on that wise disease brought infamy.°
But none had modesty enough to 'plain°
Their want of learning, honesty, and brain,   60
The general diseases of that train.
These call themselves ambassadors of heaven
And saucily pretend commissions given;°
But should an Indian king whose small command
Seldom extends beyond ten miles of land   65
Send forth such wretched fools in an embassage,°
He'd find but small effects of such a message.
List'ning I found the cob of all this rabble:°
Pert Bays, with his Importance Comfortable.°
He being raised to an Archdeaconry   70
By trampling on religion's liberty,
Was grown too great, and looked too fat and jolly
To be disturbed with care and melancholy,
Tho' Marvell has enough exposed his folly.
He drank to carry off some old remains   75
His lazy dull distemper left in's veins.°
Let him drink on, but 'tis not a whole flood
Can give sufficient sweetness to his blood
To make his nature or his manners good.
Importance drank too tho' she'd been no sinner   80
To wash away some dregs he had spewed in her.°
Next after these a fulsome Irish crew
Of silly Macks were offered to my view.°
The things did talk but th'hearing what they said
I did my self the kindness to evade: 85

Nature has placed these wretches beneath scorn;
They can't be called so vile as they are born.
Amidst the crowd, next I my self conveyed,
For now were come, white wash and paint be'ng laid,
Mother and daughter, mistress and the maid,   90
And squire with wig and pantaloon displayed;°
But ne'er could conventicle, play, or fair°
For a true medley with this herd compare:°
Here lords, knights, squires, ladies, and countesses,
Chandlers, mum-bacon women, seamstresses°   95
Were mixed together, nor did they agree,
More in their humours than their quality.°
Here waiting for a gallant, young damsel stood,
Leaning on cane, and muffled up in hood.
The would-be wit, whose bus'ness was to woo,   100
With hat removed, and solemn scrape of shoe,
Advanceth bowing, then genteely shrugs
And ruffled foretop into order tugs°
And thus accosts her: 'Madam, methinks the weather
Is grown much more serene since you came hither.   105
You influence th'heavens; and should the sun
Withdraw himself to see his rays outdone
By your bright eyes, they would supply the morn
And make a day before the day be born.'
With mouth screwed up, conceited winking eyes,   110
And breasts thrust forward, 'Lord! sir,' she replies,
'It is your goodness and not my deserts
Which makes you show this learning, wit, and parts.'°
He puzzled bites his nails, both to display
The sparkling ring, and think what next to say,   115
And thus breaks forth afresh, 'Madam, egad,
Your luck at cards last night was very bad:
At cribbage fifty-nine, and the next show
To make the game and yet to want those two!°
God damn me, Madam! I'm th'son of a whore   120
If in my life I saw the like before.'
To pedlar's stall he drags her, and her breast°
With hearts and such like foolish toys he drest,

And then more smartly to expound the riddle
Of all his prattle gives her a Scotch fiddle.° 125
Tired with this dismal stuff, away I ran
Where were two wives with girl just fit for man,°
Short-breathed with pallid lips and visage wan.
Some courtesies passed, and the old compliment
Of being glad to see each other spent, 130
With hand in hand they lovingly did walk
And one began thus to renew the talk:
'I pray, good Madam, if it may be thought
No rudeness, what cause was't hither brought
Your ladyship?'; she, soon replying, smiled, 135
'We have a good estate but have no child
And I'm inform'd these wells will make a barren
Woman as fruitful as a cony warren.'°
The first returned, 'For this cause I am come
For I can have no quietness at home: 140
My husband grumbles tho' we have got one
(This poor young girl) and mutters for a son;
And this is grieved with headache, pangs, and throes,
Is full sixteen, and never yet had those.'°
She soon replied, 'get her a husband, Madam! 145
I married at that age, and ne'er had had 'um;
Was just like her; steel waters let alone:°
A back of steel will bring them better down.'°
And ten to one, but they themselves will try
The same means t'increase their family! 150
Poor foolish Fribble, who by subtlety°
Of midwife (truest friend to lechery)°
Persuaded art to be at pains and charge
To give thy wife occasion to enlarge
Thy silly head; for here walk Cuff and Kick° 155
With brawny back, and legs, and potent prick,
Who more substantially will cure thy wife
And on her half-dead womb bestow new life:
From these the waters got the reputation
Of good assistants unto generation. 160

Some warlike men were now got into the throng
With hair tied back, singing a bawdy song.
Not much afraid I got a nearer view
And 'twas my chance to know this dreadful crew:
They were cadets that seldom can appear,°   165
Damned to the stint of thirty pounds a year;
With hawk on fist or greyhound led in hand,
The dogs and footboys sometimes they command.
But now having trimmed a cast-off spavined horse,°
With three hard-pinched-for guineas in the purse,   170
Two rusty pistols, scarf about the arse,°
Coat lined with red, they here presume to swell:°
This goes for Captain, that for Colonel.
So the beargarden ape, on his steed mounted,°
No longer is a jackanapes accounted°   175
But is by virtue of his trumpery then°
Called by the name of 'the young Gentleman'.
Bless me, thought I, what thing is man that thus
In all his shapes he is ridiculous!°
Ourselves with noise of reason we do please   180
In vain; humanity's our worst disease.
Thrice happy beasts are, who because they be
Of reason void, are so of foppery.
Faith I was so ashamed that with remorse
I used the insolence to mount my horse;   185
For he doing only things fit for his nature
Did seem to me, by much, the wiser creature.

Of Marriage

Out of stark love, and arrant devotion,
Of marriage I'll give you this galloping notion.
'Tis the bane of all bus'ness, the end of all pleasure,
The consumption of wit, youth, virtue, and treasure;
'Tis the rack of our thoughts, night-mare of our sleep   5
That calls us to work before the day peep,°
Commands us to make brick without stubble or straw.°
A cunt has no sense of conscience or law.

If you needs must have flesh, take the way that is noble:
In a gen'rous wench there's nothing of trouble;° 10
You come on, you come off, say, do what you please,
And the worst you can fear is but a disease,
And diseases, you know, will admit of a cure;
But the hell-fire of marriage the damned do endure.

Upon Nothing

Nothing, thou elder brother even to shade,
Thou had'st a being ere the world was made
And (well fixed) art alone of ending not afraid.

Ere time and place were, time and place were not,
When primitive nothing something straight begot;° 5
Then all proceeded from the great united what.

Something, the general attribute of all,
Severed from thee, its sole original,
Into thy boundless self must undistinguished fall.

Yet Something did thy mighty power command 10
And from thy fruitful emptiness's hand
Snatched men, beasts, birds, fire, water, air, and land.

Matter, the wicked'st offspring of thy race,
By Form assisted, flew from thy embrace,
And rebel Light obscured thy reverend dusky face. 15

With Form and Matter Time and Place did join;
Body (thy foe) with these did leagues combine
To spoil thy peaceful realm and ruin all thy line.

But turn-coat Time assists the foe in vain
And (bribed by thee) destroys their short-lived reign, 20
And to thy hungry womb drives back thy slaves again.

Though mysteries are barred from laic eyes,°
And the divine alone with warrant pries°
Into thy bosom where the truth in private lies,°

Yet this of thee the wise may truly say: 25
Thou from the virtuous nothing tak'st away,
And to be part of thee, the wicked wisely pray.

Great negative, how vainly would the wise
Enquire, define, distinguish, teach, devise,
Didst thou not stand to point their blind philosophies!°   30

Is, or is not, the two great ends of fate,
And true or false, the subject of debate
That perfect or destroy the vast designs of state,

When they have wracked the politician's breast,
Within thy bosom most securely rest,   35
And, when reduced to thee, are least unsafe and best.

But, Nothing, why does something still permit
That sacred monarchs should at council sit
With persons highly thought, at best for nothing fit,°

Whilst weighty Something modestly abstains   40
From prince's coffers and from statesman's brains,°
And nothing there, like stately something, reigns?°

Nothing, who dwell'st with fools in grave disguise,
For whom they reverend shapes and forms devise,
Lawn sleeves and furs and gowns, when they like thee look wise,° 45

French truth, Dutch prowess, British policy,°
Hibernian learning, Scotch civility,°
Spaniard's dispatch, Dane's wit are mainly seen in thee;°

The great man's gratitude to his best friend,
Kings' promises, whores' vows—towards thee they bend,   50
Flow swiftly into thee, and in thee ever end.

To the Post Boy

Son of a whore, God damn you, can you tell
A peerless peer the readiest way to Hell?
I've out swilled Bacchus, sworn of my own make°
Oaths would fright furies and make Pluto quake;°
I've swived more whores more ways than Sodom's walls°   5
E'er knew or the college of Rome's cardinals.
Witness heroic scars—look here—ne'er go:
Cerecloths and ulcers from the top to toe.°
Frighted at my own mischiefs I have fled
And bravely left my life's defender dead,   10
Broke houses to break chastity, and dyed
That floor with murther which my lust denied.°
Pox on't, why do I speak of these poor things?
I have blasphemed my God and libelled kings.°
The readiest way to Hell? come quick, ne'er stir!°   15
BOY. The readiest way, my Lord,'s by Rochester.°

From 'An Essay on Satire'
[by John Sheffield, Earl of Mulgrave, assisted by John Dryden]

Rochester I despise for his mere want of wit,°
Though thought to have a tail and cloven feet.
For while he mischief means to all mankind,
Himself alone the ill effect does find,
And so, like witches, justly suffers shame   5
Whose harmless malice is so much the same.
False are his words, affected as his wit,
So often he does aim, so seldom hit.
To ev'ry face he cringes, whilst he speaks,
But when the back is turned, the head he breaks.   10
Mean in each motion, lewd in ev'ry limb,
Manners themselves are mischievous in him.
A proof that chance alone makes ev'ry creature,
A very Killigrew without good nature.°
For what a Bessus hath he always lived°   15
And his own kicking notably contrived?

For there's the folly that's still mixed with fear:°
Cowards more blows than any hero bear;
Of fighting sparks some may their pleasure say°
But 'tis a bolder thing, to run away.°   20
The world may well forgive him all his ill,
For every fault does prove his penance still.°
Falsely he falls into some dangerous noose,°
And then as meanly labours to get loose.
A life so infamous, it's better quitting,°   25
Spent in base injuring and low submitting.
I'd like to have left out his poetry,
Forgot almost by all as well as me.
Sometimes he hath some humour, never wit,
And if it ever (very rarely) hit,   30
'Tis under so much nasty rubbish laid,
To find it out's the cinder-woman's trade,
Who for the wretched remnants of a fire
Must toil all day in ashes and in mire.
So lewdly dull his idle works appear,°   35
The wretched text deserves no comment here,
Where one poor thought's sometimes left all alone,
For a whole page of dulness to atone;
'Mongst forty bad's one tolerable line
Without expression, fancy, or design.°   40

My Lord All-pride

Bursting with pride the loathed impostume swells,°
Prick him he sheds his venom straight and smells;
But 'tis so lewd a scribbler that he writes°
With as much force to nature as he fights.°
Hardened in shame, 'tis such a baffled fop°   5
That every schoolboy whips him like a top.
And with his arm and heart his brain's so weak
That his starved fancy is compelled to rake
Among the excrements of others' wit
To make a stinking meal of what they shit.   10

So swine for nasty meat to dunghill run,
And toss their gruntling snouts up when they've done.
Against his stars the coxcomb ever strives,
And to be something they forbid contrives.
With a red nose, splay-foot, and goggle eye,   15
A ploughman's looby mien, face all awry,°
With stinking breath, and every loathsome mark,
The Punchinello sets up for a spark.°
With equal self-conceit too he bears arms,°
But with that vile success his part performs°   20
That he burlesques his trade, and what is best
In others turns, like Harlequin, to jest.°
So have I seen at Smithfield's wondrous fair°
(When all his brother monsters flourish there)°
A lubbard elephant divert the Town°   25
With making legs and shooting off a gun.°
Go where he will, he never finds a friend,
Shame and derision all his steps attend;
Alike abroad, at home, i'th' camp and court
This knight o'th' burning pestle makes us sport.°   30

Ephelia to Bajazet
[by Sir George Etherege?]

How far are they deceived who hope in vain
A lasting lease of joys from love t'obtain!
All the dear sweets we promise or expect,
After enjoyment, turns to a cold neglect.°
Could love a constant happiness have known,   5
The mighty wonder had in me been shown.
Our passions were so favoured by fate,
As if she meant 'em an eternal date;°
So kind he looked, such tender words he spoke,
'Twas past belief such vows should e'er be broke.   10
Fixed on my eyes, how often would he say
He could with pleasure gaze an age away!
When thoughts too great for words had made him mute,
In kisses he would tell my hand his suit.

So great his passion was, so far above   15
The common gallantries that pass for love,
At worst I thought if he unkind should prove,
His ebbing passion would be kinder far
Than the first transports of all others are.
Nor was my love or fondness less than his,   20
In him I centred all my hopes of bliss;
For him my duty to my friends forgot,
For him I lost—alas! what lost I not?
Fame, all the valuable things of life,
To meet his love, by a less name than wife.°   25
How happy was I then, how dearly blest,
When this great man lay panting on my breast,
Looking such things as ne'er can be expressed!
Thousand fresh looks he gave me ev'ry hour,
Whilst greedily I did his looks devour,   30
Till quite o'ercome with charms I trembling lay,
At ev'ry look he gave melted away.
I was so highly happy in his love,
Methoughts I pitied them that dwelt above!
Think then, thou greatest, loveliest, falsest man,   35
How you have vowed, how I have loved, and then,
My faithless dear, be cruel if you can!
How I have loved, I cannot, need not tell—
No! ev'ry act has shown I loved too well.
Since first I saw you, I ne'er had a thought   40
Was not entirely yours; to you I brought
My virgin innocence, and freely made
My love an off'ring to your noble bed.
Since when, y'ave been the star by which I steered,
And nothing else but you I loved or feared.   45
Your smiles I only live by, and I must,
When e'er you frown, be shattered into dust.
Oh! can the coldness that you show me now
Suit with the gen'rous heat you once did show?°
I cannot live on pity, or respect: 50
A thought so mean would my whole love infect;
Less than your love I scorn, sir, to expect.

Let me not live in dull indiff'rency,
But give me rage enough to make me die!°
For if from you I needs must meet my fate,   55
Before your pity I would choose your hate.

A Very Heroical Epistle in Answer to Ephelia

Madam,
If you're deceived, it is not by my cheat,
For all disguises are below the great.
What man or woman upon earth can say
I ever used 'em well above a day?   5
How is it then that I inconstant am?
He changes not, who always is the same.
In my dear self I centre every thing:
My servants, friends, my mistress, and my king,
Nay Heaven and Earth, to that one point I bring.   10
Well-mannered, honest, generous and stout°
(Names by dull fools to plague mankind found out)°
Should I regard, I must my self constrain,°
And 'tis my maxim to avoid all pain.°
You fondly look for what none e'er could find,°   15
Deceive your self, and then call me unkind,
And by false reasons would my falshood prove,
For 'tis as natural to change as love.
You may as justly at the sun repine
Because alike it does not always shine.   20
No glorious thing was ever made to stay;
My blazing star but visits and away.°
As fatal too, it shines as those i'th'skies;°
'Tis never seen but some great Lady dies.
The boasted favour you so precious hold   25
To me's no more than changing of my gold.°
What e'er you gave, I paid you back in bliss,
Then where's the obligation, pray, of this?
If heretofore you found grace in my eyes,
Be thankful for it, and let that suffice.   30

But women beggar-like still haunt the door
Where they've received a charity before.
O happy sultan! whom we barbarous call,°
How much refined art thou above us all!
Who envies not the joys of thy serail?°   35
Thee, like some god, the trembling crowd adore,
Each man's thy slave, and woman kind thy whore.
Methinks I see thee underneath the shade
Of golden canopies supinely laid,
Thy crouching slaves all silent as the night,°   40
But at thy nod all active as the light.
Secure in solid sloth thou there dost reign,°
And feel'st the joys of love without the pain.
Each female courts thee with a wishing eye,
While thou with awful pride walk'st careless by,   45
Till thy kind pledge at last marks out the dame
Thou fanciest most to quench thy present flame.
Then from thy bed submissive she retires,
And thankful for thy grace no more requires.°
No loud reproach, nor fond unwelcome sound   50
Of women's tongues thy sacred ear dares wound.
If any do, a nimble mute straight ties
The true love knot, and stops her foolish cries.°
Thou fear'st no injured kinsman's threat'ning blade°
Nor midnight ambushes by rivals laid;°   55
While here with aching hearts our joys we taste,
Disturbed by swords like Damocles his feast.°

An Epistolary Essay, from M. G. to O. B.
upon their Mutual Poems

Dear friend, I hear this Town does so abound
With saucy censurers that faults are found°
With what of late we, in poetic rage°
Bestowing, threw away on the dull age;
But howsoever envy their spleen may raise   5
To rob my brows of the deserved bays,

Their thanks at least I merit since, through me,
They are partakers of your poetry.
And this is all I'll say in my defence:
T'obtain one line of your well-worded sense   10
I'd be content t'have writ the *British Prince*.°
I'm none of those who think themselves inspired,
Nor write with the vain hope to be admired;
But from a rule I have (upon long trial)
T'avoid with care all sort of self-denial,   15
Which way so e'er desire and fancy lead,
(Contemning fame) that path I boldly tread.
And if exposing what I take for wit,°
To my dear self a pleasure I beget,
No matter though the cens'ring critics fret.   20
Those whom my muse displeases are at strife
With equal spleen against my course of life,
The least delight of which I'll not forgo,
For all the flatt'ring praise man can bestow.
If I designed to please, the way were then   25
To mend my manners rather than my pen:
The first's unnatural, therefore unfit,
And for the second, I despair of it,
Since grace is not so hard to get as wit.
Perhaps ill verses ought to be confined,   30
In mere good breeding, like unsav'ry wind.°
Were reading forced, I should be apt to think
Men might no more write scurvily than stink.
But 'tis your choice whether you'll read or no;
If likewise of your smelling it were so,   35
I'd fart just as I write, for my own ease,
Nor should you be concerned, unless you please.
I'll own that you write better than I do,°
But I have as much need to write as you.
What though th'excrements of my dull brain   40
Runs in a harsh insipid strain,°
Whilst your rich head eases itself of wit—
Must none but civet cats have leave to shit?°
In all I write should sense and wit and rhyme
Fail me at once, yet something so sublime°   45

Shall stamp my poem that the world may see
It could have been produced by none but me;
And that's my end, for man can wish no more
Than so to write as none e'er writ before.°
Yet why am I no poet of the times?°   50
I have allusions, similes and rhymes,
And wit—or else 'tis hard that I alone
Of the whole race of mankind should have none.
Unequally the partial hand of heav'n
Has all but this one only blessing giv'n.   55
The world appears like a great family
Whose Lord, oppressed with pride and poverty,
That to a few great plenty he may show,
Is fain to starve the numerous train below.°
Just so seems Providence, as poor and vain,   60
Keeping more creatures than it can maintain;
Here 'tis profuse, and there it meanly saves,
And for one prince it makes ten thousand slaves.
In wit alone 't has been magnificent,°
Of which so just a share to each is sent   65
That the most avaricious are content;
For none e'er thought (the due division's such)
His own too little, or his friend's too much.
Yet most men show or find great want of wit,
Writing themselves, or judging what is writ.   70
But I, who am of sprightly vigour full,
Look on mankind as envious and dull;
Born to myself, myself I like alone°
And must conclude my judgment good or none.
For should my sense be naught, how could I know   75
Whether another man's were good or no?
Thus I resolve of my own poetry
That 'tis the best, and there's a fame for me.
If then I'm happy, what does it advance
Whether to merit due or arrogance?   80
Oh! but the world will take offence thereby;°
Why then the world shall suffer for't, not I.
Did e'er this saucy world and I agree
To let it have its beastly will on me?

Why should my prostituted sense be drawn   85
To ev'ry rule their musty customs spawn?°
But men will censure you, 'tis two to one;
When e'er they censure, they'll be in the wrong.
There's not a thing on earth that I can name
So foolish and so false as common fame.°   90
It calls the courtier knave, the plain man rude,
Haughty the grave and the delightful lewd,
Impertinent the brisk, morose the sad,°
Mean the familiar, th'reserved one mad.°
Poor helpless woman is not favoured more: 95
She's a sly hypocrite, or public whore.
Then who the devil would give this—to be free°
From the innocent reproach of infamy.°
These things considered make me, in despite
Of idle rumour, keep at home and write.   100

EXPLANATORY NOTES

SONGS AND LOVE LYRICS

3 *The Discovery*. First printed in *A Collection of Poems, Written upon several Occasions, By several Persons* (1672) but probably written while R. was on the Grand Tour in 1664 and still writing in a heavily conceited style 'palpably influenced by Donne' (Love). In 'Harbin', though, the poem comes between 'The Mistress' and 'Absent from thee I languish still', two of R.'s most mature and complex lyrics. The 'discovery' is the acknowledgement of her lovers which the speaker presses the lady to make at ll. 26–8.

l. 3. *ideas*. Ideals.

l. 14. *challenges*. Asks for.

l. 26. *own*. Claim responsibility for.

4 l. 33. *to my state*. In my condition.

Song [Give me leave to rail at you]. The first stanza was printed with a vocal setting in *Songs for 1, 2 & 3 Voyces composed by Henry Bowman* (1677). Together with 'The Answer', the poem forms a musical dialogue, jointly composed by R. and his wife.

l. 8. *would not*. Do not want to.

ll. 11–12. *Anger . . . Love*. Alluding to the myth of Venus seducing Mars, a favourite subject for painters.

The Answer [by Elizabeth Wilmot, Countess of Rochester]. The 'Portland' copy, in the handwriting of R.'s wife, includes only the first two stanzas; ll. 17–24, added in *1680*, derive from scriptorium copies and may not be by her.

l. 1. *fond fire*. 'Fire of devotion'; but also perhaps 'foolish passion', since it needs scorn to sustain it.

l. 5. *insulted on*. Exulted over.

5 ll. 15–16. *Ah! forgive . . . to gain*. 'Forgive me for practising the one form of deviousness that love (which has otherwise rendered me wholly ingenuous) has left me through which to win your love.'

ll. 17–24. *You that could . . . in your arms*. Not in 'Portland'.

l. 18. *pretend*. Aspire.

Song [While on these lovely looks I gaze]. First printed in *A New Collection of the Choicest Songs* (1676). In most of the manuscript sources, as well as *1680* and *1691*, the poem is placed next to 'Love and Life' and 'The Fall'. But it may be an early piece, or a consciously nostalgic one, to judge from its use (at ll. 1–2) of the so-called 'lovers' babies' conceit, popular in Elizabethan lyric, and the Donne-like tautness of its argumentative structure.

5 l. 2. *a wretch*. The speaker himself, reflected in his mistress's eyes.

l. 5. *move*. Plead, in a court of law.

l. 16. *dies*. Reaches orgasm.

6 *Song [Phyllis, be gentler I advise]*. Undatable. First printed in *1680*. Its placement there, after the polite dialogue 'Give me leave to rail at you' and 'The Answer', and before 'To Corinna' reflects the poem's semi-libertine character as a 'persuasion to love' with a sting in the tail. 'Hartwell' has the same sequence. But in 'Gyldenstolpe' it is interposed in the group comprising 'The Fall', 'Love and Life', and 'While on these lovely looks I gaze'.

l. 4. *'Tis high time to repent*. i.e. of the abstinence which constitutes her 'time misspent'.

l. 5. *your*. Referring to women in general.

l. 6. *old so soon*. In the Restoration, a court beauty was considered past her best in her early twenties.

l. 15. *scandal*. Scandalous reputation.

The Mistress. Undatable. The final stanza is present only in 'Harbin', and Love argues that it was cut from the other two sources, *1691* and 'Hartwell', because 'of its "Popish" tendency or simple impiety'. But it might equally have been dropped for aesthetic reasons, by readers who registered its coarse rhythms and diction as an attack on the lyricism of the conclusive-sounding l. 36. Whether this attack formed part of R.'s original scheme for the poem, or was the result of sceptical second thoughts is not clear.

7 l. 16. *Short ages, living graves*. Oxymorons representative of the fantastical quality of the speaker's thought in the first three stanzas.

l. 17. *Whene'er*. If ever.

l. 20. *had*. Would have.

l. 29. *Fantastic fancies fondly move*. 'Extravagant imaginations are foolishly suggestible.'

ll. 33–6. *Kind jealous doubt . . . blest at last*. Cf. Matthew 6: 19–21: 'Lay not up for yourselves treasure upon earth, where moth and rust doth corrupt, and where thieves break through and steal: | But lay up yourselves treasures in heaven, where neither moth nor rust doth corrupt, and where thieves do not break through nor steal: | For where your treasure is, there will your heart be also.'

8 *Song [Absent from thee I languish still]*. Undatable. Similarities of phrasing, as well as the shared theme of absence, suggest a close link with 'The Mistress', which is reflected in the contiguity of the poems in two out of the three sources containing both, 'Hartwell' and *1691*.

l. 6. *prove*. Experience.

[Song] [Version 1: 'How happy, Chloris, were they free']. The three surviving versions of this lyric 'provide a rare opportunity to see a poem by

Rochester in the process of revision' (Walker). But whether R. was improving the poem towards a final state, or recalibrating it for different audiences, is not certain. This version is the one in 'Harbin' and 'Hartwell': either an early draft which R. later expanded, or a censoring of the longer poem to make it fit for family consumption.

l. 3. *formal*. Inflexible, officious.

l. 7. *Bottle*. Personified, as if a character in a Restoration comedy.

l. 9. *brisk insipid*. Brash yet vapid.   *spark*. Foppish young man.

l. 10. *flutters*. Gads about.

9 *[Song] [Version 2: 'How perfect, Chloris, and how free']*. The version in R's handwriting in 'Portland'.

10 l. 31. *ideas*. Cf. 'The Discovery', l. 3 and n.

To a Lady, in a Letter. The version printed in *A New Collection of the Choicest Songs* (1676), where it is entitled 'Against jealousy', and also in *1691*. The only known manuscript copy is in 'Houghton', which takes the epistolary claim in the title literally by placing the poem after 'An Epistolary Essay, from M. G. to O. B. upon their Mutual Poems'.

l. 13. *that*. Her vagina.

11 l. 24. *cods*. Testicles.

Against Constancy. First printed in *A New Collection of the Choicest Songs* (1676). One of the two surviving manuscript copies is also a musical setting, and the lack of any sardonic or obscene twist in the poem's argument (the 'Haward' copy reads 'And' instead of 'But' at l. 13) suggests R. may have been aiming for a classic treatment of this staple 'Cavalier' song theme. The title given here is from the printed edition.

l. 2. *pretence*. Deceptive claim.

l. 4. *sense*. Physical responsiveness.

l. 9. *idle*. Lacklustre.

12 *Love and Life*. Written some time before 1677, when it was set to music in Henry Bowman's *Songs for 1, 2 & 3 Voyces*. The best-known title of this most famous of R.'s lyrics has fostered a belief that it articulates his personal philosophy, but in some manuscripts the poem is called 'To Phyllis' or just 'Song'. Modern editors have generally put it next to 'The Fall', a linkage for which contemporary precedent exists in 'Hansen', as well as on the more private wing of the textual tradition in 'Harbin' and 'Hartwell'. However, in 'Gyldenstolpe', the two are separated by the semi-libertine 'Phyllis, be gentler I advise', while 'Houghton' pairs 'Love and Life' not with the spiritually elevated 'The Fall' but with the flagrantly obscene 'Love to a Woman'. The extremely high level of textual stability among the surviving manuscript copies of the poem perhaps indicates that R., recognizing its singular quality, took particular care over its transmission.

l. 9. *got*. (i) Obtained; (ii) begotten (cf. 'Upon Nothing', ll. 4–5).

12 l. 14. *livelong*. 'An intensified form of *long* . . . Chiefly in the *livelong day*
    (also *night*)' (*OED*) and so, when applied to 'minute', a witty paradox. But
    R.'s only other use of 'livelong' ('Could I but make my wishes insolent',
    l. 16) is pejorative, and here too 'going on and on' would fit with the sar-
    donic side of 'by miracle'. After 1675, when second hands started being
    added to clocks and watches, the minute was no longer the shortest visible
    unit of time.

    Song [As Chloris full of harmless thought]. First printed as one of the
    collection of songs in *The Wits Academy or, The Muses Delight* (1676),
    the poem was set to music more often than any other of R.'s lyrics by
    Restoration and eighteenth-century composers. No manuscript copies
    survive. Modern editors usually put it next to 'Fair Chloris in a pig-sty'.
    But unless ll. 21–2 describe a fantasy, this particular Chloris is not a real
    shepherdess but a court lady on a pastoral day out, like the 'gallant ladies
    and people, come with bottles and baskets and chairs to sup under the
    trees by the waterside' whom Pepys ogled at Barn Elms in 1667. The only
    one of R's love poems in which 'actual sexual satisfaction as a result of
    heterosexual intercourse is described' (Thormählen).

13 l. 15. *let me*. Let me go.

    A Dialogue between Strephon and Daphne. First printed in *1691*. Possibly
    written in 1674. 'Strephon' is a soubriquet R. applied to himself in
    another pastoral dialogue he wrote as a compliment to the Duchess of
    Portsmouth in the summer of that year, while visiting Bath as a member of
    her entourage.

14 l. 17. *Love like other little boys*. Cupid, the god of love, was represented as
    a young boy.

15 l. 56. *trading*. Workmanlike.

    l. 66. *practice*. (i) Habit; (ii) trick.

16 *Song [Fair Chloris in a pig-sty lay]*. Undatable. Love's copy-text:
    'Houghton'. First printed in *1680* and included in the more genteel *1691*
    though without the obscene final stanza. In 'Gyldenstolpe', this libertine
    mock-eclogue unexpectedly precedes 'Love and Life'. More striking still
    is its placement in 'Houghton', where it leads off an isolated grouping
    of three poems by R. whose other members are 'Seneca's *Troas*. Act. 2.
    Chorus' and 'A Satire against Reason and Mankind'. This juxtaposi-
    tion puts a frame of anticlerical philosophy around the lyric, identifying
    Chloris's shame over her sexuality (evident in her dreamy elision of her
    'gruntling' pigs with a human lover) as an instance of the false moral con-
    sciousness propagated by the clerical 'Rogues' of the Seneca translation
    and the 'Satire'.

    l. 8. *ivory pails*. Swill-buckets would hardly be made of ivory, so either the
    pails are just 'made of some light-coloured wood, suggesting ivory' (Love)
    or Chloris is romanticizing them in her dream (as Ellis suggests).

    l. 9. *love-convicted*. Conquered by love.

l. 13. *bosom*. Darling.

l. 14. *gate*. A common seventeenth-century euphemism for 'vulva' (cf. 'cave' at l. 15).

17 ll. 36–40. *Frighted she wakes . . . innocent and pleased*. Not in *1691*.

l. 37. *Nature thus kindly eased*. 'Having thus satisfied her natural appetites.'

A Letter [by Sir Carr Scroope]. Love's copy-text: 'Gyldenstolpe'. Initially affiliated with R. and the Buckingham group, the minor court wit Sir Carr Scroope had defected to the rival Mulgrave faction by the winter of 1676–7 when he began his pursuit of the court beauty Cary Frazier to whom one manuscript copy claims this poem was addressed.

l. 4. *that poor swain*. The speaker, Amintor.

18 *Answer*. R. had taken a passing swipe at Scroope in 'An Allusion to Horace' (cf. ll. 115–17 and n.) but Scroope upped the stakes by alluding to R.'s ignominious role in the Epsom affray (cf. headnote to 'To the Post Boy') in his 'In Defence of Satire', which was circulating in autumn 1676. In 'Gyldenstolpe' and the other manuscript sources, as well as in modern editions, the poem is put next to R.'s other lampoons on court figures. But classing it among the 'Songs and Love Lyrics' brings out R.'s particular achievement, which is to turn Scroope's poem into a savage lampoon against him whilst preserving its (rather fey) lyricism.

l. 6. *forty*. An ironic use of the biblical number for a multitude.

l. 15. *rage*. Passion.

To Corinna. Undatable. First printed in *1680*. The third stanza is missing from the scriptorium copies including 'Gyldenstolpe' but present in the private sources 'Harbin' and 'Hartwell'. In 'Gyldenstolpe', the poem breaks into the normally stable pairing of 'Love and Life' and 'The Fall'. 'Hartwell' makes the more obvious link with 'Phyllis, be gentler I advise', another semi-libertine assault on a coy mistress. In 'Harbin', the poem follows a sequence of ten letters from R. to his wife and young son Charles.

l. 2. *force*. Produce by force.   *harmless*. Ineffectual.

l. 4. *Love cannot lose his own*. 'Love cannot forfeit what is rightfully his' (Corinna's face).

ll. 9–12. *Poor feeble tyrant . . . rules of honour*. See headnote.

l. 9. *tyrant*. i.e. Corinna. She is a tyrant in two senses: because she is attempting to usurp Nature, and because the illegitimate regime she hopes to install, that of Honour, is an authoritarian one.

19 l. 13. *bears*. (i) Displays; (ii) endures (she is her own worst enemy).

Song [At last you'll force me to confess]. Love's copy-text: 'Portland'. First printed in *A New Collection of the Choicest Songs* (1676). R.'s latest biographer relates the poem to his courtship of Elizabeth Malet, on the grounds of its presence in 'Portland', which includes their lyric dialogue. But its immediate neighbour in the manuscript is 'Leave this gaudy gilded stage', which R. probably addressed to his mistress Elizabeth Barry a decade later.

19 l. 5. *surprise*. Take by storm.

ll. 6–7. *give my tongue the glory | To scorn*. 'Allow me at least to boast in conversation about being indifferent to your charms.'

l. 7. *unfaithful*. To the speaker, because they reveal his devotion to the addressee.

Grecian Kindness. First printed in *1691*, and otherwise preserved only in 'Hartwell' and 'Harbin', surprisingly in the case of the latter given the poem's brutally misogynistic manner. The rape of the Trojan women by the conquering Greeks is the subject of tragedies by Euripides and Seneca (cf. 'Seneca's *Troas*. Act 2. Chorus') but neither offers a precedent for R.'s anti-heroic claim that their menfolk were complicit in their violation.

l. 6. *baggage*. (i) Supplies; (ii) 'worthless woman ... so called, because such women follow camps' (Johnson).

l. 9. *This*. The latter.   *that*. The former.

l. 11. *punk*. Concubine.

Love to a Woman. Undatable. First printed in *1680*, but only publishable in *1691* in a censored version. Its status as a textbook case of libertine posturing is confirmed by its placement in *1680*, immediately after 'Régime de Vivre' (once thought to be by R.) which recounts a day in the life of a rake: 'I rise at eleven, I dine about two, | I get drunk before seven, and the next thing I do; | I send for my whore, when for fear of a clap, | I spend in her hand, and I spew in her lap', etc. The compiler of 'Houghton' came up with a more provocative juxtaposition, putting it after 'Love and Life' (with no other poems by R. in the immediate vicinity). The title means 'Love of woman'; the poem is of course addressed to a man.

20 l. 6. *designed for*. Created to be.

l. 7. *Drudge*. 'Copulate in an unfeeling, mechanical way' (Love).

ll. 13–16. *Then give me healthy . . . forty wenches*. This stanza is found in 'Gyldenstolpe' and 'Houghton' but omitted in *1691*.

l. 14. *intrenches*. Butts in.

The Platonic Lady. Undatable. Included in neither *1680* nor *1691*. Both the surviving manuscript copies occur in sources which feature no other work by R. Love's copy-text: Oxford, Bodleian Library, MS Rawlinson D 361. Poems guying 'platonic' or spiritually pure love had a long history, but R.'s use of the adjective is especially outrageous. For his 'Platonic Lady' all forms of sex play short of consummation itself qualify as spiritually elevated. In that sense, the poem also harks back to the so-called 'anti-fruition' lyrics of the early seventeenth century, and therefore 'seems to belong stylistically to the generation of Rochester's father rather than to his own' (Love). But prolonging a mode that was on the point of 'dying' would be wittily apposite given the speaker's sexual tastes.

l. 3. *press*. Urge.

l. 6. *I'd understand*. Probably 'I want to learn', but possibly an elision of 'I do understand'.

l. 7. *the thing is called.* i.e. improperly so, in the Lady's view.   *enjoy-ment.* Consummation.

l. 18. *flat.* Outright. But also a transferred epithet, describing the object of her 'disdain' after she has 'obtained' it.

21 *The Fall.* First printed in *1680*. Closely linked in all the printed and manuscript sources with 'Love and Life' and 'While on these lovely looks I gaze'. The title equivocates between the Christian sense of the noun and its colloquial applications to sexual intercourse (as in 'a tumble' in modern English) and even the detumescence of the penis afterwards. But these are not reasons to reject a possible link with *Paradise Lost*. Indeed, that link may suggest a date for the poem. Milton's epic enjoyed something of a libertine vogue in 1674, following the appearance of the second edition, with its commendatory poem by R.'s favourite non-courtier poet, Marvell. The first draft of Dryden's adaptation of the epic, foregrounding paradisal sexuality, circulated in manuscript at this time. But the extent of R.'s interest in Milton should probably not be exaggerated. Love suggested, in light of the poem's structuring conceit about court attendance, that its original function was as 'a courtly brush-off to a too demanding lover'. If so, the elevated Miltonic atmosphere may have been designed to let the over-eager duchess or countess keep her dignity.

l. 4. *We need not fear another hell.* i.e. 'Life is so hellish that any hell we may go to after death will seem tame by comparison.'

l. 6. *waited on.* 'Stood ready to fulfil Desire's wishes' (Love). In an undated and fragmentary letter to his wife, R. complained of the 'disproportion 'twixt [human] desires & what [heaven] has ordained to content them', invoking the condition of 'dependence and attendance' at court as his prime illustration.

l. 8. *Nor could a wish set pleasure higher.* 'Nor did they have anything left to wish for which could have augmented their pleasure.'

l. 13. *duly.* Only 'Houghton' has this reading, which is also audible as 'dully' and so brings out the link with 'dull' at l. 12. The other manuscripts, whether professional like 'Gyldenstolpe' or private like 'Harbin' and 'Hartwell', as well as *1680* and *1691*, give 'duty'.

l. 15. *severe.* 'Harbin' and 'Hartwell' have 'sincere'.

Upon his Leaving his Mistress. Undatable. Entitled 'To Celia, for inconstancy' in 'Harbin' and 'Hartwell'. In the latter it follows 'A Dialogue between Strephon and Daphne', another defence of inconstancy which shares the third stanza's natural imagery. Unlike Strephon, though, the male speaker here seems prepared to grant his mistress the same sexual freedoms he demands for himself. However, the misogyny latent in his vision of her as 'the mistress of mankind' is brought out by the poem's placement in 'Houghton', where it comes after 'Love to a Woman', and particularly in 'Gyldenstolpe', where it is preceded by an anonymous lampoon 'On Marriage': 'The clog of all pleasure, the luggage of life | Is the best can be said of a very good wife; | But if she prove whorish and peevish beside | Her fortune but narrow & her cunt very wide | Marriage then seems by the devil invented | In the height of his malice when over tormented; | And the portion he gave with madam his daughter [i.e. Eve] | Is a hell upon earth worse than any hereafter.'

21 l. 3. *face*. (i) 'Boldness, impudence, effrontery' (*OED* 3); (ii) 'artificial or assumed expression' (*OED* 14). 'Design' belongs grammatically with 'To damn' but the idea of designing a face is irresistibly suggested (cf. 'To Corinna', ll. 1–2).

l. 6. *By merit or by inclination*. 'Either because you deserved it, or out of sheer liking for you.'

22 l. 9. *perplex*. Entangle, complicate.

l. 12. *impartial sense*. Unpossessive sensuality.

A Young Lady to her Ancient Lover. Undatable. The only complete copies are 'Hartwell' and *1691*; the 'Harbin' scribe stopped at l. 4. Poems addressed by young women to older male lovers were a staple of the seventeenth-century lyric repertoire. 'Advice to the Old Beaux', by R.'s friend Sir Charles Sedley, is typical: 'Scrape no more your harmless chins, | Old beaux, in hope to please; | You should repent your former sins, | Not study their increase'. R.'s 'Young Lady' seems uniquely accommodating, but male commentators have been more readily moved than female ones by her self-presentation as a natural principle of fertility. Certainly, R. cannot have been unaware of the often brutish social realities in such cases: his own niece Anne Lee was apparently deflowered for a fee in her early teens by the middle-aged Lord Peterborough. How far the 'Young Lady' is consciously feeding her beau's vanity is a question posed by her repetitions of 'art', her potentially glacial reference to him as 'person', and the textual variants at l. 2 and l. 25.

l. 1. *Ancient*. (i) Antiquated, out of date; (ii) having the experience, wisdom of age.

l. 2. *flutt'ring*. Fidgety. *1691* has 'flatt'ring'.

23 l. 21. *All a lover's wish can reach*. In *1691*, this stanza and the one which precedes it are run together, resulting in a progressive elongation of verses across the poem which may mimic the erection promised to the ancient lover.

l. 25. *I'll*. A promise or aspiration for the future, by contrast with *1691*'s 'I', a statement of present fact.

Song [By all Love's soft yet mighty pow'rs]. Ellis connected this Rochesterian song of innocence and experience with a local Oxfordshire rumour, reported to the antiquarian Thomas Hearne in 1726, that R. 'used the body of one Nell Browne of Woodstock, who, though she looked pretty well when clean, yet she was a very nasty, ordinary, silly creature'. But the poem combines extreme grossness of content with extreme delicacy of manner, and Love argued that it was addressed to 'a woman recently arrived at court, but not yet aware of the enhanced standards of personal deployment made fashionable by French imports'. His suggested candidate Nell Gwyn was possibly R.'s mistress shortly before she became the King's, and the two remained on friendly terms until the poet's death. She joined the court full-time in 1671, but was still being lampooned for her poor personal hygiene in 1676, a more likely date for this most accomplished of R.'s lyric lampoons.

l. 3. *time of flow'rs*. Menstrual period.

l. 5. *nasty*. Dirty.

ll. 7–8. *behind*. i.e. for when the 'smock's beshit'.   *before*. i.e. in time of flowers.

l. 8. *sponges*. 'A more sophisticated, and no doubt more expensive, solution than the "double clout" [cf. 'On Mrs Willis', l. 7 and n.]. Sponges, while they might be reused, had to be imported from the Eastern Mediterranean' (Love).

l. 10. *close*. Encounter.

l. 14. *cleanly sinning*. Cf. 'An Allusion to Horace', l. 61.

l. 15. *fresh*. (i) Inexperienced; (ii) unjaded.

24 *[Song] [Leave this gaudy gilded stage]*. Preserved only in 'Portland'. Perhaps written in the winter of 1676–7, if the poem was addressed to the actress Elizabeth Barry, whose increasing fame was by then causing problems in her affair with R. In the spring of 1677, Barry did indeed temporarily retire from acting after having been made pregnant by R. However, the 'stage could just as easily be a metaphorical one, such as the court' (Love).

l. 2. *use*. 'Any benefit it might confer.'

l. 3. *either . . . age*. 'The two ages were "the last age", that of the court of Charles I and Henrietta Maria, which still had numerous survivors, and "the present age"—that of the generation that had grown to maturity since the Restoration' (Love).

l. 4. *see themselves presented*. i.e. in stage characters who share their experiences and preoccupations. But the phrase applied more literally in the case of Restoration celebrities: R. himself was widely recognized as the model for Dorimant in Etherege's *The Man of Mode* (1676).

l. 9. *Love and War*. Cf. 'Give me leave to rail at you', ll. 11–12 and n.

STAGE ORATIONS AND DRAMATIC MONOLOGUES

25 *[Could I but make my wishes insolent]*. Undatable. Love's copy-text: 'Portland'. He saw the poem 'as a ritualized expression of devotion to a highly-placed court beauty, perhaps the Duchess of Portsmouth, with whom Rochester was intriguing outrageously at Bath in the summer of 1674', and so put it next to the ornately Petrarchan 'The Discovery'. But the dramatization of the speaker and prevailing air of theatricality (cf. ll. 13–16), as well as the link between the opening lines and the epilogue

'What vain unnecessary things are men' connect this unfinished piece with R.'s experiments in dramatic lyric from the early 1670s.

25 l. 2. *force some image*. 'Get myself to visualize', probably as an aid to masturbation (cf. 'What vain unnecessary things are men', ll. 22–3).

l. 8. *familiar with merit*. 'Insolently at their ease in distinguished company.'

l. 9. *Phaeton*. Son of Helios, the sun god, who rashly stole his father's chariot but then proved unable to control it.

l. 14. *would have*. Was determined to acquire.

l. 16. *idle*. Foolish.   *livelong day*. The whole day long (cf. 'Love and Life', l. 14).

l. 18. *unrelenting*. Relentlessly.

l. 21. *claims*. Such misalignments of plural subjects and singular verbs, or vice versa, were still tolerated in Restoration English.

ll. 21–4. *Such fears . . . lead me to despair*. The misfit between these four lines and the surrounding syntax marks the poem as unfinished.

26 *[What vain unnecessary things are men!]*. This unfinished work survives only in R.'s working draft in 'Portland'. Originally intended as the epilogue for a play performed by an all-female cast while the male actors were on strike between March and November 1672. But Love's suggestion that it 'had grown beyond its intended length and been laid aside for later reworking as a satire' is borne out by the piece's close links with 'A Letter from Artemiza in the Town to Chloe in the Country' and the complexity of the ironies in its final section.

ll. 6–8. *To make men wish . . . drawing-room*. Cf. 'A Letter from Artemiza in the Town to Chloe in the Country', ll. 54–8.

l. 8. *drawing-room*. The Great Withdrawing Room in the Palace of Whitehall, a favourite networking place for the nobility and the gentry.

l. 9. *coursers*. Hunters.

l. 10. *chaffer*. Haggle. The women are horses at a market.

l. 12. *pretending*. Presumptuous.

l. 13. *Huff*. Bluster. A generic name for a yobbish loudmouth.

l. 14. *de God*. Fashionable drawl for 'dear God'.

l. 16. *tawdry*. Cf. 'A Letter from Artemiza in the Town to Chloe in the Country', l. 208 and n.

l. 17. *take upon her*. Put on airs.

l. 22. *humouring my self*. 'Indulging myself', with strong sexual undertones.

l. 23. *former days*. The early seventeenth century, particularly the reign of Charles I.

l. 24. *pensive*. Melancholy.   *ends*. Bits. Either the old plays are fragmentary, or she reads only those parts which feed her courtly love fantasy.

l. 26. *Was fain to*. Had to.

l. 27. *But*. Dependent on 'I'd' at l. 21.   *insulting*. Exultant.

l. 28. *his—*. The speaker draws the line at writing the word 'whore'.

l. 31. *you*. Women.

l. 36. *we*. The all-female cast.

27 l. 38. *tinsel*. Insubstantial glitter.

l. 39. *properties*. Stage props.

l. 46. *Hart*. Charles Hart, the leading actor in the King's Company. *Rollo*. The lead in Fletcher's *Rollo, Duke of Normandy*, one of Hart's most celebrated roles.

l. 49. *go home and practise*. i.e. Love with a capital 'L', or possibly less exalted forms: 'go home' recalls 'at home' (l. 21) and so draws 'practise' towards 'humouring myself alone'.

ll. 50–2. *Just as in other preaching places . . . atheists*. The actors commit abuses in their actual love affairs which they preach against while in character on stage.

l. 53. *These two*. i.e. Love and religion.

l. 54. *Live up to half the miracles they teach*. Cf. 'Addition', l. 46 and n.

The Disabled Debauchee. One manuscript copy is dated 15 February 1673. Some of the titles conferred on the poem by copyists ('The Earl of Rochester to his Companions when he lay sick'; 'Upon his lying in and could not drink'; 'The Lord Rochester upon himself') characterize it as confessional. R. certainly had much in common with the speaker: he was now retired from naval service, and may have suspected from the worsening of his syphilis that his best days as a rake too were behind him. But the poem is also notable for its high level of artifice: its complex time scheme, and its formal self-consciousness, beginning with R.'s choice of the *abab* quatrain or 'heroic stanza' most recently employed by Dryden in his praise poem on English naval victories during the Second Anglo-Dutch War, *Annus Mirabilis* (1667). The large number of surviving manuscript copies reflects contemporary awareness of the poem's quality; the high level of textual instability among those copies testifies to its innovativeness. Uncertainty about the tone and mode of the poem persist to this day. Walker placed it among the 'Satires and Lampoons', Love in the category he called 'Libertine Lyrics and Shorter Satires'. But the dramatized fullness of the debauchee's character and the scenic feel of the poem has led more than one critic to call it a 'dramatic monologue'. It is not clear whether, as in Victorian dramatic monologues, there is a silent auditor for the debauchee's speech ('your' at l. 30 conflicts with 'they' at l. 28, and the direct address to Chloris at l. 37 gives way to 'him' at l. 43). But the poem can productively be compared with Tennyson's 'Ulysses' or 'Bishop Blougram's Apology' and 'The Bishop orders his tomb' by Browning.

ll. 1–6. *As some brave admiral . . . the fight*. An epic simile based on the scenario of philosophic detachment in Book II of Lucretius' *De Rerum Natura*: "Tis pleasant, safely to behold from shore | The rolling ship, and

hear the tempest roar; | Not that another's pain is our delight, | But pains
unfelt produce the pleasing sight' (Dryden's translation).

27 l. 2. *pressed.* (i) Spurred on; (ii) conscripted.

l. 8. *glory.* Exalted position, with a secondary implication of 'glorying' or
empty boastfulness.

28 ll. 15–16. *Forced from . . . lazy Temperance.* The capitals are retained
because this is an allegorical landscape, mockingly reminiscent of noncon-
formist narratives of spiritual development such as *The Pilgrim's Progress*.

l. 21. *scars.* From brawling in taverns or venereal disease, rather than actual
battle.

l. 25. *hopeful.* Promising (as future rakes).   *worth being drunk.*
Deserving to have toasts drunk to them.   *nice.* Too delicate.

l. 27. *Vice.* 'Depravity . . . Personified' (*OED*). The debauchee now pic-
tures himself as the villain in a medieval morality play.

l. 28. *If, at my counsel, they repent and drink.* In several manuscript copies,
the poem ends here; and in one of those which does have the full poem this
stanza is positioned last, after ll. 45–8.

ll. 33–6. *I'll tell of whores attacked . . . contrivance done.* Parodying lines
from Waller's 'A Panegyric to my Lord Protector' (1655) where the muses
assure Cromwell they will 'Tell of Towns storm'd, of Armies over-run, |
And mighty Kingdomes by your Conduct won'.

l. 33. *whores.* Promiscuous aristocratic women.

l. 34. *Bawd's quarters beaten up.* Brothels laid waste.

ll. 37–40. *Nor shall our love fits . . . I the boy.* Omitted from *1691* and some
manuscript copies.

l. 38. *When each the well-looked link-boy strove t'enjoy.* The young boys
carrying torches, hired by well-to-do Londoners to light them through
the streets at night, were commonly supposed to moonlight as rent-boys.

29 *Epilogue to Love in the Dark.* The minor courtier Francis Fane dedicated
his comedy *Love in the Dark* (1675) to R. in gratitude for his 'partial rec-
ommendations and impartial corrections'. That remark, and Fane's subse-
quent contribution of a masque to R.'s re-write of Fletcher's *Valentinian*,
constitute the main evidence for R.'s authorship of this epilogue, which
was first published as his in *1691*. Love used the 1675 printing as his copy-
text, supplementing it with a passage (ll. 46–59) not in either of the printed
texts but written alongside the epilogue in his copy of the play by John
Verney, a neighbour and associate of R's mother. Fane wrote his comedy
for the King's Company, whose rivalry with their competitors, the Duke's,
had intensified sharply over the early 1670s, as the latter capitalized on
the technological superiority of their new theatre at Dorset Garden by
staging a series of lavish operatic dramas. The epilogue's advocacy of the
French-influenced, ritualistic performance style of the King's, as against
the new informal manner practised at the Duke's, fits with the courtly

Francophile side of R.'s identity but conflicts with the line he took a few months later when, tutoring the actress Elizabeth Barry, he urged her to prize expressive realism over formal correctness in gesture and pronunciation. However, ll. 24–7 suggest that R. was not seeking to adjudicate between formality and informality but rather to define an ideal commingling of the two, much as he did where poetic style was concerned in the closely contemporaneous 'An Allusion to Horace'.

l. 1. *charms*. Magic spells.

l. 3. *scenes*. Spectacular scenery, as depicted on the painted side-boards newly installed in Restoration theatres.

l. 4. *takes*. Succeeds with the audience.   *two-eyed Cyclopes*. Homer's Cyclopes, of course, were one-eyed. In Act III of Shadwell's semi-opera *Psyche*, the monstrous blacksmiths perform a dance, before Vulcan enters to lead them in a drinking song.

l. 5. *machines*. Theatre machinery used to produce special effects.

l. 7. *discreetly*. Prudently.

l. 12. *clouts*. Old bits of linen.

l. 13. *losing loadum*. Any card game in which the object is to lose.

l. 16. *But of such awkward actors we despair*. 'We despair of finding any actors who can rival yours for awkwardness.'

l. 20. *unweighed action*. Ill-considered gesture, one not sufficiently adapted to its dramatic context.

l. 23. *fribbling*. Either muttering or stammering.   *free speaking*. Informal conversational manner.

l. 24. *False accent*. Misplacing the rhythmic stress when speaking lines of verse.

l. 25. *both so nigh good, yet neither true*. Referring either just to 'accent' and 'action', or to 'false accent' and 'neglectful action', implying that these have the potential to be virtues of acting style. Graceful negligence is usually a virtue in R.'s work. 'False accent' could be positive too, if it means pronouncing lines against the grain of their prosody in pursuit of expressive realism. As tutored by R., Elizabeth Barry was celebrated for 'perfectly changing herself as it were into the person, not merely by the proper stress or sounding of the voice [i.e. 'accent'], but feeling really, and being in the humour, the person she represented, was supposed to be in'.

l. 26. *an ape's mock face*. Cf. 'A Letter from Artemiza in the Town to Chloe in the Country', ll. 143–4.

l. 28. *Th'rough-paced*. Thoroughly.

l. 31. *the great wonder of our English stage*. Michael Mohun, one of the King's Company's two leading men. He was in his mid-fifties (hence, 'expose the age' at l. 31).

30 l. 35. *Mimic his foot*. Move as awkwardly as Mohun, who suffered from gout.

30 l. 36. *the Traitor or Volpone*. Mohun gave famous performances in the title roles of Ben Jonson's *Volpone* (in 1665) and James Shirley's *The Traitor* (in 1674).

l. 38. *Cethegus, or . . . Cassius*. Two more of Mohun's celebrated parts, in Jonson's *Catiline* (revived in 1675) and Shakespeare's *Julius Caesar* (revived in 1672) respectively.

l. 40. *monsters' heads*. In Act III of *Psyche* a dragon's head is brought on stage and a song performed with the refrain 'For the monster is dead, | And here is his head'.   *Merry Andrew*. 'A name applied to a quack doctor's zany who contorted himself [hence, 'dances'] and pulled faces to attract customers' (Love); here punningly applied to the French dancing master St André who choreographed *Psyche*.

l. 42. *But they were blighted, and ne'er came to bear*. 'They were cursed at birth, and so never proved productive.'

l. 43. *dressed*. Adorned.

l. 45. *patched*. Patched up; adapted. Shadwell's *The Tempest* (1674) was a revision of Dryden and Davenant's operatic adaptation of Shakespeare.   *twice o'er*. 'The same prostitute, posing as a virgin, would be sold to several men' (Love).

l. 47. *at-all-positive*. Sir Positive At-all is a know-all in Shadwell's first play, *The Sullen Lovers* (1668).

l. 49. *Epsom Wells*. Shadwell was rumoured to have had help from one or more of the 'wits' in the Duke of Buckingham's circle with his break-through comedy *Epsom Wells* (1673).

l. 51. *The Humorists, the Shepherdess, and Hypocrite*. Titles of three unsuccessful early plays by Shadwell.

l. 55. *Since Samson-like his locks are grown again*. Possibly Shadwell 'had worn a wig for a while but then reverted to his natural hair' (Love).

l. 57. *another Miser*. Shadwell's adaptation of Molière's *Tartuffe* had been performed by the King's Company in 1671–2.

l. 59. *Our house was burnt for playing of his last*. Shadwell's *The Miser* was the last play performed at the King's House in Drury Lane before it was severely damaged by fire on 25 January 1672.

l. 61. *swelled so high to hector you*. 'Become so presumptuous as to start bullying their audience.'

l. 63. *keeps out ten*. Draws away ten potential customers of the Duke's Company.

l. 65. *substantial trades*. Solid tradesmen.

ll. 66–7. *Who love our muzzled boys . . . great nephew Aeolus*. During the finale of Shadwell's *Tempest*, a chorus of thirty Tritons is silenced by Neptune's command 'Great nephew Aeolus, make no noise, | Muzzle your roaring boys'—i.e. the winds, here invoked in their traditional connection with vacuous stylistic bluster or 'tearing' (cf. 'An Allusion to Horace', l. 72 and n.).

l. 68. *citizen*. The site of the Duke's Company's new theatre in Dorset Garden, near St Paul's, made it vulnerable to association with the reputed philistinism of 'city' audiences.

l. 70. *"Psyche, the goddess of each field and grove"*. The opening line of the first vocal number in *Psyche*.

31 *Epilogue to Circe*. The effects-laden semi-opera *Circe*, by Charles Davenant, co-manager of the Duke's Company, premiered on 12 May 1677, with Elizabeth Barry in the cast. The epilogue was attributed to R. in the printed edition which appeared later that year.

l. 1. *from wit . . . got*. 'Deduced, through their intelligence.'

l. 16. *would be*. Aspire to be.

l. 18. *theirs*. Their enemies too.

l. 21. *stand or fall*. Phallic innuendoes.

TRANSLATIONS AND IMITATIONS

32 *Translation from Lucretius, De Rerum Natura, ii. 646–51*. First printed in *1691*, the only contemporary source, this translation was drafted before the spring of 1673 when R. showed it to Dryden. Lucretius' philosophical epic was much admired by seventeenth-century free-thinkers for its materialist account of natural causation, its Epicurean analysis of human psychology, and its sceptical vigour. This passage particularly typifies the work's 'atheistical' tendency, in the contemporary sense not of denying the existence of deity altogether but of denying God's providential action in the universe. Dryden responded to being shown the piece by complimenting R. in Lucretian terms, as the serenely disinterested deity of the Restoration poetic world—a compliment which was to be given the lie in their coming power struggle (cf. headnote to 'An Allusion to Horace').

Translation from Lucretius, De Rerum Natura, i. 1–4. Undatable, although generally connected by editors with R.'s other translation from Lucretius. But in 'Portland', the only contemporary source, it lies next to another poem which invokes Venus: 'Leave this gaudy gilded stage' (cf. l. 9 and n.).

l. 1. *mother of Aeneas*. Venus bore Aeneas from her union with Anchises.

l. 3. *all beneath*. Direct object of 'dost bless' at l. 7.

l. 7. *fruitful earth*. A further object of 'dost bless'.

Upon his Drinking a Bowl. Presumably written soon after June 1673 when the military affairs detailed at ll. 11–12 were fresh news. The title is chosen from a number of variants in the printed and manuscript copies as the one which best brings out the poem's relation to Anacreon, the putative author of a collection of lyrics from the Hellenistic age which advocate a life of bibulous hedonism. R. adapts two of these 'Anacreontea', as mediated either through the French translation by Ronsard or Thomas

Stanley's English versions, which, along with a series by Cowley, gener-
ated a vogue for Anacreon in English poetry in the 1650s. A literal transla-
tion of the relevant ode by Ronsard (IV. xxiii) reads as follows:

32 'Vulcan, I pray you, hasten and fashion for me a cup more capacious
than that of old Nestor. I don't want it to be in gold; just make mine out
of oak or ivy or ash; and don't carve on it those great nodding plumes,
breast-plates, helmets or weapons: of what concern to me are alarums
and excursions and fights? And don't engrave the sun or the moon on
it, nor daylight nor the darkness of night, nor the bright stars: what do
I care about the skies and their constellations, the Bear, the Wain, Orion
or Bootes? Instead, depict for me, if you would, the tendrils of a vine as
yet unharvested; depict a vine heavy with grapes and raisins; depict men
treading the grapes; depict Venus and Cassandra; let Bacchus festoon my
cup with ivy; and depict on it the Graces and Cupid; depict the reddened
nose and cheeks of Silenus or a drunkard.'

The two Stanley translations involved are these:

XVII	XVIII
Vulcan come, thy hammer take,	All thy skill if thou collect,
And of burnished silver make—	Make a cup as I direct:
Not a glittering armour, for	Roses climbing o'er the brim,
What have we to do with war?—	Yet must seem in wine to swim;
But a large deep bowl, and on it	Faces too there should be there,
I would have thee carve no planet,	None that frowns or wrinkles wear,
Pleiads, wains nor waggoners	But the sprightly Son of Jove,
(What have we to do with stars?)	With the beauteous Queen of Love;
But to life exactly shape	There, beneath a pleasant shade,
Clusters of the juicy grape;	By a vine's wide branches made,
Whilst brisk Love their bleeding heads	Must the Loves (their arms laid by)
Hand in hand with Bacchus treads.	Keep the Graces company;
	And the bright-haired God of day
	With a youthful bevy play.

l. 1. *Vulcan*. The blacksmith god.

l. 2. *Nestor*. The oldest of the Greek heroes in the *Iliad*.

l. 4. *Damask*. Inlay.

l. 7. *toasts*. Spiced bits of toast floated in wine or beer.

33 l. 11. *Maastricht*. City in the Netherlands stormed by Anglo-French forces
in June 1673.

l. 12. *leaguer*. Camp. In the summer of 1673, troops gathered at Yarmouth
for an invasion of the Netherlands which was subsequently called off.

l. 15. *Sir Sidrophel*. Gullible astrologer in Samuel Butler's anti-Puritan
mock-epic *Hudibras* (1662–3).

l. 20. *type*. Prophetic emblem. The term is from biblical exegesis, used of
events in the Old Testament which prefigure the life of Christ.

l. 24. *Phill*: This abbreviated form of Phyllis is the reading in 'Gyldenstolpe'. *1691* gives 'Love', while 'Houghton' and *1680* have 'Cunt'. See Introduction, pp. xiv–xv.

Seneca's Troas. Act 2. Chorus. Thus Englished by a Person of Honour. In a letter to R., dated 7 February 1680, Charles Blount records his receipt of a copy of this translation. It is not certain R. himself sent it, though Blount presumably had the poet's permission to print the poem later that year in his *The two first books of Philostratus, concerning the life of Apollonius Tyaneus.* Because of R.'s close association with Blount, Love chose that printing as his copy-text. But the translation may have been drafted as early as 1674, when the 'Haward' copy was apparently transcribed. The original passage, from Seneca's tragedy about the aftermath of the Trojan war, was admired by free-thinkers like Blount and R. for its demystifying rationalism and anticlerical animus. In *1680*, the piece immediately precedes 'Upon Nothing', a conjunction emphasized by commentators who see in R. a forerunner of modern nihilism. For alternative placings of the poem in the manuscript sources, see the headnotes to 'The Disabled Debauchee' and 'Fair Chloris in a pig-sty lay'. R.'s translation has been called 'close' by one editor (Ellis) and 'a creative reworking' by another (Love). Literally translated, the original reads: 'After death there is nothing, and death itself is nothing, the finishing post of life's rapid course. Let the ambitious give up their hopes, the anxious their fears: ravenous time and chaos devour us all. Death does not discriminate: it destroys the body, and is as unsparing to the soul. Taenarus [i.e. hell] and the kingdom of the harsh tyrant [i.e. Pluto] and the guard [dog] Cerberus making access through the gate to the underworld difficult are all idle rumours and empty words, a nightmarish fable. You ask where you will lie when you are dead? Where the unborn lie.'

l. 13. *foul fiend*. Satan.

34 l. 16. *grim grisly dog*. Cerberus, guardian of the gates of the underworld in Roman poetry and of Hell in Dante's *Inferno*.

l. 18. *Dreams, whimsies, and no more*. Cf. 'The Fall', l. 4 and n.

An Allusion to Horace. The Tenth Satire of the First Book. First printed in *1680* but omitted from *1691*, presumably because its publisher Jacob Tonson was then working closely with the target of R.'s satire, Dryden. The poem can be dated to the winter of 1675–6 on the evidence of its various literary allusions. In his 'Life of Rochester', Samuel Johnson defined 'allusion' as a sub-category of literary imitation 'in which the ancients are familiarised by adapting their sentiments to modern topics'. Precedents for the technique (though not the term itself) existed in the versions of Horace, *Odes* I. v and *Satires* II. vi by R.'s beloved Cowley in his *Verses upon Several Occasions* (1663). The Horatian poem to which R. alludes is *Satires* I. x, which had previously been invoked by Dryden in his 'Defence of the Epilogue' to *The Conquest of Granada* (1672). There Dryden used Horace's criticism of the old-fashioned style of the pre-Augustan poet

Lucilius to validate his own controversial attacks on Ben Jonson's style as crude by Restoration standards. Thereafter, Horace's work became ever more central to debates about the nature of poetic 'wit' in the Restoration, an age which prided itself on its urbane modernity. Since the early 1670s, Dryden had been attempting to position himself, in his capacity as Poet Laureate, as the primary arbiter on that and other questions of literary taste, thereby introducing strains into his relationship with his patron R., who adhered to a traditional understanding of the court as the centre of the nation's cultural life. 'An Allusion to Horace' brought these tensions out into the open, initiating a power struggle between the two which represents a watershed in English literary history. Dryden's major response came in the dedication of *All for Love* (1678), where he presented R. as the last of the dying breed of courtier poets, and himself as the first of the evolving species of professionals destined to rule the cultural world.

34 l. 3. *patron.* R. had been replaced as Dryden's patron by John Sheffield, Earl of Mulgrave, his personal and political enemy.

l. 7. *paper.* A manuscript lampoon.

l. 9. *loose.* Poorly structured, or generally slapdash.

l. 11. *Crowne's tedious scenes.* Thomas Crowne's masque *Calisto*, acted at court in 1675, was notoriously boring.

l. 13. *Hits.* Strikes a chord with.

l. 15. *crack.* Burst into applause, but also fart (*OED* 4)—with 'load' completing the excremental conceit.

l. 18. *blundering Settle.* Elkanah Settle's play *The Empress of Morocco* (1673) had been attacked by Dryden for its 'blundering hobbling verse' and 'blundering kind of melody'.

l. 19. *puzzling Otway.* Thomas Otway's first play *Alcibiades* (1675) was awkwardly plotted.

l. 25. *Your rhetoric with your poetry unite.* 'Ensure that the pitch of your poetic style conforms to the dramatic situation.'

35 l. 32. *refined Etherege.* The playwright George Etherege epitomized courtly polish—but was also regarded even by his friends, who included R. both before and after 'An Allusion to Horace', as prone to over-dressing.

l. 33. *sheer original.* Either 'glorious one-off' or 'utter anomaly'.

l. 34. *swift pindaric.* Pindaric odes were sometimes associated with inspired rapidity.   *strains.* Melodies; but the verbal sense too is suggested.

l. 35. *Flatman, who Cowley imitates.* The syntax is inverted: it was Thomas Flatman, the lawyer-poet, who imitated Cowley's *Pindarique Odes* (1656) not vice versa.

l. 36. *jaded.* Worn out.   *whipped with loose reins.* The energy of Flatman's pindarics is self-defeating because it is not reined in by discretion.

l. 37. *Lee.* Nathaniel Lee was beginning to acquire a reputation for hyperbolic tragic 'rant'.   *temperate Scipio fret and rave.* Actually, Lee, in his presentation of Scipio Africanus in his heroic tragedy *Sophonisba* (1675), mostly upheld the stoic self-restraint for which the Roman general was famous.

l. 39. *fustian*. Bombastic.

l. 40. *Busby's*. Richard Busby, the famously strict headmaster of Westminster School.

l. 43. *hasty Shadwell*. R. had transferred his patronage from Dryden to Thomas Shadwell, who was given to bragging in prefaces about how quickly he wrote his comedies. *slow Wycherley*. There had been a gap of three years between Wycherley's first two comedies, *Love in a Wood* (1671) and *The Gentleman Dancing-Master* (1672), and his masterpiece *The Country Wife* (1675).

l. 44. *unfinished*. Unpolished.

l. 51. *judgment*. Discretion; literary tact.

l. 54. *Waller*. Edmund Waller, whom R.'s stage alias Dorimant enters quoting at the beginning of Etherege's *The Man of Mode* (1676). *bays*. Poetic laurels.

l. 56. *does excel mankind*. (i) Outdoes all other poets; (ii) offers praise beyond what any human being could merit.

l. 57. *inforce*. Add force to, 'perhaps in the sense of conferring a heroic character on unheroic actions' (Love).

l. 58. *conquerors*. Waller had written panegyrics on Oliver Cromwell.

l. 59. *Buckhurst*. Charles Sackville, Lord Buckhurst, boon companion of R., earned his name as a satirist through his contribution to a volume of mock-complimentary verses on Edward Howard's disastrously bad epic poem *The British Princes* (1669).

l. 61. *mannerly obscene*. Decorously offensive.

l. 62. *springs*. Sources (with innuendo).

l. 63. *the queen*. Catherine of Braganza, who would need to be warmed without recourse to flagrant obscenities since her court was notoriously staid.

l. 64. *Sedley*. Sir Charles Sedley, R.'s close friend and fellow libertine 'wit'. *gentle*. Refined.

l. 65. *resistless*. Irresistible.

36 l. 68. *declining*. (i) Saying 'no'; (ii) weakening in its resistance.

l. 71. *nice*. Delicate; precise.

l. 72. *tearing blade*. Rowdy man-about-town.

l. 75. *dry bawdy bob*. Ejaculation producing no semen.

l. 76. *Squab*. (i) Short and stout; (ii) young and undeveloped. Dryden was in fact forty-four in 1675, and had already been Poet Laureate for seven years.

36 l. 82. *Fletcher and Beaumont*. Elizabethan dramatists criticized by Dryden in his breakthrough critical work, *An Essay of Dramatic Poesy* (1668).

l. 83. *lewd*. Crude, in a grammatical sense. Dryden had accused Fletcher of committing solecisms.

l. 84. *Stiff and affected*. Shakespeare's particular failings, according to Dryden, were far-fetched punning and stylistic pomposity.

l. 89. *gross faults*. Glaring lapses into crudity.

l. 90. *judgment*. Discrimination.   *wit*. Verbal sophistication.

l. 91. *lumpish*. (i) Clumsy; (ii) earth-bound.   *fancy*. Imagination.

l. 92. *slattern*. Slovenly.

l. 96. *Mustapha*. A tragedy by Roger Boyle, Earl of Orrery, written in 1665 but revived in 1675 in a production including R.'s mistress Elizabeth Barry in a leading female role.   *The English Princess*. A tragedy by John Caryll, written in 1667 but published in a new edition in 1673.

37 l. 108. *cunning*. Knowledgeable.

l. 109. *drawing-room*. The so-called 'wits' drawing-room' in the palace of Whitehall where fashionable courtiers, including R., would gather after performances of new plays.

l. 111. *Betty Morris*. The prostitute mentioned in 'A Letter from Artemiza in the Town to Chloe in the Country', l. 184.

l. 112. *Buckley's*. Henry Bulkeley, Master of the Household at the court of Charles II.

l. 115. *purblind knight*. Sir Carr Scroope, whom R. would soon attack for more than being shortsighted (cf. headnotes to 'A Letter [by Sir Carr Scroope]' and 'Answer').

l. 118. *poor led*. Like horses, led by the nose.

l. 121. *Sheppard*. Fleetwood Sheppard, an occasional poet and critic in R.'s circle.

l. 122. *Godolphin*. Sidney Godolphin, a courtier and successful politician whose only major literary effort was the last act in a collaborative version of Corneille's *Mort de Pompée* (1663) in which Buckhurst and Sedley also participated.   *Butler*. Samuel Butler, the author of the wildly popular anti-Puritan mock-epic *Hudibras* (1662–3).   *Buckingham*. George Villiers, second Duke of Buckingham, R.'s close friend and fellow 'wit', the main author of *The Rehearsal* (1671), a burlesque on Dryden in which R. too may have had a hand.

An Allusion to Tacitus. De Vita Agricolae. Not included in either *1680* or *1691*, this piece was ranked by Love among the 'disputed works' despite its presence in both 'Hartwell' and 'Harbin'. But it can now be confidently assigned to R. following the discovery by Paul Hammond and Nicholas Fisher of additional manuscripts in reliable sources. Its references to the fall of Danby in December 1678 establish it as a late work, part of the remarkable flowering of R.'s genius in the last eighteen months of his life.

It supports the claim made by R.'s friend Robert Wolseley that the poet was in his final years 'inquisitive after all kind of histories, that concerned England, both ancient and modern'. But how far it supports Wolseley's further claim that R. put his newfound historical learning to Whiggish use in poems intended 'to stop the progress of arbitrary oppression' is open to debate. R.'s attempt to segregate Charles from blame for the quasi-absolutist policies of his minister Danby seems strained in places (cf. l. 19). Moreover, controversy raged in R.'s lifetime about whether Tacitus, the most tonally elusive of the Roman historians, was a defender of liberty and an opponent of arbitrary rule or a Machiavellian instructor in the art of retaining power through cunning and deception. The work of Tacitus to which R. alludes, his biography of Agricola, governor of the Roman province of Britain from AD 78 to 85, could be used to substantiate either view. Much depends on quite what R. meant by calling the poem an 'allusion'. Unlike 'An Allusion to Horace', this poem is only in direct contact with its Latin source for its opening nine lines. They stem from a single sentence in Tacitus which, literally translated, reads: 'The Britons themselves discharge fully the taxes and tributes and imperial duties levied upon them, always provided there is no wrongdoing: for that they have no tolerance, and whilst they submit to the point of loyal obedience, they will not go so far as to enslave themselves.' But if R. had the source text more generally in mind, then his celebration of the liberty-loving spirit of his countrymen takes on a number of ironies (cf. ll. 29–30). On that reading, the poem would rank as a precursor of the mature Augustan art of allusion as practised by Pope, as avant-garde in its mode as the contemporaneous 'An Epistolary Essay from M. G. to O. B., upon their Mutual Poems' is in that of the Horatian epistle.

l. 1. *generous*. Great-hearted.

l. 7. *with*. By.

l. 10. *still*. Always.

l. 12. *Kings are least safe in their unbounded will*. 'Kings are most at risk [of being rebelled against] when they tolerate no limits to their power.'

38 l. 18. *Catiline*. Lucius Sergius Catilina attempted unsuccessfully to seize control of the Roman republic.

l. 19. *stake*. Risk; gamble. Charles II was a notoriously heavy gambler.

l. 20. *vassals*. Servants; slaves.

l. 21. *some base favourite's*. The Earl of Danby, Lord Chancellor from 1674 until his impeachment in December 1678.   *pretence*. Presumption.

l. 22. *tyrannize at the wronged king's expense*. Danby's particular crime had been to negotiate secret subsidies from Louis XIV, in an effort to circumvent parliament's hold over the finances of the crown. When these negotiations came to light, Buckingham and Danby's other enemies accused him of planning to convert England's constitutional monarchy into an absolutist tyranny on the French model.

38 ll. 23–4. *Let France grow proud . . . lick the dust.* Cf. 'A Satire on Charles II',
    ll. 6–7.

l. 25. *genius.* National character.

l. 26. *Ambitious slavery.* Enslavement of the people resulting from the
expansionist ambitions of their king (cf. 'A Satire on Charles II', l. 5).

l. 27. *servile yokes.* The 'Norman yoke' was a slogan commonly invoked in
the seventeenth century by radicals who argued that English law retained
fundamental inequities put in place at the Norman conquest.

l. 29. *pretend.* (i) Claim; (ii) feign. The verb could potentially govern '[to
have] made' as well as 'to have enslaved'. Tacitus ascribes Agricola's suc-
cess in pacifying Britain to his politic strategy of cultural softening up:
'He began to train the sons of the chieftains in the liberal arts . . . As a
result the nation which used to reject the Latin language began to aspire
to rhetoric; further, the wearing of Roman dress became a mark of distinc-
tion, and the toga came into fashion; and little by little the Britons were
seduced into the alluring vices of the lounge, the bath, the dinner table
provisioned with delicacies. And this was called "culture" by the subju-
gated Britons, when in fact it was a form of slavery.'

SATIRES AND EPISTLES

39 *Song [Quoth the Duchess of Cleveland to Councillor Knight].* Written
    between 1671 and 1672 on the evidence of topical references in l. 1 and
    l. 12, these primarily anapaestic verses have an impromptu air about them,
    which may explain the very high level of textual variation among the sur-
    viving manuscript copies, and also the absence of any authorial attribu-
    tion in those copies. The poem's claim to be R.'s rests on its inclusion in
    1680 and general agreement among modern editors. Collaboration is once
    again a possibility, but the computational analyses carried out by Love's
    colleague John Burrows ranked the piece in category '2' out of five 'in
    descending degrees of resemblance to Rochester'.

l. 1. *Duchess of Cleveland.* Barbara Palmer, countess of Castlemaine,
Charles's principal mistress throughout the 1660s.   *councillor
Knight.* Mary Knight, a celebrated singer and court pimp in whose apart-
ment in Pall Mall Cleveland conducted her affair with the playwright
Wycherley in 1671.

l. 4. *nice.* Fastidious.

l. 5. *Sodom.* Red-light district in London, between Fleet Street and the
Thames.

l. 6. *porters.* Cf. 'A Ramble in St. James's Park', l. 120 and n.   *black
pots.* Beer-mugs.

l. 7. *case.* (i) mask, such as court ladies often wore in public; (ii) plea,
legal argument—for 'relief' from the 'abuse' referred to at l. 12; (iii)
vagina.

l. 10. *key that unlocks the back-door.* A familiar run of innuendo; but there were actual 'back stairs' at court which allowed Cleveland to come and go unseen from her apartments.

l. 12. *abused.* Left unsatisfied.   *Churchill.* John Churchill, later Duke of Marlborough and the victor at Blenheim, was Cleveland's lover in 1670–1.   *Jermyn.* Henry Jermyn, Master of the Horse to the Duke of York, whom Pepys reports hearing had impregnated the Duchess in 1667.

The Imperfect Enjoyment. First printed in *1680* but inevitably excluded from *1691*. The allusion in l. 18 (first pointed out by Jeremy Treglown) dates the poem to 1671–2, and connects it with the Buckingham circle's parodic assault in *The Rehearsal* (1671) on the grandiose idioms of Dryden's early heroic tragedies. Poems about premature ejaculation formed a recognizable sub-category of seventeenth-century love lyric, originating in the French libertine school and imported into England at the Restoration. Other examples by major poets of the period include Aphra Behn's 'The Disappointment' and George Etherege's 'The Imperfect Enjoyment'. But R. varies the theme by hybridizing it with lampoon. Etherege's speaker blames the woman for his premature climax, but R.'s turns away from his (actually very understanding) mistress, and devotes the second half of the poem to lampooning his own penis. The resulting instability of tone is reflected in the liminal positioning of the poem in contemporary manuscript miscellanies where, like 'The Disabled Debauchee', it usually comes just after the opening section of satires. In 'Gyldenstolpe' it is between 'Seneca's *Troas*. Act. 2. Chorus' and the anonymous 'On Marriage' (see headnote to 'Upon his Leaving his Mistress').

l. 11. *fluttering.* (i) Hovering; (ii) 'excited with hope, apprehension, or pleasure' (*OED* 5).

ll. 11–12. *sprung . . . pointed . . . hovering.* An extended hunting conceit: to 'spring' is to flush out a game-bird from cover, and to 'point' is to bring potential quarry to the attention of the hunter.

40 l. 18. *Her hand, her foot, her very look's a cunt.* Parodying a line in Dryden's heroic play *Conquest of Granada* (1672): 'Her tears, her smiles, her every look's a Net'.

l. 27. *swive.* Fuck.

l. 35. *limber.* Supple.

l. 38. *has dyed.* Several manuscripts, including 'Gyldenstolpe', read 'have', but the apparently illogical 'has', found in 'Houghton' among other sources, may be preferable: the speaker needs to see his penis as the subject, dyeing the maids rather than being dyed by them.

l. 42. *Woman, nor man.* The reading in 'Gyldenstolpe'; 'Houghton' has 'Woman, or man', and *1680* gives 'Woman or boy'.

l. 50. *oyster.* Oyster-seller.   *cinder.* A woman who raked through heaps of ashes looking for re-usable cinders.

41 l. 54. *hector*. Roisterer.

l. 59. *stew*. Brothel.   *small*. Cheap.

l. 61. *recreant*. Deserter.   *to*. From.

l. 63. *Town*. The area around Covent Garden and Drury Lane, newly developed following the Great Fire and associated particularly with theatricality and sexual vice; as distinct from the trading districts of the 'City' inside the walls, and the 'Court' at Westminster.

l. 66. *shankers*. Chancres; ulcers from venereal disease.

l. 67. *weepings*. Discharges.

l. 68. *strangury*. Painful urination, caused by kidney stones or syphilis.

l. 69. *spend*. Ejaculate.

A Ramble in St. James's Park. In circulation by 20 March 1673 when the Earl of Huntingdon received a copy from one of his London agents. R.'s is probably the first so-called 'ramble poem', a minor offshoot of satire which enjoyed a brief vogue in the 1670s and early 1680s. A 'ramble' is 'an expedition by a disreputable male into the city by night in search of drink and prostitutes' (Love); hence R.'s choice of the octosyllabic line synonymous with Samuel Butler's mock-epic of chivalric questing, *Hudibras* (1662–3). Further mock-heroic energies are generated through the poem's engagement with Waller's 'A Poem on St. James's Park as Lately Improved by His Majesty' (1661), which celebrated Charles II's development of the park into a modern pleasure garden, complete with a canal, in the most rarefied terms of Caroline pastoral. The speaker is unlikely to have been modelled on a single individual (least of all R. himself), but his situation as an aristocratic male co-habiting with a whore has precedents in social fact (cf. headnote to 'On Mrs Willis').

l. 4. *the Bear*. Possibly the Bear and Harrow on Drury Lane, noted for its French cuisine, although l. 7 may imply a venue closer to St James's Park, and there were several 'Bear' taverns in Restoration London.

l. 6. *relieved by*. Alternates with.

l. 9. *St. James has the honour on't*. It is dedicated to St James.

l. 14. *pict*. Ancient Briton.

42 l. 18. *his Mother's face*. The ground.

l. 19. *mandrakes*. Mandrakes were reputed to grow from spilt blood or semen.

l. 22. *fold of Aretine*. Pietro Aretino wrote a series of sonnets to accompany sixteen illustrations by Giulio Romano, first published in 1524 and much reprinted, depicting sexual positions. A sequence of paintings based on these so-called 'postures'—or 'folds'—hung on the walls of R.'s bachelor retreat at Woodstock.

l. 26. *bulk*. A bulkhead outside a shop, used for selling goods during the day and for assignations by prostitutes at night.   *alcove*. Recess in a royal bedchamber housing the bed of state.

l. 28. *rag-picker*. A woman who scavenged in old clothes and bundles of rags.

l. 29. *Car-men*. Drivers of horse-drawn carts.

l. 32. *promiscuously*. Without respect for boundaries of status or class. *swive*. Fuck.

l. 43. *knights o'th'elbow and the slur*. Gambling cheats. 'To shake the elbow' was to play at dice, while 'slurring' involved throwing the dice in such a way as to prevent them from turning over.

l. 45. *Whitehall blades*. Dashing young men at court—but these ones are wannabes.

l. 46. *th'Mother of the Maids*. Governess to the queen's maids of honour—not a fashionable connection (cf. 'An Allusion to Horace', l. 63 and n.).

l. 48. *th'waiters' table*. Dining-table for those who attended the King in the Presence Chamber, the least restricted area of the court.

l. 49. *Edward Sutton*. A court official in Charles II's Privy Chamber.

l. 50. *Banstead mutton*. Meat from sheep grazed on Banstead Downs in Surrey was prized for its sweetness.

43 l. 62. *birthday coat*. An elaborate coat worn to celebrate a royal birthday. The Whitehall blade cannot afford not to re-use his.

l. 63. *Gray's Inn wit*. Gray's Inn was one of the Inns of Court, where well-off young men studied law, or else pretended to whilst seeking to launch their literary careers.

l. 72. *Against*. Before.

l. 74. *A most accomplished tearing blade*. Cf. 'An Allusion to Horace', l. 72 and n.

l. 86. *salt-swoll'n*. In heat.

l. 87. *more patient*. i.e. than the speaker himself.

l. 90. *taste so much of*. 'Savour so strongly of'; or possibly 'sample so much'.

l. 92. *parson*. A country parson, by convention an idiotic figure.

44 l. 93. *job*. Either 'abrupt stab' or, more likely, 'operation'.   *sluice*. valve, pipe.

l. 98. *gen'rous*. Heroic.   *mere*. Sheer.

l. 99. *jade*. Unreliable woman.

l. 103. *played booty . . . with*. Ganged up with.

l. 110. *nice*. Exact.

l. 116. *surfeit-water*. Medicinal beverage to relieve the after-effects of over-eating or over-drinking.

l. 120. *brawn*. Legs. Strong legs and 'backs' were both considered marks of sexual potency.

l. 122. *grace-cup*. Final drink of a meal, served after grace has been said.

44 l. 125. *make . . . away*. (i) Hand over to someone else; (ii) destroy.

l. 126. *colours*. Soldier's uniform.

l. 130. *Wrapped*. Spelled 'wrapt' in both the manuscripts and the printed versions, which keeps in view 'rapt'.

45 l. 136. *whiffling*. To 'whiffle' is 'to move inconstantly, as if blown by a puff of wind' (Johnson).

l. 138. *go mad for the North Wind*. As mares in heat were believed to do.

l. 143. *rant*. Boast in heroic style.

l. 148. *cod*. Testicle.

l. 149. *Physicians shall believe in Jesus*. In 1669, R. had suffered excruciating torments under the care of Monsieur Forcade, the king's physician, while taking mercury treatment for syphilis.

l. 150. *disobedience*. By 1673, opposition to Charles II's religious policies was escalating in parliament.

l. 154. *limed*. Mated with (*OED* 8).

l. 155. *that most lamentable state*. Parodying the description of marriage in the Book of Common Prayer as 'an honourable estate'.

l. 160. *whines like a dog-drawn bitch*. During mating, the bitch's vagina contracts to prevent the dog from withdrawing; the dog may drag the bitch along with him, causing both considerable pain.

l. 166. *profane*. Desecrate.

46 *On Mrs Willis*. Sue Willis was a prostitute who started out in 'Mother' Moseley's brothel (cf. 'Timon', l. 77) and subsequently worked the theatres, before becoming the mistress of Thomas, Lord Colpeper. This lampoon may have been written after the couple's return from a trip to Paris in June 1673, if 'precise in words' at l. 17 is a mocking allusion to the putative effects on Willis of visiting the high-minded salons of the Parisian *précieuses*.

l. 7. *double clout*. Sanitary towel, made from a piece of old linen, folded double.

l. 8. *flowers*. Menstrual blood.

l. 16. *spends*. Comes.

l. 17. *precise*. Fastidious.

l. 20. *common shore*. Open sewer.

A Satire on Charles II. During the Christmas festivities at court in 1673, R. accidentally put a copy of this lampoon into the king's hands. His resulting banishment sealed the poem's celebrity, but its circulation was clandestine, apparently involving much memorial reconstruction. Love gave up the attempt to reassemble a single 'authorial' text from the mass of fundamentally discrepant surviving copies, and instead presented four versions, each representative of a main branch of the poem's transmission. The text given here is from 'Group A', the best in my aesthetic judgement.

The title conferred on the poem by modern editors has been retained for its convenient descriptiveness.

l. 4. *easiest*. Most affable.

l. 6. *the French fool*. Louis XIV.

l. 8. *Peace is his aim*. Charles was constantly looking for ways to limit his expensive involvement in Louis's long-running conflict with the Protestant powers in Europe, but the specific reference here may be to the negotiations in the winter of 1672–3 which eventually put an end to the Second Anglo-Dutch War.

47 l. 13. *his brother*. James, Duke of York, whose reputation for political stupidity had lately been confirmed by his marriage to the Roman Catholic duchess Mary of Modena, at a time when Charles was suspected of crypto-Catholicism.

l. 15. *hector*. Bully.   *cully*. Dupe.

l. 16. *The hector wins towns by money, not trenches*. Cf. 'Timon', ll. 155–64.

l. 20. *buffoons at court*. R. probably includes himself among these witty triflers who pandered to Charles's irresponsibility. For other candidates, cf. 'From "An Essay on Satire"', l. 14 and n.

l. 26. *With dog and bastard always going before*. Charles was famous for taking daily walks with his spaniels in St James's Park, at a brisk enough speed to outpace his ministers.

l. 28. *easy*. (i) Promiscuous; (ii) irresponsible.   *poor*. Charles's difficulties in extracting funds from an increasingly oppositional parliament, coupled with his failure to rein in his lavish expenditure, led in 1672 to the 'Stop of the Exchequer', when all payments to crown officials were suspended. R.'s own salary as Gentleman of the Bedchamber was more than two years in arrears at this time.

l. 29. *Carwell*. Louise de Kéroualle, Duchess of Portsmouth, Charles's principal mistress since October 1671.

l. 30. *declining years*. Charles was forty-three, but the reference here is to his waning sexual potency as a result of over-indulgence. Some manuscript copies of the poem make the reference explicit by reading 'Grown impotent' instead of 'An easy monarch' in their versions of l. 28.

l. 33. *tarse*. Prick.

l. 34. *hang an arse*. 'To be tardy, sluggish, or dilatory' (Johnson).

l. 36. *painful*. Painstaking.   *laborious*. Hard-working.   *Nelly*. Nell Gwyn, former orange-seller and actress, had become the King's mistress in the summer of 1669.

Timon. Written between March and July 1674, when the military manoeuvrings described at ll. 152–4 were in process. So this loose imitation of Boileau's 'Satire III' is closely contemporaneous with the other two of R.'s major satires which are influenced by Boileau, 'A Satire against Reason and Mankind' and 'A Letter from Artemiza in the Town to Chloe in the Country'. Boileau's third satire itself depends on Horace, *Satires* II. viii, the origin of the so-called *repas ridicule* subset of the genre. Horace's main emphasis was on the hideous food and drink; Boileau introduced a concern with taste more largely, including in literature; R. adds the military and nationalistic themes, pushing the tone over towards the coarser end of the satiric spectrum. In three manuscripts the poem is attributed to R.'s friend and fellow wit Sir Charles Sedley, but it is not within Sedley's ken, as the stylometric analyses of John Burrows confirm. The two copyists who assigned it to R. were almost certainly better informed, but an element of collaboration is possible.

47   *Timon*. Only one of the nine surviving manuscript copies has the name of the speaker Timon in the title, but that reading has been preferred for the sake of convenience. 'Although Restoration readers were familiar with the misanthropic Timon of Athens (through Shakespeare's play, and Shadwell's adaptation of 1678), they would also know of Timon as a name for an honest critic of a corrupt society' (Hammond).

l. 1. *A*. Abbreviation of 'auditor' or 'adversary'.

l. 3. *on tick*. On credit.

48   l. 14. *a libel of a sheet or two*. A lampoon of between four and eight pages, either in the form of a printed broadside, or a manuscript 'separate'.

l. 16. *Shadwell's unassisted former scenes*. Cf. 'Epilogue to *Love in the Dark*', l. 51.

l. 20. *unblest*. Not blessed with talent.

l. 22. *pintle*. Cock.

l. 24. *a revenge so tame*. Either the particular lampoon, or the general practice of lampooning one's enemies, as against the nobler course of challenging them to a duel.

l. 34. *Sedley*. Cf. 'An Allusion to Horace', l. 64 and n.   *Buckhurst*. Cf. 'An Allusion to Horace', l. 59 and n.   *Savile*. R's close friend Henry Savile, an especially unlikely guest at this jingoistic dinner party, since he had recently served as diplomatic envoy at the court of Louis XIV and was a confirmed Francophile.

l. 35. *Huff*. Cf. 'What vain unnecessary things are men!', l. 13 and n.

l. 36. *Kickum*. i.e. Kick 'em.   *Ding-Boy*. To 'ding' is to pummel (*OED*).

l. 37. *brave*. Splendid.

l. 40. *tam Marte quam Mercurio*. 'Pledged to both Mars [the god of war] and Mercury [the god of eloquence].'

49   l. 43. *salute*. Exchange greetings.

l. 51. *As cocks will strike although their spurs be gone*. i.e. once their cock-fighting careers, during which they would have been armed with artificial 'spurs', were over.

l. 57. *the French King's success*. During the spring and summer of 1674, Louis XIV enjoyed a run of dazzling military triumphs in his war against the United Provinces.

l. 59. *two women at one time*. At this time, Louis's mistresses were Mme de Montespan and Mme Scarron.

l. 62. *gelt*. Castrated.

l. 71. *tierce*. Claret.   *the Bull*. Generic name for a tavern.

l. 73. *kickshaws*. Delicacies.   *Sellery*. Sillery, a still white wine from the Champagne region.   *Champoone*. Champagne had only recently become available in London (the spelling reflects the Host's franglais).

l. 77. *Moseley*. 'Mother' Moseley, a famous brothel madam.

l. 78. *The coach-man*. i.e. the beef is too heavy to be carried by one of the indoor servants.   *ridden by a witch*. Combining 'hag-ridden', meaning 'having a nightmare', with an allusion to the reputed sexual voraciousness of witches. Thus: 'having nightmarishly protracted sex'. Eating the gargantuan joint of beef will also involve drawing out what should be a pleasurable experience to a grotesque extent.

l. 80. *tool*. Dildo.

50 l. 82. *flaming head*. 'Dildos were sometimes made with pink or red tips' (Love).

l. 83. *capon*. Chicken.

l. 85. *eighty-eight*. 1588, the year of the defeat of the Spanish Armada. The sauces are quintessentially English but outdated.

l. 88. *clout*. Dishcloth.

l. 89. *brimmer*. A large glass brim-full.

l. 90. *Small beer*. Weak beer.

l. 92. *safe six old Italians place*. If 'safe' means 'easily', then the allusion is probably to the Roman habit of reclining full-length at table. But if it means 'without risk', then perhaps the reference is to the vengefulness of Italian characters in Jacobean ('old') tragedy.

l. 93. *Porter*. George Porter, who served alongside R. as a Groom of the Bedchamber to Charles II.   *Blunt*. Charles Blount (cf. headnote to 'Seneca's *Troas*. Act 2. Chorus').

l. 94. *Harris*. Henry Harris, an actor.   *Cullen*. Elizabeth Cockayne, wife of Viscount Cullen, was notoriously promiscuous.   *bushel*. Capable of holding eight gallons.

ll. 100–1. *He talked much of a plot . . . In Cromwell's time*. Apparently the Host fought on the royalist side in the Civil War (l. 96), and contributed funds to the campaign in the form of a loan which Charles neglected to repay at the Restoration.

l. 103. *small*. Low-grade.   *players*. Actors.

l. 106. *Too rotten*. i.e. as a result of venereal disease.

50 l. 107. *Falkland*. Lucius Cary, second Viscount Falkland (1610–43), cavalier poet and royalist war-hero.   *Suckling*. Sir John Suckling (1609–42), author of courtly ('easy') love lyrics admired by R.

l. 108. *parts*. Qualities, both literary and sexual.

l. 109. *the best*. Wife, or possibly 'cunt' (cf. 'A Satire on Charles II', l. 2).

l. 113. *my Lord of Orrery*. Cf. 'An Allusion to Horace', l. 96 and n.

l. 114. *how well Mustapha, and Zanger die*. Sons of the Turkish emperor Solyman, who commit suicide in fine Stoic style at the end of *The Tragedy of Mustapha*.

ll. 117–18. *And which is worse . . . to me*. Actually a misquotation from Orrery's *The Black Prince* (1667).

51 l. 121. *God zounds*. 'By God's wounds!'

ll. 122–5. *Etherege writes . . . without one plot*. Cf. 'An Allusion to Horace', ll. 32–3.

l. 125. *talking plays without one plot*. Full of witty conversation but lacking action.

l. 126. *Settle . . . Morocco*. Cf. 'An Allusion to Horace', l. 18 and n.

ll. 128–30. *Whose broad-built Bulks . . . Tituan*. R. has beefed up the alliterative bombast of the passage, which in the original reads: 'Their lofty Bulks the foaming Billows bear, | Saphee and Salli, Mugadore, Oran, | The fam'd Arzille, Alcazer, Tituan'.

l. 131. *braver*. (i) Grander; (ii) more hectoring.

l. 132. *Crowne*. Cf. 'An Allusion to Horace', ll. 11 and n.

l. 134. *Pandion . . . Charles the Eight*. Respectively, *Pandion and Amphigenia* (1665), a prose romance, and the *History of Charles the eighth of France* (1672), a heroic drama.

ll. 139–40. *Fitting their Oars . . . rising Sun*. Accurately quoted from *The History of Charles the eighth*.

l. 144. *The Indian Emperor*. Dryden's *The Indian Emperor* (1667), the sequel to *The Indian Queen* (cf. 'A Letter from Artemiza in the Town to Chloe in the Country', l. 99 and n.).

ll. 145–6. *As if our Old World . . . a new*. Correctly quoted from *The Indian Emperor*.

l. 148. *withdrawing room*. Chamber prepared for a woman about to give birth.

l. 152. *Zouches . . . Champoone*. In the spring of 1674, Ludwig de Souches, general of the Imperial army on the Rhine, seemed on the point of invading the region of Champagne.

l. 153. *Turene*. Henri de la Tour d'Auvergne, Vicomte de Turenne, commander of the French forces defending Champagne.

ll. 155–6. *the French cowards are . . . Swiss make war*. Louis XIV funded England's naval war against the Dutch, as well as employing Scottish, Irish, and Swiss mercenaries in his armies.

52 l. 171. *joins*. Either 'sides with' or 'fights against' (with these ham-fisted combatants there is little difference).

l. 172. *safe*. Out of reach.

l. 174. *treat*. Negotiate a peace, by buying each other drinks.

A Satire against Reason and Mankind. R.'s most famous and controversial poem was circulating in manuscript in 1674 (the date given on two copies) and immediately drew ripostes, most notably from the star Anglican preacher Edward Stillingfleet, a possible model for the 'formal band and beard' (cf. l. 73 n.) in a sermon delivered on 24 February 1675. But the letter which precedes the text in 'Hartwell' implies the poem existed in a private draft as early as 1672, and the initial impetus may date even further back to R.'s stay in Paris in 1669 when he had the opportunity to read Boileau's newly published *Satires* (1668). Boileau's 'Satire VIII', featuring a debate between a poet and a clerical 'adversarius' about the relative merits of animality and human nature, was from the first recognized as a precedent for R.'s 'Satire', though Thomas Rymer was right to observe in the preface to *1691* that the debt was limited to plot as opposed to phrasing or tone. The title's original spelling of *Satyr* invokes the priapic hybrid of man and goat sometimes identified in this period with the figure of the satirist, an especially pertinent connection in this case: 'If it is a satyr speaking, then a creature half-man and half-animal is saying that he would rather be all animal' (Ellis). The 'paradox' ('Addition', l. 48) of mankind's inferiority to animals had in fact been asserted regularly since classical times, and was especially current amongst seventeenth-century French writers whose work R. knew well, including Montaigne and the libertine poets Mathurin Régnier and Théophile de Viau. More specific to the contemporary English context of the 'Satire' is R.'s treatment of its other target, 'Reason'. Ownership of this term had been keenly contested since the Restoration. Clerical moderates ('latitudinarians'), who brandished the 'Reasonableness of Christianity' as a means of dissociating themselves from the anarchic anti-rationalism of the radical sects of the Civil War era, met opposition from a loose alliance of secularizing thinkers like Thomas Hobbes and Charles Blount and 'wits' like R., for whom championing 'reason' meant embracing the new sceptical empiricism of the age. R.'s poem stages an episode in this territorial dispute in which neither the protagonist nor his clerical opponent is finally permitted to vindicate his claim. For the former (a dramatized character who should not be confused with R.) 'reason' boils down to a brutish reliance on the senses; for the latter, it expands into a gaseous fantasy of omniscience.

l. 8. *The senses are*. i.e. 'That vain animal, Man, thinks that the senses are . . . '   *gross*. (i) 'Coarse, inferior, common' (*OED* 12a); (ii) 'Material . . . as contrasted with what is spiritual, ethereal, or impalpable' (*OED* 8c); (iii) 'Palpable, striking; plain, evident, obvious' (*OED* 3).

l. 12. *ignis fatuus*. 'A phosphorescent light seen hovering or flitting over marshy ground . . . called Will-o'-the-wisp . . . When approached, the

ignis fatuus appears to recede, and finally to vanish, sometimes reappear-
ing in another direction. This led to the notion that it was the work of
a mischievous sprite intentionally leading benighted travellers astray'
(*OED*).

53 l. 15. *Error*. Capitalized since, together with 'Doubt' at l. 19 and 'Age' and
'Experience' at l. 25, it makes up a miniature allegorical narrative.

l. 19. *like*. Likely.

l. 21. *bladders*. Buoys.

l. 31 *bubbles*. Dupes.

l. 46. *band and beard*. Churchman. At this stage, a composite portrait
seems intended: 'bands', a clerical collar with two hanging strips, were
worn by Puritans and Anglicans alike.   *formal*. 'Rigorously obser-
vant of forms; precise; prim in attire; ceremonious' (*OED* 8), encompass-
ing the stereotypes of the Puritan (fastidious over points of doctrine and
ostentatiously plain in dress) and the Anglican (a stickler for the minutiae
of church ceremony).

l. 50. *Likes*. Pleases.   *you take care*. You ought to take care.

54 l. 53. *smart*. Caustic.

ll. 68–9. *Dive into mysteries . . . the universe*. An echo of Lucretius' paean
to the philosopher Epicurus for explaining natural phenomena with-
out recourse to religious myth. If the reference is intentional, the priest
is clumsily aligning himself with the classic ancestor of the 'atheistical'
wits (cf. headnote to 'Translation from Lucretius, *De Rerum Natura*,
ii. 646–51'). This links him more specifically with the new breed of urbane
Anglican clerics like Stillingfleet and Samuel Parker (cf. 'Tunbridge
Wells', l. 69 n.).

l. 73. *Ingelo*. Nathaniel Ingelo, author of a prose romance *Bentivoglio and
Urania* (1660), which includes the claim that 'Reason . . . doth make us
capable of converse with God' (Ellis).

l. 74. *Patrick's Pilgrim*. *The Parable of the Pilgrim* (1664), by the latitudin-
arian divine Simon Patrick, typified the latitudinarian style of urbane
'reasonableness'.   *Sibbes*. The puritan divine Richard Sibbes
(1577–1635) who extolled 'reason' as 'a beam of God'.   *Soliloquies*.
Sermons. Some manuscripts have 'Stillingfleet's replies', almost certainly
a later revision by R. in light of the 1675 sermon (see headnote).

l. 76. *mite*. Worm.

l. 83. *Bedlams*. The Bethlehem Hospital, popularly known as 'Bedlam',
was a madhouse in Bishopsgate.   *Schools*. Universities.

l. 86. *charming ointments*. Witches were said to rub themselves down with
magical lotions as a preparative to flying.

55 l. 90. *whimsical philosopher*. Diogenes, who argued that shunning physical
pleasure was the key to the good life, and lived in a tub to prove his point.

l. 110. *your doubt secures*. Should leave you in no doubt.

l. 112. *for*. Either 'as for' or 'in favour of'.

l. 119. *Jowler*. Generic name for a hunting dog.

l. 120. *Meres*. Sir Thomas Meres MP, a frequent committee chair in Restoration parliaments.

56 l. 127. *bring it to the test*. Put the case.

l. 146. *for the which*. For which.

l. 150. *screws . . . in*. Crams into.

l. 162. *play upon the square*. Play fair.

57 *Addition*. These lines circulated separately in manuscript, in the aftermath of Stillingfleet's sermon attacking the 'Satire', before being combined by R. with the main body of the poem at some later date. In outlining the ideal opposite of the 'formal band and beard' (an otherworldly fideist who has no truck with modish rationalism), they bring the composite poem into line with the Horatian practice of ending satires on a positive note. Apart from the introductory sentence and the concluding couplet, the lines constitute a single vast period of conditional syntax: 'If' (l. 6), 'If' (l. 12), 'Is there a' (i.e. 'If there is'; l. 18), 'If upon earth there dwell' (l. 47)—then 'I'll here recant' (l. 48). But the illogical full-stops which break up that period in the original manuscripts and printings have been left in, since removing them would further obscure the structure.

l. 2. *pretending*. (i) Grasping; (ii) deceptive.

l. 4. *holy cheats*. Frauds perpetrated against superstitious believers. *formal*. Relating to church ceremony.

l. 8. *needful*. Unavoidable.

l. 11. *that unhappy trade*. Attendance at court.

ll. 16–17. *Nor while . . . close bribes*. 'And does not accept bribes in secret, whilst being too vain to be openly avaricious.'

l. 20. *prelatic*. Priestly. Originally, 'prelates' were Roman Catholic cardinals and bishops.

l. 21. *for*. Instead of.

l. 22. *pretence*. Pretext (governing 'to' in l. 24).

l. 23. *saucy*. Upstart.

58 l. 27. *gossiping*. Gathering of women to celebrate the birth of a child.

l. 31. *good livings*. Lucrative church appointments.

l. 46. *conceive*. (i) Understand; (ii) invent. See Introduction, p. xl.

l. 48. *paradox*. Unconventional teaching: the 'theriophilic' argument of the 'Satire'. *them*. All priests.

A Letter from Artemiza in the Town to Chloe in the Country. First printed in a pirated edition of 1679 and then in *1680* within the opening sequence of six major satires. The 'Haward' copy was almost certainly transcribed either late in 1674 or early in 1675, and a date of composition around then would make this 'most complex of R.'s longer satires' (Love), which partly depends on Boileau's 'Satire I', contemporaneous with his two more systematic imitations of Boileau (see headnote to 'Timon'). Another intertext for the poem is Dryden's comedy *Marriage-à-la-Mode* (1671) which R. evidently saw in draft and which features a ludicrously Frenchified female character, Melantha, similar in many respects to R.'s 'fine Lady'. Dryden thanked R. in the dedication for improving the play, so the direction of influence remains unclear. Certainly, though, R. can claim priority in adapting the Horatian mode of the verse epistle to the distinctive cultural circumstances of the 1670s, when improvements to the road network and the advent of a regular postal service fed the ever-increasing appetite of country-dwellers for news from the metropolis (not least of R.'s latest shocking activities). So artfully does the poem mimic the rambling informality of familiar correspondence that Rachel Trickett's account of its 'chinese-box structure' (in Christopher Ricks (ed.), *English Poetry and Prose 1540–1674* (London, 1970), 325) bears repeating, supplemented so as to bring out R.'s interweaving of the three female characters' voices in this his most advanced experiment in cross-gender ventriloquism (cf. 'A Young Lady to her Ancient Lover', 'The Platonic Lady', and 'What vain unnecessary things are men'):

> the most interior narrative of the Chinese box is the tale of Corinna (ll. 189–255) who is ruined by a man of wit, but survives prostitution to become the mistress of a booby squire; her bastard succeeds to the squire's estate when she poisons the squire [the fine lady narrating or commenting: ll. 189–227, 228–35?, 240–55; Corinna's reported speech, 228–35?, 236–9];
>
> the interior narrative is the monologue of the fine lady (ll. 73–188) who on principle has married 'a diseased, ill-favoured fool' (l. 84) rather than a man of wit [the fine lady's direct speech: ll. 85–91, 95–135, 143–5, 169, 171–88; Artemiza narrating or commenting: ll. 73–84, 92–5, 135–42, 145–68];
>
> the frame story is Artemiza's report to Chloe in the country about the latest fashions in 'the loves of the Town' (ll. 1–264).

58 *Artemiza*. In some manuscripts she is 'Artemisia' or 'Artemisa'. There were two famous Artemisias in classical culture: Artemisia of Caria, who was synonymous with marital fidelity, because of her devotion to the memory of her dead husband Mausolus, and Artemisa of Halicarnassus, who was a byword for female heroism but also possibly craftiness, because of her role in helping Xerxes defeat the Greeks at the battle of Salamis. A third probable reference is to the Latin name of mugwort, a plant reputed to cure women's illnesses.   *Chloe*. Deriving from the Greek for 'young plant' or 'green shoot'.   *the Town*. Cf. 'An Imperfect Enjoyment', l. 63.

l. 2. *astride*. i.e. like a man.

59 l. 7. *bays*. Laurel leaves, the conventional reward for poetic excellence.

l. 17. *Bedlam has many mansions*. A profane echo of Christ's reference to heaven as 'my father's house' where there 'are many mansions' (John 14: 2).

l. 21. *fiddle*. Plaything, laughing-stock.

l. 24. *arrant*. Absolute.

l. 31. *I stand on thorns*. 'I am on tenterhooks.'

l. 44. *cordial*. Medicinal; recalling the Latin root *cor*, meaning 'heart'.

60 l. 46. *one only*. Single.

l. 47. *subsidies*. Taxes.

l. 51. *play*. Gambling at cards.

l. 52. *rooks*. Sharpsters.

l. 57. *gypsies*. 'A contemptuous term for a woman, as being cunning, deceitful, fickle' (*OED* 2b).

l. 58. *And hate restraint, though but from infamy*. 'And hate restraint, even when all they are being restrained from is making themselves infamous.'

l. 59. *common*. Open to all; trashy.   *nice*. Choosy; elitist.

l. 63. *action*. (i) Behaviour, with strong implications of theatricality; (ii) 'the sex act'.   *passion*. Feeling, particularly of a painful strength (cf. 'The Mistress', ll. 31–2).

l. 68. *Fashions grow up for taste, at forms they strike*. 'Fashions come to replace independent taste, and people surrender [*strike*: a metaphor from one ship striking sail to another as a mark of respect] to codes and conventions of behaviour' (Hammond).

l. 69. *would*. Want to.

l. 70. *Bovey*. Sir Ralph Bovey, son of a London merchant, who seems to have epitomized the moneyed grossness of the 'citizen'.

l. 83. *had been*. Wanted to be.

l. 84. *ill-favoured*. Ugly.

61 l. 90. *lemon pill*. Lemon peel, chewed to hide bad breath.

l. 92. *necessary thing*. A 'necessary woman' in Restoration English was a maidservant. But the husband may also be 'necessary' as cover for the fine lady's sexual adventuring.

l. 94. *antic*. Bizarre and antiquated.   *postures*. Theatrical poses.

l. 96. *Let me die*. Also Melantha's catch-phrase in Dryden's *Marriage-à-la-Mode*.

l. 99. *Indian queen*. Dryden and Sir Robert Howard's play *The Indian Queen* (1665) helped launch a cult of oriental primitivism in the 1660s.

l. 100. *is strangely seen*. Combining 'seems out of place' with 'gets odd looks'.

l. 104. *incommode*. Inconvenient. The rhyme 'à la mode' | 'incommode' occurs in Boileau's 'Satire I', where it is not wits but poets who are 'incommode'.

61 l. 109. *what may should not please*. 'What might be a source of pleasure [i.e. any woman whatsoever] ought not to be enjoyed.'

62 l. 124. *kind*. Forgiving.   *easy*. Indulgent.

l. 127. *his proper*. His own.

l. 138. *monkey*. Kept as pets by fashionable courtiers, including R. himself.

l. 144. *japan*. Exotic.

l. 161. *parts*. Accomplishments.

63 l. 169. *Pug*. A generic name in this period for monkeys as well as dogs.

l. 180. *pit-buffoon*. Show-off in the pit at the theatre, where low-rent prostitutes plied for trade.

l. 182. *fond*. Eager.

l. 183. *Foster*. A woman of this name, who was the daughter of a Kensington inn-keeper, apparently masqueraded as a court lady; elliptical references in R.'s correspondence suggest he may have had sex with her before realizing his error and seeking to palm her off on to another well-born lover (the 'Irish Lord').   *Nokes*. The actor James Nokes specialized in clown roles.

l. 184. *Betty Morris*. A prostitute (cf. 'An Allusion to Horace', ll. 111–14).   *City Cokes*. A gullible 'citizen', after Bartholomew Cokes in Ben Jonson's *Bartholomew Fair*.

l. 188. *lewd*. (i) Debauched (Corinna); (ii) simple-minded (the fool). *abandoned*. (i) Deserted (Corinna); (ii) 'devoted' (*OED* 2; the fool).

l. 191. *Cozened*. Deceived.

l. 192. *too-dear-bought trick*. It often resulted in venereal disease for which the only cure—mercury treatment—was both excruciating and expensive.

64 l. 199. *Who found 'twas dull to love above a day*. Cf. 'A Dialogue between Strephon and Daphne', l. 56.

l. 204. *mortgage*. Pawn.   *mantua*. A modishly loose blouse.

l. 208. *tawdry*. Dolled up in tasteless glamour.

l. 209. *Easter term*. Easter term of the lawcourts, 'when country gentlemen, with the Spring planting complete, would come to London to conduct legal business and enjoy themselves' (Love).

l. 210. *worship*. A polite form of address for a countryman.

l. 214. *Conquest*. The Norman Conquest.

l. 216. *crossing of the strain*. Interbreeding, with a lower class.

l. 217. *booby-breed*. Ancestral line of idiots.

l. 222. *Dunghill*. 'Old-fashioned manor houses would still have a dung-hill in the centre of the stable yard' (Love).   *pease*. Not 'peas', but an abbreviation of 'pease-pudding', here as a catch-all term for a rustic diet.

l. 228. *Pretends*. Claims.

l. 231. *prove*. Experience.

ll. 232–3. *no pains . . . But what*. Pangs of love, as opposed to syphilis pains.

l. 235. *libels*. Writes and circulates lampoons against.   *kind*. (i) Compassionate; (ii) sexually accommodating.

65 l. 240. *unbred*. Gauche.

l. 250. *owl*. Blithe idiot.

l. 254. *kind-keeping fools*. Tolerant benefactors.

ll. 254–5. *Wisely provides . . . wear out*. The men of wit cast aside Corinna and her ilk like worn-out clothes, but the fools patch them up and wear them second-hand (cf. l. 102).

Tunbridge Wells. First printed in Richard Head's guide to low life *Proteus Redivivus*, which was licensed for publication on 10 November 1674, the poem was probably written at some point during the summer of that year, when the references to the controversy between Samuel Parker and Andrew Marvell and borrowings from Shadwell's play *Epsom Wells* remained topical, and R. was himself holidaying at another spa—Bath—in the retinue of the Duchess of Portsmouth. Count Grammont, a French exile at the Restoration court who visited Tunbridge in 1663, celebrated it some decades later in his *Memoirs* as a 'rallying-point . . . of all that is fairest and most gallant in both sexes' where 'constraint and formality are banished', and 'the tender commerce [i.e. of love] flourishes'; R.'s poem provides a splenetic gloss on those sepia-tinted recollections. Its 'casual accretive structure' (Walker) led to considerable textual confusion among the surviving manuscript copies, and whilst collaborative authorship is again likely (as with 'Of Marriage' and 'Timon'), this is a uniquely puzzling case: Love accepted the poem as wholly R.'s since it is 'solidly attributed' to him in the manuscripts, but the stylometric analyses conducted by his colleague John Burrows rated R.'s involvement in the text as minor.

l. 1. *At five this morn*. Guides for visitors to Tunbridge Wells recommended the small hours as the most advantageous time to drink the spa waters.

l. 2. *Thetis*. A sea-nymph; here a mock-epic personification of the sea.

l. 4. *praters*. Empty talkers.

l. 5. *citizens*. Residents of the 'City', merchants, conventionally associated by court writers with money-mindedness, cultural philistinism, and moral scrupulosity.

66 l. 13. *calf*. Symbolic of naivety.

l. 14. *Sir Nicholas Cully*. A character in George Etherege's first comedy, *The Comical Revenge; or, Love in a Tub* (1664), whose name derives from 'cully', meaning a dupe or simpleton.

l. 15. *Nokes*. James Nokes, the actor who took the role of Sir Nicholas and specialized in playing idiots or 'naturals'.

l. 22. *crabfish*. A cheap whore (so named after the crab-lice with which she might well be infested).

66 l. 30. *fundament*. Arsehole.

l. 32. *Trulla*. Mannish woman.

l. 33. *tarses*. Penises.

l. 34. *foggy arses*. Gaping vaginas.

l. 37. *lower walk*. Two promenades led to the wells, with a tree-lined slope running between them.

ll. 38–9. *Charybdis . . . Scylla*. Sea monsters in Homer's *Odyssey*. In avoiding the former, Odysseus and his men fall prey to the latter.

l. 42. *Spanish guise*. Spaniards were associated with officiousness and pomposity.

l. 43. *buckram*. Artificially stiffened cloth.

l. 44. *woodcock*. Proverbially stupid, because so easily caught by hunters.

67 l. 48. *cabal*. Group of conspirators. The word was highly current at this time, since it happened to double as an acronym for the five members of Charles II's inner council of ministers in 1667–73: *C*lifford, *A*rlington, *B*uckingham, *A*shley, *L*auderdale.

l. 51. *upper end*. The higher of the two walks leading to the wells.

l. 53. *canonical elves*. Vindictive and toadying junior clerics.

l. 56. *strangury*. Painful urination.

l. 57. *spleen*. Melancholia, or chronic irascibility.

ll. 57–8. *To charge . . . brought infamy*. Spleen was often used as a cover for syphilis.

l. 59. *'plain*. Lament.

l. 63. *saucily pretend*. Arrogantly lay claim to.

l. 66. *embassage*. Embassy.

l. 68. *cob*. Leading man.

l. 69. *Bays*. Abusive nickname given to Samuel Parker, a conservative churchman, by Andrew Marvell during their polemical exchanges over repeal of the laws which compelled nonconformists to attend Anglican worship. Parker led the campaign against repeal (hence, 'trampling on liberty' at l. 71).   *Importance Comfortable*. Parker's wife. Referring to his impending marriage in 1674 as the reason for discontinuing his debate with Marvell, Parker had pompously claimed he would be busy with 'matters of a closer and more comfortable importance'.

l. 76. *lazy dull distemper*. Another injudicious phrase of Parker's, which Marvell interpreted as meaning that the cleric had syphilis.

l. 81. *spewed*. Ejaculated.

l. 83. *Macks*. Sons.

68 l. 91. *squire*. Country landowner.   *pantaloon*. Wide-legged breeches. The squire is foolishly aping the latest French clothing trends.

l. 92. *conventicle*. Nonconformist religious meeting, officially outlawed by the Conventicle Act of 1670.

l. 93. *medley*. Rabble.

l. 95. *Chandlers*. Candle-makers.   *mum-bacon-women*. Women who sold bacon and beer.

l. 97. *humours*. Tempers, dispositions.   *quality*. Social class.

l. 103. *foretop*. Front part of his wig.

l. 113. *parts*. Personal accomplishments.

ll. 118–19. *At cribbage fifty-nine . . . yet to want those two!* On a cribbage-board, the sixty-first is the winning hole.

l. 122. *pedlar's stall*. 'Here, at the place where the Wells are, the visitors gather every morning. This is a spacious avenue, bordered by shady trees under which they stroll while taking the waters. Along one side of it runs a lengthy range of booths, garnished with all kinds of jewellery, laces, stockings and gloves, and at which gambling goes on at a fair' (*Memoirs of the Count de Gramont*, ed. Henry Vizetelly, 2 vols. (London, 1889), ii. 151–2).

69 ll. 124–5. *And then more smartly . . . Scotch fiddle*. Either 'He bought her a cheap violin as a brilliantly witty means of making his intentions plain' (because violins symbolized the vagina) or 'To cut to the chase of this tediously involved story, he succeeded in making her horny'.   *Scotch fiddle*. (i) A cheap violin; (ii) the 'itch' of sexual excitement (*OED*).

l. 127. *just fit for man*. Pubescent.

l. 138. *cony*. Rabbit.

l. 144. *those*. Menstrual periods.

l. 147. *steel waters*. The waters at Tunbridge are rich in iron ores.

l. 148. *back of steel*. Cf. 'A Ramble in St. James's Park', l. 120 and n.

l. 151. *Fribble*. A character in Thomas Shadwell's play *Epsom Wells* (1673), along with the 'cheating, sharking, cowardly bullies' Cuff and Kick. Fribble's wife ends up in bed with Cuff.

l. 152. *midwife (truest friend to lechery)*. Midwives were often suspected of helping women to cover up their sexual peccadilloes, particularly by passing off bastards as legitimate children.

ll. 154–5. *enlarge | Thy silly head*. By adding to it the horns which traditionally symbolized the cuckold.

70 l. 165. *cadets*. Younger sons, who often had to make do on small yearly allowances, while their elder brothers inherited the family estate.

l. 169. *trimmed*. Saddled.   *spavined*. Bandy-legged.

l. 171. *scarf*. Regimental sash.

l. 172. *swell*. Strut about.

l. 174. *beargarden ape, on his steed mounted*. The diarist John Evelyn recorded a performance at the Bear Garden in Southwark on 16 June 1670 which 'ended with the Ape on horse-back'.

70 l. 175. *jackanapes*. Someone who apes about or apes his betters.

l. 176. *trumpery*. Foolish antics.

ll. 178–9. *what thing is man . . . he is ridiculous*. An ironic echo of Psalm 8, in the popular version by Sternhold and Hopkins: 'What thing is man (Lord) think I then | that thou dost him remember? | [. . .] Thou hast preferred him to be Lord | of all thy works of wonder: | And at his feet hast set all things, | that he should keep them under. | As sheep, and neat, and all beasts else | that in the fields do feed: | Fowls of the air, fish in the sea, | and all that therein breed.'

ll. 186–7. *For he . . . the wiser creature*. Cf. 'A Satire against Reason and Mankind', ll. 112–40.

Of Marriage. First published, without attribution, in *London Drollery: or, The Wits Academy. Being a Select Collection of the Newest Songs, Lampoons and Airs alamode* (1673), and attributed to R. in only one of the surviving six manuscript copies, this libertine mock-sonnet is one of three poems included in the present edition whose place in R.'s canon remains in doubt (cf. headnotes to 'Timon' and 'Tunbridge Wells'). Editors have always found it Rochesterian, but its 'galloping' anapaestic rhythm, and preponderance of separable epithets and bon mots suggest it may have originated as an impromptu exercise involving several members of R.'s circle during a night's drinking.

l. 6. *work*. Cf. 'Love to a Woman', l. 7 and n.

l. 7. *Commands us to make brick without stubble or straw*. In Exodus 5: 6–19, the Israelites, enslaved in Egypt, are punished by Pharaoh for complaining about their working conditions by being ordered to make bricks without straw.

71 l. 10. *gen'rous*. Cf. 'A Ramble in St. James's Park', l. 98.

Upon Nothing. The manuscript copy dated 14 May 1678, and the appearance of two pirated editions in 1679, support what has been the general view of this as one of R.'s latest poems. It belongs to the mode of 'mock-encomium' or 'paradoxical eulogy', in which entities or qualities usually considered unworthy of praise are celebrated. Nothingness had received such treatment from previous early-modern poets, most recently in the anonymous ballad 'Much A-do, about Nothing' (1660), from which R. may have borrowed the verse form of tercets made up of two pentameters followed by an alexandrine. 'R. is also presenting an ironic inversion of recent accounts of creation' (Hammond), though what phrasal allusions have been detected involve Cowley's now forgotten epic the *Davideis* rather than *Paradise Lost*. The placement of the poem alongside 'Seneca's *Troas*. Act. 2. Chorus' in *1680* suggests it was being credited as philosophically serious, but its positioning in front of 'On Mrs Willis' in 'Gyldenstolpe' sets its nihilism in a less cerebral light. The copy with emendations in the hand of Rochester's mother, probably dating from the period between the poet's death and the publication of *1691* when she was working to rehabilitate his memory, implies the possibility of viewing the poem as a Christian expression of *contemptus mundi*.

l. 5. *primitive*. Original, primary.

l. 22. *laic*. Laymen's.

l. 23. *divine*. Priest.

l. 24. *lies*. (i) Rests; (ii) deceives.

72 l. 30. *point*. (i) Lend point to; (ii) guide, direct.   *blind*. Ignorant.

l. 39. *thought*. Thought of.

l. 41. *prince's coffers*. Cf. 'A Satire on Charles II', l. 28 and n.

l. 42. *like stately something*. The contrary logic of the poem deteriorates into confusion in this line which is short of two syllables. This reading is found in five copies including 'Haward' and 'Houghton'; *1680* and most of the surviving manuscripts have 'stately nothing'.

l. 45. *Lawn*. Fine linen, worn by bishops.   *furs and gowns*. Worn by judges.

l. 46. *prowess*. Courage.   *policy*. Diplomacy.

l. 47. *Hibernian*. Irish.

l. 48. *dispatch*. Promptness to action.

73 *To the Post Boy*. Written after the summer of 1676, following the Epsom affray which is referred to in ll. 9–12. Post-boys were coaching-inn servants paid a few pence per stage to accompany well-to-do travellers who were 'riding post', that is, switching to fresh horses at each break in their journey. The poem is set at one such staging-post, as R. negotiates to hire horses for the next leg of his headlong retreat from Epsom back to London.

l. 3. *make*. Invention.

l. 4. *furies*. The three furies, Tisiphone, Megaera, and Alecto, were responsible for executing the vengeance of the gods.   *Pluto*. King of the underworld.

l. 5. *swived*. Fucked.

l. 8. *Cerecloths*. Waxed bandages.

ll. 9–12. *Frighted . . . my lust denied*. These couplets, which are absent from some manuscript copies of the poem, refer to an incident which took place on 17 June 1676 at Epsom where R. and his cronies, including a certain Captain Downs, were enjoying a day out at the races. According to a contemporary report: 'They were tossing some fiddlers in a blanket for refusing to play, and a barber, upon the noise, going to see what [was] the matter, they seized upon him, and, to free himself from them, he offered to carry them to the handsomest woman in Epsom, [but] directed them to the constable's house, who demanding what they came for, they told him a whore, and he, refusing to let them in, they broke open the doors and broke his head, and beat him very severely. At last, he made his escape, called his watch [officers]. But presently after, the Lord Rochester drew upon the constable; Mr. Downs, to prevent his pass, seized on him, the constable cried out "Murder!", and the watch returning, one came behind Mr. Downs and with a staff cleft his skull. The Lord Rochester and the rest run away, and Downs, having no sword, snatched up a stick and striking at them, they run him into the side with a half-pike, and so bruised his arm that he was never able to stir it after' (letter from Charles Hatton to his brother, 29 June 1676, in *Correspondence of the Family of Hatton*, ed. E. M. Thompson, 2 vols. (London, 1878), i. 133–4). Downs died of his injuries shortly afterwards.

73 l. 14. *libelled kings*. Cf. headnote to 'A Satire on Charles II'.

l. 15. *ne'er stir*. Some copies of the poem attribute these words to the post-boy, as in 'there's no need to move, my Lord, you're already in Hell' (cf. Satan's realization at *Paradise Lost*, 4. 75: 'Which way I fly is Hell; myself am Hell'). If spoken by Rochester himself, they represent a second effort, after 'ne'er go' at l. 7, to prevent the post-boy from leaving in horror.

l. 16. *by Rochester*. Dropped to the line below in some manuscripts, making the poem into a signed confession.

From 'An Essay on Satire'. Love's copy-text: 'Haward'. This is the concluding passage of an ambitious and incisive satire, circulating in London by the autumn of 1679, which opened up a literary-critical front in the war between the circle of 'wits' grouped around R. and Buckingham, hostile to the Duke of York, and Mulgrave's new stable of 'Yorkist' writers. Probably a joint effort by Mulgrave and Dryden, it was originally reckoned to be by Dryden alone, and R. shared this view. But the subsequent cudgelling of the upstart Laureate in Rose Alley, Covent Garden on 18 December 1679 was probably carried out by agents of the Duchess of Portsmouth, another of the essay's targets, rather than on the orders of R. himself.

l. 1. *mere*. Absolute.

l. 14. *Killigrew*. Henry Killigrew, a courtier and close friend of R.'s well known for his high-spiritedness, or else his father Tom, the manager of the King's theatre company, whom R. once struck in the presence of the King.

l. 15. *For what*. Why.   *Bessus*. A cowardly soldier in Fletcher's tragi-comedy *A King and No King*. Mulgrave had challenged R. to a duel in 1669, and when R. turned up on horseback, in what may have been intended as a parodic gesture, Mulgrave spread it abroad that he had been unwilling to fight.

74 l. 17. *still*. Always.

l. 19. *their pleasure say*. Say whatever they want.

l. 20. *bolder*. Cf. 'A Satire against Reason and Mankind', l. 158.   *run away*. Cf. 'To the Post Boy', ll. 9–12.

l. 22. *For every fault does prove his penance still*. 'Every transgression he commits brings with it its own punishment.'

l. 23. *Falsely*. Through his treachery.

l. 25. *it's better quitting*. 'It would be better to put a stop to it altogether' (through suicide).

l. 35. *idle*. Trivial.

l. 40. *expression*. 'Character; expressive quality' (*OED* 5a), a sense not recorded before the eighteenth century.   *fancy*. Imagination. *design*. Form.

My Lord All-pride. This lampoon against John Sheffield, third Earl of Mulgrave, R.'s principal adversary in the later 1670s, is the least sophisticated of the three attacks on Mulgrave, which all seem to have circulated in 1679.

l. 1. *imposthume*. Boil, abscess.

l. 3. *lewd*. Vulgar; uninspired.

l. 4. *force to nature*. Strain against his natural disposition.

ll. 3–4. *But 'tis so lewd . . . as he fights*. On 4 July 1675, Mulgrave had been wounded in a duel by the brother of his mistress Mary Kirke.

l. 5. *baffled*. Disgraced.

75 l. 16. *looby mien*. Loutish expression.

l. 18. *Punchinello*. Puppet shows featuring characters akin to the later Punch were performed in London and at court by Italian touring companies in the 1670s.   *spark*. Young man-about-town.

l. 19. *self-conceit*. Complacency.   *bears arms*. Mulgrave particularly prided himself on his soldiery.

l. 20. *that*. Such.

l. 22. *Harlequin*. Grotesque would-be lover in Italian *commedia'dell'arte*, another Restoration literary craze.

l. 23. *Smithfield's wondrous fair*. Bartholomew Fair had been held in Smithfield every August since medieval times.

l. 24. *monsters*. Freaks.

l. 25. *lubbard*. Clumsy.

l. 26. *making legs*. Kneeling.

l. 30. *knight o'th' burning pestle*. Alluding to the title of a comedy by Francis Beaumont which parodies chivalric heroism. Mulgrave's 'burning pestle' would be his bulbous red nose, or his penis if inflamed and itchy from venereal disease.

Ephelia to Bajazet. Buckingham attributed this poem to George Etherege, whose earlier diplomatic posting to Turkey makes him a plausible source for the identification of Mulgrave with 'Bajazet', that is Bajazid I (1347–1403), the Turkish sultan defeated and captured in 1402 by Timur (Marlowe's Tamburlaine). But it may be by the pseudonymous woman poet 'Ephelia' whose *Female Poems on Several Occasions* appeared in 1679, when R.'s literary war with Mulgrave was at its height. The poem is a 'heroical epistle', on the model of Ovid's *Heroides*, letter poems of complaint addressed by betrayed or abandoned women from myth and legend to their delinquent lovers. Either Etherege was following Ovid in assuming a female voice, or 'Ephelia' was reclaiming the mode for her sex.

75 l. 4. *enjoyment*. Consummation.

l. 8. *date*. Duration.

76 l. 25. *To meet his love, by a less name than wife*. 'To reciprocate his love, without the honour of being called his wife.'

l. 49. *gen'rous*. Heroic.

77 l. 54. *rage*. Passion.

A Very Heroical Epistle in Answer to Ephelia. The title of R.'s satirical response to *Ephelia to Bajazet*, archly emphasizing its genre, suggests it was put into circulation as Mulgrave and his star literary client Dryden were preparing their multi-authored *Ovid's Epistles, translated by several hands* (1680). Details at ll. 54–5 appear to connect 'Ephelia' with Mulgrave's sometime mistress Mary Kirke, a maid-of-honour to the Duchess of York.

l. 11. *stout*. Staunch.

l. 12. *Names*. Mere words; cyphers.

l. 13. *Should I regard*. If I were to value (the qualities listed at l. 11).

l. 14. *pain*. Anxiety, avoidance of which is the primary objective in the philosophy of Epicurus, fashionable among the Restoration 'wits'.

l. 15. *fondly*. Foolishly.

l. 22. *blazing star*. (i) comet; (ii) the star of the Order of the Garter, worn by Mulgrave with notorious vanity after his admission in July 1674.

l. 23. *fatal*. Comets were widely believed to augur catastrophes.

l. 26. *changing of my gold*. The sexual pun works in modern English: 'liquefying my assets'.

78 l. 33. *happy*. Not just generally 'fortunate', but in the particular sense of having attained the condition of Epicurean 'contentment'.   *sultan*. Eastern potentate.

l. 35. *serail*. Harem.

l. 40. *silent as the night*. Because they have had their tongues cut out.

l. 42. *Secure*. Free from anxiety.

l. 49. *requires*. Asks for.

l. 53. *true love knot*. A knot made up of two intertwined loops, symbolizing true love; but here appropriated (with 'true' modifying 'knot' instead of 'love') to refer to garrotting, reputedly a favourite mode of execution at oriental courts.

l. 54. *kinsman's threat'ning blade*. Cf. 'My Lord All-pride', ll. 3–4 n.

l. 55. *midnight ambushes*. Guards posted by the Duke of Monmouth once seized Mulgrave as he was coming out of Mary Kirke's lodgings at Whitehall.

l. 57. *Damocles his feast*. Damocles's. A member of the court of Dionysius of Syracuse, Damocles was forced to sit at a feast with a sword suspended by a single horsehair over his head, as an object lesson in the precariousness of power.

An Epistolary Essay, from M. G. to O. B. upon their Mutual Poems. So fine are the ironies in this verse epistle, which appears to advocate an ethic of aristocratic self-gratification and a poetics of courtly amateurism, that it was taken by several contemporary copyists to be spoken in R.'s own person, and therefore titled 'A Letter from My Lord Rochester' or 'From the E. of R.'. Its placement at the head of *1680* gives it the look of a manifesto for the volume. Modern commentators too regarded it as an expression of R.'s own moral and aesthetic creed until 1963, when David Vieth suggested that of all the various pairs of initials attached to the poem's title in contemporary sources, the correct one was 'M. G.' and 'O. B.', for Mulgrave and Dryden ('Old Bays') respectively. This suggestion has achieved wide acceptance, but residual uncertainty about the poem's context continues to block recognition of its pioneering achievement in the epistolary mode, and as a forerunner of 'Augustan' poetic criticism.

l. 2. *saucy censurers*. Upstart critics.

l. 3. *what of late*. i.e. 'An Essay on Satire'.   *poetic rage*. Frenzy of inspiration.

79 l. 11. *the British Prince*. Edward Howard's epic poem *The British Princes* (1669) had long been a byword for hack writing.

l. 18. *exposing*. Publishing (with innuendo).

l. 31. *In mere good breeding*. 'Out of politeness, if nothing else.'

l. 38. *own*. Admit.

l. 41. *harsh insipid*. Strongly tasteless.

l. 43. *civet cats*. Musk or 'civet' was obtained from the anal glands of a species of wild cat.

ll. 44–5. *rhyme | Fail . . . sublime*. Longinus' *On the Sublime* had been translated into English in 1674, and subsequently invoked by Dryden in his 'Apology for Heroic Poetry, and Poetic Licence' (1677) to justify Milton's grand style, and in particular his abandonment of rhyme.

80 l. 49. *Than so to write as none e'er writ before*. Cf. 'An Allusion to Horace', l. 33 and n.

l. 50. *of the times*. Fashionable; successful.

l. 59. *Is fain to*. Has to.

l. 64. *magnificent*. Beneficent.

l. 73. *Born to myself*. 'Independent, through privilege of my high birth.'

l. 81. *Oh! but the world will take offence thereby*. This line (like l. 87) is spoken by an imagined interlocutor.

81 ll. 85–6. *Why should . . . customs spawn.* 'Why should what I write be debased—constrained to fit every measure which has acquired the force of a law, though it is actually just the product of long-running convention?'

l. 90. *common fame.* Public opinion.

l. 93. *brisk.* Lively.   *sad.* Serious.

l. 94. *Mean.* Indiscriminately sociable.   *familiar.* Affable.

l. 97. *this—.* The dash indicates a physical action: a snap of the fingers or a fart.

l. 98. *innocent.* Ineffectual.

INDEX OF MANUSCRIPTS

Gyldenstolpe   Stockholm, Kungliga Biblioteket, MS Vu. 69

A de luxe miscellany of Restoration verse, 314 pages long and containing 29 poems by R.: all the major satires and lampoons and a wide selection of his libertine and polite lyrics. Produced by scribes employed in a 'scriptorium' and sold to order in an attractive binding. Once owned by Count Nils Gyldenstolpe (1642–1709), the Swedish ambassador at The Hague in the 1670s. Like those of other 'professional' anthologies, its texts are generally free from the garbled readings found in some 'private' sources, and on that basis were treated with respect by the first modern scholars of R.'s manuscripts. But Love argued that, far from indicating any proximity to the authorial wording, the cogency of scriptorium texts was the result of editorial intervention on the part of the copyists or the manager of the scriptorium. Such editorializing might have involved either accentuating obscenity or toning it down, depending on the particular requirements of the purchaser.

Harbin   Wiltshire, Longleat House, Library of the Marquess of Bath, Thynne Papers, vol. XXVII

A loose collection of R.'s polite lyrics and family correspondence, but also including 'A Letter from Artemiza in the Town to Chloe in the Country' and a partial text of 'An Epistolary Essay from M. G. to O. B., upon their mutual Poems'. Probably copied by a member of the extended family of R.'s wife, the Somersetshire Malets, shortly after the poet's death, from an anthology held in the Adderbury household. Named after the priest George Harbin who acquired the collection in the early eighteenth century from his nephew Alexander Malet. The 'Harbin' texts, like those in the closely related 'Hartwell', are crucial 'private' sources which have been used to authenticate a number of lyrics whose attribution to R. was previously insecure. The copyist, almost certainly a woman, was called 'prudish' by Love, but if she censored the Adderbury texts she did not do so consistently (see the headnotes to 'The Mistress', 'Grecian Kindness', and 'A Young Lady to her Ancient Lover').

Hartwell   Yale University Library, Beinecke Library, MS Osborn b 334

A collection of 24 poems by R. and one prose work almost certainly by him (see headnote to 'A Satire against Reason and Mankind'), along with Francis Fane's masque for R.'s *Valentinian* adaptation (see headnote to 'Epilogue to *Love in the Dark*'). Copied from the same Adderbury source as 'Harbin' but apparently incorporating material from other sources too, since it includes more of the major satires. Unique among surviving manuscript sources in being exclusively devoted to R.'s work and featuring a title-page announcing the fact: 'Poem's | By The Right Honourable | John Earle | of | Rochester'. The copyist's interest in R. appears, then, to have been more literary than that of 'Harbin'. He or she may have been a member of the Lee family, descendants of the first husband of Rochester's mother. The manuscript later resided among their papers at Hartwell House, Buckinghamshire.

Haward   Oxford, Bodleian Library, MS Don. b 8

A massive 'personal miscellany', 738 pages long, which includes only eight poems by R. but constitutes an important 'private' source because it was compiled by Sir William Haward who enjoyed immediate access to the poet as a fellow Gentleman of the Bedchamber to Charles II. Haward was also an antiquarian scholar, so he probably took care when transcribing his manuscripts. The running order of the items in the miscellany provides crucial dating evidence for some of R.'s major poems (see headnotes to 'Seneca's *Troas*. Act 2. Chorus' and 'A Letter from Artemiza in the Town to Chloe in the Country').

Hansen   Yale University Library, Beinecke Library, MS Osborn b 105

The single most important surviving manuscript source, since it was copied from the same 'archetype' as was used to produce *1680*. Like 'Gyldenstolpe', a scriptorium miscellany including poems by a range of Restoration poets. Like 'Gyldenstolpe' too, it was almost certainly created for a diplomat, Friedrich Arnolphus Hansen, who visited England within months of R.'s death in the entourage of the elector Prince of the Palatine. As a result of its close relation to *1680*, the primary textual source for most modern editions of R., 'Hansen' has substantially conditioned our understanding of the poet, not only where individual readings are concerned (for a celebrated case, see 'Upon his drinking a bowl', l. 24 n.) but also with regard to the overall arrangement of the canon (see the headnotes to 'Seneca's *Troas*. Act 2. Chorus' and 'Upon Nothing'). Its predominance was challenged by Love, who argued for the superior trustworthiness of non-commercial sources such as 'Haward' and particularly the family manuscripts 'Harbin' and 'Hartwell'.

Houghton   Harvard University, Houghton Library, fMS Eng. 636

A 299-page miscellany of Restoration verse entitled *A Collection of Poems*. It contains twenty poems by R., including all the major satires and most famous 'polite' lyrics, but with a particular concentration on the obscene lyrics and lampoons. Although the copies are in a professional hand, this is not a commercial anthology in the conventional sense. The scribe may well have been working from sources similar to those used to create 'Hansen', but he had a 'greater tolerance for apparent error' (Love) in those sources and was less inclined to tidy them up. Another feature of the manuscript reminiscent of 'private' collections rather than commercial miscellanies is its eccentric approach to arranging R.'s work. Some of the copyist's non-standard conjunctions look merely haphazard; others are suggestive of considerable poetic insight (see the headnote to 'Fair Chloris in a pig-sty lay').

Portland   University of Nottingham Library, Portland Collection,
             MS PwV 31

The only surviving source of copies of R.'s poems in his own hand, containing ten of his politest lyrics, as well as a number of pieces by his wife Elizabeth (see headnote to 'Give me leave to rail at you'). The texts of these copies have accordingly been treated with special respect by modern editors. But their authority is limited to their specific domestic context. It is clear that Rochester circulated some of his lyrics in two or more versions, tailored to different audiences at home and at court (see the headnotes to 'How happy, Chloris, were they free', 'How perfect, Chloris, and how free', and 'To a Lady, in a Letter').

INDEX OF TITLES

INDEX OF FIRST LINES